Law Comes to Lawless

OTHER FIVE STAR WESTERN TITLES BY RAY HOGAN:

Soldier in Buckskin (1996)
Legend of a Badman (1997)
Guns of Freedom (1999)
Stonebreaker's Ridge (2000)
The Red Eagle (2001)
Drifter's End (2002)
Valley of the Wandering River (2003)
Truth at Gunpoint (2004)
The Cuchillo Plains (2005)
Outlaw's Promise (2006)
Fire Valley (2007)
Panhandle Gunman (2008)
Range Feud (2009)
Land of Strangers (2010)
Desert Rider (2011)
Apache Basin (2012)
Against the Law (2013)

LAW COMES TO LAWLESS

A WESTERN DUO

RAY HOGAN

FIVE STAR

A part of Gale, Cengage Learning

GALE
CENGAGE Learning·

Farmington Hills, Mich • San Francisco • New York • Waterville, Maine
Meriden, Conn • Mason, Ohio • Chicago

GALE
CENGAGE Learning

LIBRARY OF CONGRESS CATALOGING-IN-PUBLICATION DATA

Hogan, Ray, 1908–1998.
  Law comes to Lawless : a Western duo / by Ray Hogan. —
First Large Print Edition.
    pages cm.
  ISBN-13: 978-1-4328-2768-7 (hardcover)
  ISBN-10: 1-4328-2768-5 (hardcover)
  1. Large type books. I. Hogan, Ray, 1908–1998. Ryker. II. Title.
PS3558.O3473L297 2014
813'.54—dc23   2013050376

First Edition. First Printing: May 2014.
Published in conjunction with Golden West Literary Agency.
Find us on Facebook– https://www.facebook.com/FiveStarCengage
Visit our website– http://www.gale.cengage.com/fivestar/
Contact Five Star™ Publishing at FiveStar@cengage.com

Printed in the United States of America
1 2 3 4 5 6 7 18 17 16 15 14

CONTENTS

* * * * *

Ryker

* * * * *

I

Jake Ryker was in the Lordsburg jail when the letter caught up with him. It was the third of a ten-day sentence for taking apart the Montezuma Saloon and for cracking a few heads during the process. The penalty had been a light one at that, the judge having taken into consideration that it was Ed Virden along with his younger brother Chuck, and their dark-faced friend, Lenny Gault, who actually started it. However, the jurist wasn't so generous that he felt Ryker, six feet of red-headed toughness, should be excused for shattering half the mirrors in the place, smashing five tables and double that number of chairs, as well as tossing the blackjack dealer, who somehow got in the way, through a front window. In retrospect, Ryker guessed it hadn't been necessary, but, what the hell, at a time like that who keeps track?

The Virdens had been packing a grudge for him ever since Wichita, more than six months back, when he'd sided with a soldier they'd crowded into a fight. There'd been four of them then to the Army boy's one. Things changed when Ryker evened up the odds a bit by declaring himself in. Finally matters had turned deadly when the fourth member of the Virden bunch— Tolly somebody—had gone for his gun. Jake Ryker beat him to the draw. That had started problems with the Virdens and Lenny Gault; they'd been dogging his tracks ever since.

But they had been careful. Ryker's gun was known to be fast and sure, and while Wichita had created a festering sore, the

9

three men were prudent enough to seek redress only when they felt they had Ryker at a disadvantage. So far they'd had small success. Jake Ryker, despite the fact he had just passed his thirtieth birthday, carried the trail and town experience of double that number of years under his thatch of red, and never permitted himself to be caught off guard. It was a trait that was as much a part of him as a leg or hand, for the life he led, that of drifter, paid gun, trail boss, gambler, shotgun rider, and a dozen other similar vocations had educated him early to the fact that in such a world only the wary and the quick lived to ripe old ages. And while Ryker never expected to reach the foot-long beard and rocking chair category, there were still a few places he hoped to see, and things he'd like to do before he started bucking for the graveyard.

"This here letter," Town Marshal Borden said, studying the soiled and creased envelope thoughtfully, "sure has done some traveling around. Been clean up to Miles City, appears."

Ryker, sprawled on the cell's hard cot, stirred disinterestedly. The drunk who'd shared the barred cubicle with him the first three days had been turned loose the night before and he'd finally managed to get some sleep. "Can't think of nobody who'd be writing me," he said.

"How about some woman? Looks like a female's handwriting. You leave a little filly in a family way somewheres along the line?"

"Not as I can recollect," Ryker drawled, and pulled himself to a sitting position. He yawned, stretched, scratched at the scruff of red beard making itself noticeable along his jaw. "You going to let me see it or you just aiming to stand there and guess about it?"

Borden shrugged, stepped in close to the bars, and flipped the envelope to Ryker. The tall rider grabbed for it, missed, knocked it under the cot on the opposite side of the cell.

Mumbling a curse, he hunched forward, fished it out from under the narrow bench. Some previous occupant had forgotten a sock he noticed while he was bent over—a black one with the heel worn through.

Settling back, he slid a finger under the flap of the envelope, not bothering to ascertain the postmarks under the smudges, and removed the sheet of lined and folded paper. "From Callie," he said, glancing at the waiting marshal. "My brother Tom's wife."

The lawman's expectant face dropped, reflecting keen disappointment. "Family, eh?" he said grudgingly. "Where they live?"

"Got a ranch east of here. On the Pecos near Haystack Mountain. Pa started it a long time back. When he died, he left it to Tom and me . . . only I never was much for nursing cows. Just let Tom take over, after he and Callie got married up, and moved on."

"What's it doing going to Miles City?"

"Was forwarded up there. Had a job on a ranch just outside of the town for a spell. Folks there sent it on down here, knowing I figured to hang around for a time. Looks like it's been to quite a few places," Ryker said, examining the face of the envelope. Then he fell silent, sitting motionlessly, moody eyes on the floor, the still unread letter in his hands.

"Ain't you going to read it? Could be something mighty important."

Ryker shrugged, straightened. "Anything Callie's got to say to me sure'd not be important, far as I'm concerned," he said, and again leaned back against the bars of his cell. Unfolding the sheet a second time, he began to decipher the cramped writing.

Dear Jacob:

I'm sending you this letter and hoping it will find you somewheres. Your brother Tom has been hurt. He'll never walk again the doctors tell us. He was thrown from a horse.

I can't run the ranch by myself and things are getting worse, especially the rustling. I think you ought to come home and do your share. Lord knows Tom has always done his. It's time you settled down.

Your sister-in-law,
Callie Ryker

A nice, friendly letter, Ryker thought, folding the sheet—with about the same depth of affection and warmth a money-lender would exhibit when he foreclosed on a one-legged widow. But that was Callie's way. She was right, however. If Tom had been made a cripple, it was up to him to do something about it. He swore softly. It was a hell of a thing to consider, ranching. Being tied down to raising cattle and having Callie looking over his shoulder, griping and criticizing and bitching at him all day long. But he guessed there was no way around it. He'd have to ride over and see Tom, and at least talk about it.

Rising, he moved to the front of his cell. Borden had moved away and now stood in the doorway of the building, soaking up a little of the cooling breeze that was drifting in from the Gila River to the north. It was hot for August, hotter than usual.

"Marshal, like for you to read this."

The lawman turned, sauntered lazily back to the cell-block, extended his hand.

"Why? It got something to do with me?"

"Reckon so. Need to get out of here . . . now."

The older man brushed Ryker with a speculative glance, dropped his eyes to the letter. He read slowly, laboriously, his lips moving with each word. Finished, he passed it back to Ryker. "Reason you're in here's because you didn't have the cash to pay your fine. Can't expect me to just up and turn you loose on account of a letter."

"There's a way to collect that fine. I get to the ranch, I'll send the twenty-five dollars first off."

The lawman clawed at his chin. "Something to that, maybe. Your paying off, I mean. Costing the town aplenty to keep you. How'll I know you'll send the money?"

"Because I'm telling you I will. Now, don't get me wrong, Marshal. I'd a hell of a lot rather stay right here in jail, eating three squares a day and taking it easy, than go back to that ranch. But once in a while something turns up that a man plain has to do. That's what I'm looking in the face right now . . . something I've got to do. Anyway, you know where I'll be."

Borden continued his thoughtful consideration. "The judge ain't in town. Won't be back for another three, maybe four weeks. You figure you can have that money here before then?"

Ryker said: "I'll put it on the first stage headed this way."

The marshal turned, picked up the ring of keys on his desk. Moving back to the cell, he unlocked the door.

"I'm agreeing," he said, once again turning to his desk. "And I'm betting that you're a man who'll keep his word. Otherwise, I'm going to come looking for you." Opening a drawer, he pulled out Ryker's belt and holster, added to them the pistol that he'd placed in a different drawer.

"My word's something I've never gone back on yet," Ryker said, strapping on his gear. "Don't aim to start now." He paused, a stillness coming over him. "What happened to the Virdens and Gault?"

Borden shrugged. "Took off, I expect. While I was busy with you, they slipped out the back door of the Montezuma. Ain't seen them since." The lawman studied Ryker through narrowing eyes. "Why? You aiming to look them up?"

"Not 'specially. Just hoping they've had enough. Where'd you put my horse?"

"Gabaldon's stable. Tell Chico I'll settle with him later."

Ryker, about to head for the door, hesitated again. He extended his hand. "Obliged to you, Borden."

The lawman clasped Ryker's hand in his own, nodded curtly. "Just hoping you'll stay obliged."

"Don't fret over it. You'll get your money," Ryker said, and stepped through the doorway into the brilliant sunlight.

He swung his glance up and down the street, located Gabaldon's livery barn at the lower end. Immediately he headed for it, walking in the short, mincing way of a man who detested that mode of travel.

Gabaldon frowned when Ryker stated his desire, glanced toward the jail. Borden evidently gave the stableman a confirming wave, for he turned immediately, headed back into the runway until he came to the stall quartering Ryker's sorrel.

"This is the one, *señor*?" he asked in heavily accented English.

Ryker nodded. Moving to the separating partition upon which his gear had been racked, he saddled and bridled the sorrel, made him ready for the ride. That done, he unhooked his canteen, filled it from the water bucket outside the office door. He had a fair amount of trail grub in his saddlebags—enough, he figured. There would be ranches and a few small towns along the way; he'd depend on them for meals.

Taking the sorrel's headstall in hand, he backed the gelding into the runway, swung him about, and moved to the doorway. In the better light he ran his eye over the horse, nodded appreciatively to Gabaldon, lounging now against the wall, sucking at a thin, brown cigarette.

"You took good care of him."

"A fine animal," the stableman said, shifting his shoulders. Abruptly a frown covered his dark features. He straightened slowly. "*Amigo* . . . those men. . . ."

Ed Virden's shout cut into Chico Gabaldon's words. "Come on out, Mister Gunslinger! This here's one time you ain't dodging me!"

II

Jake Ryker became a nerveless figure in the half light of the stable. He looked beyond the sorrel's head. Ed Virden, Chuck, and the cold-eyed Lenny Gault were in the shadowy rectangle of the passageway lying between the two buildings directly opposite. They could see him easily but were barely visible to him. He sighed heavily. He'd hoped they'd given it up.

"Ryker, you hear me?"

Ryker scanned the area of the street fronting Gabaldon's. There was no cover of any sort. If he tried to make a run for it, they'd have him cold. "I hear you!"

"What's holding you back, Ryker? It'll be just you and me. The boys'll stay out of it."

Ryker reached for the sorrel's reins. He glanced to Chico Gabaldon, standing rigidly against the wall just inside the livery stable's entrance. "There a back door to this place?"

"The end of the runway, to the left. You will not face them?"

"No sense to it . . . and I've got enough trouble with the marshal."

"You coming out, Ryker?"

Ryker turned his attention back upon the dim figures in the passageway. "Forget it, Ed. You've got no call to . . . !"

"Forget, hell!" Virden shouted. "Had me a hunch you was a four-flushing son-of-a-bitch when the chips were down! Giving you one more chance. You don't come out, then I'm coming in after you."

"Let it drop, Virden! I'm not . . . !"

The blast of Ed Virden's pistol drowned Ryker's words. The lean rider sprinted into the street, crouched low, triggering his weapon as he came. His first bullet struck Chico Gabaldon, broke the stableman's arm. The second caught the sorrel in the head, killing the big horse instantly. As the third bullet plucked at Ryker's sleeve, he dropped to one knee, coolly pressed off a shot. Ed Virden paused in mid-stride. A yell ripped from his throat, and then, throwing both arms wide, he fell forward into the dust.

Ryker, not moving, snapped a bullet into the ground a stride ahead of Gault, another at Chuck Virden's feet as they charged from the passageway. Both hauled up short.

"Both of you, drop your irons!"

The two complied slowly. Men were now yelling in the street, and Ryker could hear someone approaching at a run. The marshal, he guessed, and groaned quietly. He'd be lucky if he didn't wind up in a cell again.

"Now, back off!"

Virden and Gault began to move away. Ryker swung a glance to Gabaldon. The stableman was sitting in the doorway to his office. There was a dazed look on his face, and he was moaning softly as he clutched his arm.

"You hit bad?"

"The arm, *señor*. It is broke, I fear. And I bleed."

"I'll get you the doc. . . ."

"Ryker? You still in there?" It was Borden's angry voice.

"Come ahead, Marshal!" Ryker called back. "Somebody get the doc. Gabaldon's been hit."

A cry went up in the street for Vipperman, the local physician. Immediately after, Borden's distinct, nasal voice cut across the hush. "You two! Keep standing right there with your hands up. I got business with you soon as I take care of what's there in the barn. Some of you men tote the dead one over to Vipperman's office. Ryker?"

Ryker, kneeling beside the sorrel, loosening the cinch, glanced up. The lawman was standing just outside the wide doorway, a double-barreled shotgun in his hands. Beyond him, onlookers were venturing closer with cautious steps, not certain yet that it was safe.

"You been shot?"

"No, I was lucky," Ryker replied. "He got Gabaldon in the arm. Killed my horse. Wasn't much else I could do, Marshal, but cut him down. Virden was throwing lead like he'd gone loco."

The lawman cradled his weapon. "No, suppose not. Reckon I ought to feel good there wasn't three, four others hurt by such crazy shooting. In there, Doc," he added as a second figure hurried into the doorway. "It's Chico."

A small, balding man, coatless, green garters pinning back his sleeves, bustled into the runway. He touched Ryker with curious, impersonal eyes, crossed to the stableman, and hunched down beside him.

Ryker, the saddle free, turned his attention to the sorrel's bridle. "This mean I'm back in the jug?"

Borden glanced to the street. Ed Virden's body had been removed. Two or three volunteers were standing near the dead man's companions as if keeping them in hand until the lawman could take charge. "Naw, reckon not," he said. "Even a gunslinger's got a right to defend himself . . . only I wish to God you jaspers'd stay away from my town and do your calling out somewheres else."

"I was trying to dodge him," Ryker said. "Didn't get the chance."

"Sure, sure. I can just see Jake Ryker ducking a shoot-out, especially with somebody he's had trouble with, just like I can see my grandma climbing to the moon."

"*Es verdad,*" Gabaldon spoke from the doorstep. "It is the truth, Marshal. He asked for the back way from my building. But that crazy one, he start to come, shooting. . . ."

Borden grunted. "I expect he wasn't ducking out. He was just aiming to circle around, get a better crack at Virden."

Ryker straightened up, eying the lawman coldly. "I was leaving. It makes no difference to me whether you believe it or not."

Borden studied the redhead's stilled features. Somewhere in the settlement a lonely bell was ringing, tolling in slow, measured beats. Finally the lawman shrugged. "Maybe so. Well, I ain't stopping you. Sooner you're gone, better I'll like it."

"No horse."

Borden swore deeply, swung to Gabaldon, now rising unsteadily with the aid of the physician.

"Chico, the man needs something to ride. I'll see he sends you the money for it."

Gabaldon waved a limp hand toward the rear of the stable. "A chestnut is back there. It wears my brand. For fifty dollars."

"Fifty dollars . . . ?" Ryker began, frowning, and then his jaw snapped shut. He'd take the horse at any price just to get out of town while luck was still with him. "It's a deal," he said. "I'll be needing a bill of sale."

"When the money is returned, the paper will be sent," Gabaldon replied, moving into the runway with Vipperman supporting him.

"No good. Have to get it now."

"It'll be all right," Borden said. "The horse's got his brand. If he don't holler about it, who's going to question your riding it?"

"Somebody who knows him and his brand."

The lawman rubbed angrily at his neck. "God dammit, all right. I'll give you a note saying you ain't no horse thief. That ease your mind?"

"It'll do," Ryker said, lifting the saddle. Then, gathering up the bridle and blanket, he headed for the back of the stable.

He found the chestnut, looked him over casually in the half dark, and felt better about the steep price. Throwing on his gear, he led the horse into the runway, halted. A dozen or more men were gathered in the stable's entrance, talking to the marshal. The lawman saw him, broke away, and came forward, a paper in his hand.

"This here'll get you by," he said, stuffing the folded sheet into Ryker's shirt pocket. "Says you're riding the animal with my authority. Anybody wanting to know why is to get in touch with me."

Ryker nodded. "Obliged to you again, Marshal."

The lawman turned his head aside, spat. "Best way you can oblige me is to get the hell out of my town, and stay out. Trouble comes hunting you, Ryker, same as flies go after sugar. And use Gabaldon's back door. I'd as soon you'd not go riding down the street. Could be Virden's got some more relations and friends hanging around, aching to take a pot shot at you."

Ryker nodded genially. "Sure thing," he said, wheeling the chestnut around. "So long."

III

Five days later, trail-worn, gaunt, his neglected whiskers itching, with sweaty and dust-clogged beard, Jake Ryker pulled to a stop on the crest of a fair-size hill west of the Pecos River and looked to the land across the winding strip of shining silver. This was Ryker range—his actually, or at least half his forty thousand acres, most of it good grass, with year around water, plenty of trees for shade, plus winters that were always mild and summers that usually were not too hot. All in all it was a fine place on which to raise beef, to become a cattleman.

The thought of it still did not stir Jake Ryker. He was far more interested in the nearby crisscrossing trails and the places to which they led—Mexico, the lower end of Texas to the south, Fort Worth, Abilene, Wichita, Dodge City, the Indian Nations to the east; in the north the Colorado hills, and beyond them Wyoming, Montana, and the Dakotas. And to the west the new territory of Arizona, Nevada, California with its Gold Coast and wide open, hell-roaring San Francisco. A man was a fool to tie himself down to a piece of land, he thought morosely, eyes drifting aimlessly across the gray-green sea of grass. Late summer was like this; the hot sun altered the color of the growth from emerald to sage. And it hadn't been a wet spring. The Pecos, always low at this time of year, looked below normal.

He sighed, realizing that the lack or the surplus of water was to become one of his problems—if he stayed on. It seemed to Jake Ryker that every cattleman he knew was always worrying about something—the weather, disease, the market, rustlers. Rustlers! Callie had mentioned something about rustlers in her letter. Evidently they were suffering heavy losses at the hands of cattle thieves. He could see how it could be a problem for the Circle R—too small to support a large crew; it was hard to control rustling when you were short of riders.

Something else he'd have to shoulder, he thought, and touching the chestnut with his rowels, he rode down the hill. The gelding had been a good buy after all; he'd withstood the hard trip across New Mexico well. Maybe he wasn't the fastest animal on four legs but he had plenty of bottom, could stay in there and work the whole day through.

Ryker cut down for the river on a long slant, pointing for a place where he had previously forded. He was still well below Circle R's buildings which were not visible to him because of the land's rolling contours. He should arrive there around midday, right at dinnertime. He grinned at that realization. Callie would have some pointed remark to make on that. Well, she was the one who'd written the letter. His coming was her idea, and he'd never bothered them but once. That was when he needed $100 to help a friend in trouble. It hadn't seemed much to ask for. What the hell, he was half owner of the place and had never taken a penny of its profits. A lousy $100 wasn't much interest to draw for his half ownership. He smiled wryly, scratched at his beard. He needed another $75 to pay off Borden and Chico

Gabaldon. Callie would holler to beat hell when she heard about that.

He reached the bank of the Pecos, followed along its grassy edge to where it sloped down to the water. The chestnut hesitated, ears pricking. Ryker spurred the big horse gently, and he moved out into the flowing stream, lower even than it had looked from the crest of the hill.

Gaining the opposite shore, Ryker guided the gelding up through a thick stand of nodding sunflowers onto solid footing, and moved into the long band of trees that grew along the river's east bank. Shortly he was in their cooling midst, enjoying the leafy shield from the hot sun. A cottontail scooted out from under the chestnut's hoofs, bobbed off at top speed to disappear into the low brush between the tree trunks. Somewhere a dove was cooing plaintively while a jay scolded impatiently.

All about Ryker was the warm, moist smell of the soil, of saw oats, wild hay, and of the red and white flowered beard plants that grew in such profusion in the sunny places. He'd all but forgotten about them, recalled then how as a child he'd often walked through the beds, deliberately crushing the stalks with his feet to release the musky scent. That was a long time ago, twenty years or more, and since then things had changed greatly. The memory of his early life was something of a blur and there was little he could accurately recall—his ma, his pa, Tom, the bleakness of their existence—and he never forgot the wishful little ditty his father was forever humming:

> *Come some day, the great day,*
> *I'll be rich and riding a tall horse,*
> *setting high on a fine saddle.*

But the time had never come, only bad years, and a few good ones, and then there was the spring when his ma had died, and a year later when his pa had followed. That was the knife that slashed the final tie for him—the passing of John Ryker. He'd managed to get along with Tom up till then for the sake of his parents, even with Callie who had become a member of the family just after his mother had died. The day they laid Big John beside his wife on the slope east of the house, where they could look out over the land they'd loved and labored over for so long, however, was the day Jake Ryker made up his mind to get out. And he did, taking his leave before that same sun had set. Twice since then he had seen Tom and Callie. Twice too often. That's what it had amounted to, and he'd sworn never to return again, but here he was riding across Circle R range.

Ryker pulled up short. A distance ahead in a small clearing a half a dozen riders had gathered. A seventh man, hands tied behind his back and astride a lean, spotted horse, was halted beneath the extended limb of a broadly spreading tree. There was a rope around his neck and one of the riders was endeavoring to throw the loose end of it over the horizontal limb.

Ryker's mouth hardened. He'd seen enough of mob justice to know that it ordinarily was wrong, that the victim usually turned out to be innocent of the crime he was being made to pay the penalty for. Regardless, rope law was not the kind any man should adhere to. Drawing his .45, he spurred the chestnut into a fast lope down the dappled lanes between the cottonwoods. Halfway to the clearing he fired a shot into the heavily leafed tree overshadowing the men, releasing a shower of green fragments.

Startled, the riders wheeled hurriedly, angrily. One reached for the weapon on his hip. Ryker snapped a warning bullet at him, froze his arm to his side.

"All of you, hold off!" he shouted, and racing up brought the chestnut to a stiff-legged halt.

IV

The men on the ground surveyed Ryker coldly. The rider with the rope about his neck heaved an audible sigh.

"I'm thanking you, Jake."

Ryker's brows drew together. Keeping his gun drifting back and forth over the small crowd, he swung off the saddle slowly, squinted at the near victim. Nat Clover—they'd ridden shotgun together for the old Nebraska-Kansas Stage Line three or four years back, had once been fairly close friends. Then he'd quit the company and moved on. Later he'd heard that Clover had cut loose, too.

"You about to pay for your evil ways, Nat?"

"All a mistake. I. . . ."

"Mistake, hell!" An old cowpuncher somewhere in his sixties took a quick step forward. His small, dark eyes snapped angrily. "We caught this here jasper cold . . . the damned rustler! Mister, you're horning in on something that sure ain't none of your business."

"Maybe," Ryker replied quietly.

"We got proof," the man beside the old cowpuncher said. He was well up in years, also, had straw-colored hair, and a nose that had been flattened against his ruddy face. "You disbelieve us, then you just take yourself a gander at that butchered steer a-laying over in that coulée."

"I'll take your word for it," Ryker said, and shifted his attention back to Clover. "What about it?"

The man on the spotted horse shrugged. "They's a steer over there, sure enough, only it wasn't me that butchered him. Was riding through here, heading for Fort Worth. Heard somebody take off real sudden-like through the brush, so I cut in to have a look. Seen that steer a laying there. Throat'd been cut. Was just a-setting there, looking at him and wondering, when this bunch snuck in on me, holding iron. Next thing I knew I was waiting

23

to get my neck stretched. You mind untying my hands, Jake? Makes me real nervous to think what'll happen if this jughead I'm forking takes a notion to leave."

Ryker, circling the glowering cowpunchers, moved to Clover's side. Taking his belt knife from its leather sheath, he sliced through the cords that bound the man's wrists. Jaw set, he faced the others. "You aimed to hang a man on that kind of evidence?"

"Was aplenty, far as we could see," the older cowpuncher said. "We been losing us a lot of beef. . . ."

"Nothing in that proves he had anything to do with it."

"That butchered steer, reckon it's proof."

"Proves somebody did some butchering, but not that it was him. You look to see if he had a bloody knife on him? There any spots on his clothes, his boots? A man that takes it on himself to carve up a live steer has got one hell of a job on his hands, and he'd sure get a lot of blood on himself."

The two elderly men exchanged glances, swung their attention to the remaining members of their party. All were considerably younger.

"Well, maybe we was going at it a mite hasty-like. But seeing that steer, and him being there. . . ."

"Good and handy," Ryker cut in sardonically.

"Yeah, reckon that was it, but. . . ."

Ryker heard a thud behind him, looked over his shoulder.

Nat Clover had removed the rope from his neck, thrown it to the ground. "Close," he muttered, massaging his throat. "Too god-damn' close." He turned his pale eyes to Ryker. "Sure beholden to you for that one, partner. Now, maybe I'd best do me some settling up with these rope-happy holy rollers. Which one of you's got my cutter?"

One of the younger cowpunchers pulled out the pistol he'd thrust under his waistband. "Reckon I got it," he muttered, and handed it, butt forward, to Clover. He faced Ryker squarely, frowned. "You making us let him go?"

"Not making you do anything except forget lynching him. You figure you've got proof enough to take him to a sheriff or a marshal, go right ahead. I won't stop you. I'm just dead set against your using a rope on him."

The young rider glanced uncertainly at his friends. They would all be Circle R cowhands, Jake guessed. He grinned faintly, thinking of Tom's reaction when word of what had taken place reached his ears. And Callie's.

"Well, I guess we ain't got no sure-fire proof, leastwise none we could talk to the law about. Ain't nothing to do but let him go." It was one of the older men, the one who had spoken up first. He raised a bony finger, leveled it at Clover. "But you'd best remember this. This here's Circle R range you're a trespassing on, and strangers ain't welcome on it! If you're smart, you'll stay off 'cause next time maybe you won't be so lucky."

Nat Clover's dark face was cold, expressionless. He settled back on his heels as his shoulders hunched slightly. Ryker, seeing all the old signs, shook his head and stepped in front of the man. "Let it go, Nat. These boys are only doing their jobs."

The squat man's features did not change. "Nobody horses me around the way they did, throws a rope about my neck, and gets away with it."

"Let it go," Ryker said again, quietly.

Clover turned his eyes to Ryker. For a brief time their glances locked, and then he looked away, shrugged his thick shoulders. "Sure, Jake, whatever you say."

"And about riding across this range. Might be smart to stick close to the river. Nobody'll fault you for being there."

"That's what I'll do. You headed east?"

"No, not right now."

The oldster with the straw hair shifted from one foot to another, shoved his head forward. "You're mighty free telling folks what they can do on somebody else's property. Just who the hell are . . . ?"

"Who are you?" Ryker broke in.

"Me? Name's Vern Thatch, if it's any of your put in."

"Happens it is. Who're the rest?"

Thatch looked hard at Ryker for a long breath, brushed at the sweat gathered on his leathery brow. He seemed uncertain as to whether he should answer or not. Something in the tall redhead's manner brought him to a decision. Jerking a thumb at the other older man, he said: "He's Ford, Wilbur Ford. Young one there with all the hair is Sam Neff. Next to him, that's Amos Quinn. The *vaquero* calls hisself Cristobal Sanchez. Last one with the fancy vest is Carl Delaney. Now, who might you be?"

"You all work for the Circle R, I take it?"

"You take it right, else we wouldn't be here."

"Makes sense," Ryker said mildly. He swung about to Clover. "Expect you'll be riding on."

Clover, back in the saddle and settled, bobbed his head. "Reckon I will. You might as well throw in with me and come along. Hear things are mighty good around Fort Worth."

"Later maybe. Could change my mind."

Nat Clover nodded again. "Knowing you, I'll be waiting at the first town on the way," he said, and moved out. " 'Luck."

" 'Luck," Ryker replied, a slight wistfulness in his tone. Fort Worth always was a good town.

"You ain't never got around to giving me a answer," Thatch pressed testily.

Ryker pulled his attention away from Clover's departing figure. "Seems I haven't. Name's Ryker."

Thatch stared. The others stirred, glanced about. Wilbur Ford hawked, spat, clawed at his chin. "You'd be that brother of Tom's I've heard him mention now and then."

"That's me, Jake Ryker. They sent me a letter quite a spell back. Chased me all over the country, finally caught up in Lordsburg." He broke it off there, seeing no point in going into further details regarding his presence there. "Tom any better?"

"No better'n nor worse'n he'll ever be. Got hisself busted up something awful by that horse."

"Callie said he'd been thrown. Never said much else."

"You come to take over the place?" It was the youngster, Sam Neff. "If so, I reckon I'll just draw my time and move on."

Ryker's brows lifted. "Why?"

Neff shifted uncomfortably. "Was sort of high-handed, the way you took up for that rustler. Tom and his missus sure ain't going to like it."

Ryker's genial smile covered the edge to his words. "I don't give a god damn whether they do or not. Nat Clover's no rustler."

"You only got him saying that."

"Enough, far as I'm concerned. Known him for quite a spell. Been in a few tight spots together. He'd not lie to me, no more'n he'd rustle one steer. Maybe you're quitting because you don't like being caught in the wrong. I've seen a few cowhands that way . . . mostly young."

"No sense leaving," Ford said then. "Hell, we was all in on it. And if Mister Ryker says that bird's all right, it's good enough for me." The old man reached out a gnarled hand. "I'm right proud to meet you, Mister Ryker."

"Make it Jake," Ryker said, taking Ford's fingers into his own. He went through the ritual of meeting with each of the other riders. "This the whole crew?" he asked when it was done.

"The whole kit and caboodle," Ford replied. "Ain't running much stock. Things ain't been so good, what with Tom all stove up and. . . ."

"And the rustling going on," Thatch broke in.

"I was thinking about that," Ryker said. "If you're the crew, who's looking after the herd? Be a real good time for rustlers to just help themselves."

Ford looked down in embarrassment. The others shuffled about nervously, turned away.

"Expect you're right, Mister . . . uh . . . Jake," Wilbur mumbled. "Was a fool stunt, us all sashaying up here, but we allowed as how we had us a cow thief for certain." He placed his attention on the *vaquero* and the other younger men. "You boys get yourselves back to where the stock's grazing fast. Me and Vern'll rustle us up a bite to eat, then spell you off till supper."

The riders moved off at once, going to their horses at a hurried, shambling gait, mounting quickly and whirling off as if anxious to be gone.

Jake glanced at the remaining men. "Expect I'd best be riding on and tell Tom and Callie I'm here. You headed for the ranch?"

Both nodded. "We been doing the night-hawking," Vern Thatch explained. "Reason we ain't pounding leather along with the other boys. Fact is, we ought to be sleeping right now, but it was so danged hot we couldn't do it. So we rode out to see how things was. Got here just as the boys collared that rus-
. . . that friend of your'n."

"I see," Jake said, swinging to the saddle. The four Circle R cowpunchers were just topping out on a ridge a quarter mile distant. Nat Clover had long since dropped from sight. "All of you been with Tom for a long time?"

Thatch paused as he prepared to mount. "Not too long. Me and Wilbur've been here the longest, excepting for old Cocinero . . . he's the Mex cook."

"I recollect him," Ryker said, cutting the chestnut about. "Was here when I left."

"Expect he was doing the cooking even before your pa died."

"He was," Ryker said, and urged the gelding into a lope.

He had no liking for what lay ahead at the ranch, but the sooner he got there, the quicker he'd get the meeting with Tom and Callie over with.

V

The barn and the main house had been enlarged. The crew's quarters and the lesser sheds looked just the same. There were two new corrals, and the big cottonwoods that spread their welcome shade over all were even larger than he had remembered. Otherwise, there was little change, that same bleak, colorless look he'd expected. As bound by drudgery as his mother had been, even she had found time to encourage a few wildflowers around the yard in an effort to dispel the desolation. He'd thought Callie could have done the same.

He saw her then. She was standing in the doorway of the main house, hands on hips, streaked, blonde hair untidy and straggling down about her face, which had the shine of sweat upon it. She was wearing a faded, gray dress with a square-hemmed apron, one corner of which had been folded up and tucked under the waist tie for some reason. Callie Ryker had never been a beautiful woman, but she had been attractive in a severe sort of way. She could still be if she'd take the time to fix herself up a bit—that sleazy, gray dress for instance.

"So you finally got here."

She spoke even before he pulled his horse to a stop at the hitch rack. He stared at her wordlessly, temper, as always, stirring within him. It would never change, he supposed, the hostility and antagonism she felt for him.

"Letter was a long time catching up," he said, and swung from the saddle.

"Just what I thought. If you'd ever take a job somewheres, stay with it instead of running off, tramping around. . . ."

"Now, Callie," he cut in softly, firmly, shaking his head. "How's Tom?"

Callie Ryker shrugged, pushed open the screen door, and stepped out onto the porch. The door banged shut, dislodged a cloud of powdery dust that drifted slowly to the floor.

"The same."

Ryker wound the chestnut's leathers around the crossbar, started for the gallery. Behind him Thatch and Ford had curved off to the bunkhouse, were dismounting in that stiff-jointed way of men grown too old for the saddle.

"Was real sorry to hear about the accident," Ryker said halting, one foot in the yard, the other on the edge of the porch.

Callie's shoulders moved again. "Would have to happen to *him*," she said in an exasperated tone, and let her words hang.

Jake gave her a tight grin. "Instead of to some no-good saddle bum like me," he finished. "I want to see him."

"He's sleeping. Had a bad night. You'll have to wait an hour or two." She paused, considered him warily. "You here to stay or are you just passing through?" The edge to her voice was razor sharp.

"Depends. Not keen about it, but if I'm needed and it can be worked out, reckon I will. Either way it'll cost you seventy-five dollars, my coming here. Owe for my horse and . . . and another debt."

She turned, eyes flaring and sharp, gave him a long look, and then came half about, stared out over the sun-baked hardpan to the range beyond. The weariness, the worn hopelessness of her were reflected in the slack, lined planes of her face, the lassitude that gripped her. In spite of himself, Jake Ryker felt a stirring of pity for the woman.

"Wish't I could believe that, that you'd help."

"I mean what I've already said, but you know what the problem's always been."

"Callie? Who's out there?"

At the call from inside the house, she turned slowly to the door. "It's Jake. He's got here."

"Jake! Bring him in here."

Ryker stepped up onto the porch, crossed over, and entered the house without waiting for her to relay the request. Moving through the familiar kitchen, now a sort of sitting room since the cook handled all meal preparations in an adjacent cook shack, he stepped into the room that had been his parents' sleeping quarters. The small square that he and Tom had occupied lay off the opposite wall.

He moved to the head of the bed, masking the shock he felt at sight of the frail, broken man, once tall and dark and powerful enough to upend a thousand-pound steer, extended his hand. "Good to see you again, Tom."

The older Ryker responded limply. "Same here, kid. Wasn't sure you'd come when Callie decided she'd best write you."

Jake shook his head. "Hell, you ought've known I would. Just sorry it took so long. Things are looking kind of bad, I hear."

Tom nodded. Reaching back, he grasped the iron uprights of the bed's headpiece, drew himself to a sitting position. Jake leaned forward to assist, drew back when his brother frowned. "Only a few things I can do for myself. This is one of them. Callie tell you about all our troubles?"

"Some," Jake answered, sitting down on the edge of the hard mattress. "Ran into your crew out on the range. Were about to string up a fellow I know . . . for rustling."

"About to?"

"I stopped them. Man wasn't guilty."

Tom Ryker's drawn face turned grim. "They must've had proof of some kind."

"They found him near a butchered steer, figured he did it."

"Sounds to me pretty much like he might have."

Jake said: "No, I know the man. He's no rustler. Anyway, you don't lynch somebody on evidence like that. Seen too many mistakes made along those lines."

"What happened to this . . . this friend of yours?"

"Turned him loose, sent him on his way."

Tom Ryker's jaw clicked shut. "God dammit all to hell, Jake! Here we're being stole blind and you. . . ."

"He's not the man you're looking for," Jake said stubbornly. "I know Nat Clover from times back and. . . ."

"You know! Jesus God, the kind you run with, I. . . ."

Jake Ryker drew himself up slowly. A tautness had slipped into him, now held him in a firm grasp. "It'll never change will it, Tom? Just no way on this earth for you to see me except as the no-account kid brother who doesn't have a lick of sense."

"Hell, I'm sorry," the older Ryker said after a pause. "Guess this being laid up has done something to me."

"No, that's not it, and you know it. It was this way before. The years haven't changed a thing."

"Why shouldn't he feel that way?" Callie said from the doorway. "You ever do anything to prove him wrong?"

"Maybe not to your way of thinking," Jake said without turning. "But everybody doesn't look at things the same as you do. Lots of folks figure other things are important, things you think are nothing."

"Trail bums, saloon swampers, dance-hall girls, gamblers." Callie ground out the words as if they were epithets. "They're the kind of people you're talking about."

"Maybe, and there's a few others, too. But no matter. It's something we'll never see eye to eye on."

"You can be certain of that," Callie snapped. "And if you think for one minute I. . . ."

"Now, wait," Tom Ryker cut in, raising a limp hand. "We're going at this all wrong. No use us ranting at Jake. What's been is past. It's over and done with. We got no call to go raking him over the coals just because he ain't done the way we figure he ought. . . ."

Jake's shoulders lifted, settled resignedly. "See? Just what I'm talking about. But you're dead right about one thing. There's no point hashing over the past because I plain won't listen to it. That clear?"

Tom shrugged his thin shoulders, nodded. Jake swung his curt gaze to Callie. She looked away, her answer grudging but there, nevertheless.

"Then that's settled. The way I've lived my life is my business, and from here on I don't see that there's any need to complain, either one of you. I could have been ragging you regularly for my half share of everything this place has made. . . ."

"Made?" Callie interrupted. "We haven't made a dollar since the day Tom got hurt!"

"You had plenty of good years before that when you were getting the benefit of my half. But don't get me wrong. I'm not complaining. You were doing the work, you were entitled to all you made and stashed away."

"Which was damned little," Tom said bitterly. "And that's 'most gone now, what with all the doctors and all the medicines. They even brought some specialist down here all the way from Albuquerque. Cost like hell. And then me just laying here with the place going to pot."

Jake brushed at the sweat on his face, considered deeply. It wasn't what he wanted but there are times when a man is forced to accept a duty. "I'm here to stop that," he said finally, coming to a decision. "But I'll do it my way. I want that understood between us right now. I'll run this ranch the way I think best."

"And run it straight into the ground," Callie said acidly.

Jake Ryker folded his arms across his chest, jutted his bearded chin at her, and met her eye to eye. "Then why the hell did you send for me, if you think that's what I'd do?"

Her gaze wavered, broke, shifted to the open window. A light breeze was drifting in, fanning the lace curtains, relieving, to some extent, the breathless heat. "Nothing else I could think of. I . . . I wanted you to come . . . help."

"To come and take orders from you, that's what you mean, isn't it?" Jake demanded. "I can see that now. Ought've had sense enough to see it sooner, but I was thinking about Tom. Well, it won't work."

The elder Ryker pulled himself a bit higher on the bed. His sallow face showed alarm. "Won't work? That mean you . . . ?"

"Means just what I said before. If I'm to take over this ranch, I'll take it over all the way, bottle, barrel, and bung starter."

"You don't even know. . . ."

"I'll call the shots, all of them, and do the deciding and the planning. You're in no shape to. Face up to it, Tom, no man ever yet run a ranch from a bedstead or a rocking chair."

"Maybe not, but that's no reason why I can't be in on the decisions of what's to be done."

"There's plenty of reasons. The biggest one being that we don't agree on anything. We never have, expect we never will."

Both Callie and Tom were silent, admitting to themselves, no doubt, the truth of the statement. Finally the woman stirred. "Well, I don't suppose things can get much worse than they are. Either way seems we're bound to go broke and lose everything."

"We might," Jake admitted, "but I don't figure it that way. One thing you maybe don't know. All this time you've had me pegged for running around the country, drinking and raising hell and getting into shooting scrapes and the like, is not exactly true. I held a few jobs, some of them pretty good ones, in fact. Was the ramrod for a spread up Wyoming way once, one so big you could lose this cabbage patch on its south range. I'm no greenhorn when it comes to running a spread and handling cattle. Few other times, too, but there's no need going into it."

Tom studied him silently for a long minute when he finished, finally shifted his dull eyes to Callie. "I can't see as we've got a choice, and maybe we ought to be grateful."

"Don't want you to be grateful. Just want you to savvy now that if I'm to take over, it's to be with no halter ropes hanging from my neck. There's to be no cutting in, no interfering."

Tom nodded wearily. "We're agreeing. You'll run the place. Could be Callie and me'll move into town, get us a little house."

Callie flung her husband a surprised look. "Leave here . . . everything . . . to him?"

"It would be a good idea," Jake said approvingly. "Get you away from a lot of stewing and fretting."

"Just something we can think about," Tom said, continuing to ignore Callie. "What do you say?"

Jake was silent briefly, then bobbed his head. "Guess we can say it's settled. I'll take hold, get things running right. First off, I've got to put a stop to the rustling that's going on."

"No," Tom cut in flatly, "first off you're to go after some cattle I agreed to buy."

Jake Ryker's jaw tightened. Anger flashed in his eyes, and then a sort of desperation came over him. He gave his brother a long, straight look, shrugged. He should have known it would be this way.

"The hell with it," he said with finality, and turned for the door.

VI

"Now wait a damn' minute."

At Tom's anxious protest Jake Ryker never slowed but continued on for the doorway. Callie, standing squarely before him, did not stir, simply watched him with her cold eyes.

"No use. It won't work. Neither one of you'll let it," he said. "Saw a sample of that right then."

Callie bristled at once. "You think it'll be easy for him to sit back and let you or anybody else take over everything he's worked like a dog all these years to build?"

Jake, forced to halt, studied her set features. "You think it'll be easy for me to give up the kind of living I'm used to . . . and enjoy? Anyway, I think he and you had better cotton to the idea quick or there won't be anything left of the Circle R for me or anybody else to take over."

"Never meant that to sound the way it came out," Tom said gruffly. "Only with everything piling up the way it is and going sour, I. . . ."

"Which will be my worry, not yours."

Callie drew aside, placed her shoulders against the wall adjacent to the doorway. The bitterness that possessed her was like a mask, flattening her features, pocketing her eyes in deep, dark circles. "He's right, Tom," she admitted, defeated. "We've got no choice. Either we let him run it his way or we lose everything we've got. Far as I can see, the chances are about even."

Jake gave her a side look. "Thanks for the vote of confidence," he said dryly. "I expect the best thing you can do is find yourself a foreman to run things, let him handle your troubles and fight off the rustlers."

"Dammit, I said I was sorry," Tom snapped irritably. "What more you want? And there ain't no sense in you flying off the handle. Thought by now you'd have outgrown that."

"Never seem to have the problem except when I'm around you," Jake replied evenly. "You still think I'm ten years old, and until you get that out of your head, I can't see's there's any use trying to get along."

"Good God!" Tom shouted, abruptly furious. "What do you

want me to do, get down on my knees and beg?"

"Nope," Jake said quietly, turning completely about to face his brother. "I just want you to stay out of my hair. It's the only way I can help. And I'll do a job for you until I can find a good man to hire on as foreman."

"Foreman? You mean you won't stay on permanent?"

"No sense in trying. Be no satisfying you and Callie long as you're on the place. But I'll be here until I can locate the right man."

Callie's eyes held a sullen glow. Her lips moved to shape a quick, caustic remark, and then she thought better of it, and the words were never spoken.

Tom Ryker stirred, settled back resignedly. "All right, Jake, all right. Let's quit ragging over it. You take hold, run the Circle R the way you think best. Callie and me'll stay out of your way, have nothing to do with it. Leastwise we will after you've got back with the cattle I've bought."

"Bought?"

"What I was telling you. Got to pick up two hundred head from Park Justin, over on the Texas Brazos. Can get them for ten dollars a throw if I . . . we'll take them now. Next spring the same beef will bring double that price at the railhead."

Jake nodded his approval. "Sounds smart. Two hundred head all he'll let us have?"

"No, but it's all the cash we can spare."

"About all we've got, you mean," Callie corrected.

Tom Ryker said: "Yeah, guess that's closer to the truth. But that two hundred head, added to what we can afford to sell from our regular herd next spring . . . assuming we get the rustling stopped . . . will get us out of the hole and put us in pretty fair shape again."

"How much time've we got to pick up that stock?"

"Should've been there a month ago. There was no way I could

make it, and nobody I could send."

"There's not many we want to trust with two thousand dollars in cash," Callie said pointedly.

"Including me, I suspect," Jake added, unable to withhold the comment.

Callie only sniffed. Tom said: "Don't mean I wouldn't trust Will Ford or Thatch. Both of them are as honest as the day is long, but you just don't unload that kind of responsibility on a man. Don't see as there's any problem where you're concerned."

"A man packing that much cash has got himself a big problem," Jake said. "Word slips out he's carrying that kind of money and every owlhoot north of the Mexican border will be out to bushwhack him. There's got to be a better way. How about a bank draft?"

"What bank? Closest one where you can get a draft is in El Paso. Riding that far is about as chancy as the trip to Justin's, maybe more so."

Jake Ryker gave that some thought, agreed. Then: "Whereabouts on the Brazos is Justin's spread?"

"Near Ben City. Good two hundred and fifty miles from here. Figured to take Sam Neff and the *vaquero* with me. Three can handle a herd that size."

"Best not to pull anybody off the range," Jake said. "Running the place short-handed could lose us a lot of steers to the rustlers. Might cost us more'n we'd make on the two hundred."

"Hell, one man sure couldn't drive two hundred. . . ."

"I wouldn't try. Best to pick up a couple of cowhands over there, hire them on for a month. What time is left when we got back, they could spend helping us clean out the rustlers."

"It'd cost money. I'm paying thirty a month and. . . ."

"Cheap insurance." Jake was dismissing what he considered petty arguing. "You got a letter or something from this Justin? I'd hate to ride that far and have him tell me there's no deal."

"Yeah, there's a letter, but you won't need it. Justin's in the business. Done some buying from him before."

"Best I take the letter anyway, just so's there'll be no changing of the price."

An eagerness had come over Tom Ryker. "Then . . . from the way you're talking . . . you're staying on?"

"Long enough to get things back in shape and find you a good man. I'll do that if we understand there's to be no horning in and backbiting and getting in my way." The elder Ryker bobbed his head. "It's understood. I want you to say it, too, Callie."

The woman shrugged indifferently. "All right, I'll go get the money."

"No rush," Jake said, eyes narrowing cynically. "Maybe the saloons and gambling halls won't open until sundown." A half smile pulling at his lips, he glanced at Tom. His brother was studying him intently, almost with apprehension. "Don't fret," Jake said then with a laugh. "The money'll be safe, safe as it is right here in this house. But I won't be needing it until morning. I aim to pull out around sunup."

Tom relaxed. "Good enough. Meanwhile, you'd best pile your belongings in the other bedroom, the one we used to sleep in."

"All the same to you, I'll throw in with the crew in the bunkhouse. I want to get a mite better acquainted with them. Travel light, anyway. Never pack much gear."

"How about trail grub and the like? You want Callie to tell Cocinero to fix you up?"

"I'll tell him," Jake said, making a point of it. "Just as soon as I can walk through that door and get to the kitchen. After that, I'm calling the crew together, setting up a regular range watch, day and night, over the herd. Every man will be carrying a cocked Winchester, and nobody had better fall down on his job or he won't be working on this ranch."

"Now, Jake, they're all good men. You can't expect them to. . . ."

"I'll be expecting plenty," Ryker said. "Best they know that right off." Abruptly he grinned, passed through the doorway, and struck for the back entrance. "See you around suppertime."

VII

The morning was a fine one, sweet and clear, before the day's heat began to lay its shimmering blanket across the land. Jake Ryker, astride the chestnut, followed the well-marked trail that would take him eventually to Park Justin's spread on the Brazos with the attentive appreciation of a man who loved and never tired of the grandeur and solitude of the vast countryside. It would be a long, three-day ride, one that could possibly be stretched to four, depending on the big gelding's ability to stand up under the steady traveling. But the horse had pretty well proven itself on the trip from Lordsburg to the Circle R, and there should be no problem now.

They had just started, and Jake guessed he should be more concerned about the money he was carrying—$2,000 in paper and gold pieces in a belt strapped around his middle. He swore softly. It was a lousy bit of bad luck. No man with any sense would tote that much cash about on his person. It was an open invitation to robbery and death if it leaked out which, somehow, such news always seemed to do. A lot of men had been shot out of the saddle for a tenth of that amount.

He'd taken every precaution possible to avoid the word being spread. Only Tom and Callie knew of it, thus he felt fairly secure at that end of the line. That Thatch and the other Circle R cowpunchers would guess and speculate was unavoidable, but he expected to be far enough away from the Pecos country to be safe if they did spill a few hints. The main thing necessary,

he felt, was that he permit no inkling of it to escape him personally, and there was but one way to accomplish that—keep an
ordinarily tight lip buttoned even tighter.

He glanced to the warming sun, now well above the horizon
and beginning to climb into its curved canopy of flawless blue.
It would be another hot one, he could see that—but then it was
seldom the summer days weren't scorchers in the Staked Plains
country. A man simply girded himself to face them, to accept
the blistering heat, the sweat, the powdery dust, and an occasional brush with Indians. He shifted in the saddle. The horse
was moving along at an easy lope, covering the miles easily and
efficiently. If he could hold to the pace, they would make it to
Taladega, sprawled half in New Mexico, half in Texas, by
nightfall with no difficulty. He could spend the night there
quietly, getting another early start the next morning. Brushing
at the sweat already gathered on his face, Ryker grinned wryly.
He'd best be damned careful in Taladega. It was a wild, tough,
wide-open town since its divided position made law enforce-
ment practically an impossibility. It was a prevalent joke that a
man committing a crime on one side of the street had but to
cross over to the other to avoid the consequences of his act, so
distinct was the lack of co-operation between the New Mexico
and Texas law officers.

Thoughtfully Jake stared ahead into the building heat. If
something happened and he lost the $2,000 through no fault of
his own, he'd never be able to convince Callie and Tom of his
innocence. They'd believe that he'd gambled it away, lent it to
some worthless trail acquaintance, or through some act of
carelessness while in the company of such friends had allowed it
to slip through his fingers. He wasn't about to let it happen—
not under any circumstances short of being killed. It wasn't
only that Tom and his wife needed a few mistaken impressions
of him corrected—mainly that he was not a man capable of

handling any task assigned him—but, hell, when you came right down to boot heels, half of that money actually was his. And while that did not make the other half any less important, it did place a somewhat different premium upon its value. But he'd have no trouble. He knew Taladega, was fully aware of its dangers and pitfalls, and could easily avoid them. He'd be there for the one night only, anyway, and a man could hardly get himself in trouble just riding in, having a meal and maybe a drink, and then crawling into bed. He'd not even bother to look up the few friends he had there. Not that he didn't trust them, but it simply made good sense not to advertise his presence.

At noon he halted in a deep arroyo where an overhanging cedar cast a small pool of shade. He rested the chestnut for the better part of an hour, taking advantage of the break to eat a bit of the lunch old Cocinero, who had been pleased to see him again, had prepared. It was too hot to make coffee. He washed down the bread and meat with a swallow or two of water from his canteen. Afterward he gave the gelding a drink by soaking a rag and squeezing it dry into the horse's mouth. Then he rode on.

He met no one, saw no one in the distance. It was a glittering, baked land inhabited only by jack rabbits, snakes, a few horned larks, and whip-tailed lizards that were all making a point of keeping out of the sun's direct rays.

Late in the day, with the smoke of Taladega hanging in a dirty gray smudge against the horizon, he did see a coyote, a lean, shaggy, starved-looking brute that watched him from a safe distance with lowered head and yellow eyes. And then, near sundown, he encountered two riders heading west, choosing to begin their journey across the flat in the cooler night hours. They were strangers, cattlemen from their appearance and tack. Both lifted their hands in the customary, reserved salutation of passing wayfarers unknown to each other but acquainted through the fact of being mutually engaged in traversing a lonely land.

Lamps were being lit when he reached the edge of town and turned into its main street. Quite a number of horses were at the hitch racks, and he noted a good many rigs drawn up in the wagon yards. It occurred to him that the settlement was unusually busy, and then he realized it was Saturday, the customary time for ranchers and homesteaders to bring their families to town for shopping and for the cowhands who could get away to come in and slake their thirst for drink and companionship.

Riding slowly down the center of the wide lane, ankle-deep in loose dust that had not felt the kiss of rain in months, Ryker's glance cut back and forth. It had been a bit more than a year since he was last in Taladega. He noticed small change. The *LONE STAR SALOON & GAMBLING HALL—GIRLS* was still by far the largest, most active, and best-lighted edifice on the Texas side of the street. *THE CATTLEMAN'S HOTEL,* the *ACE-HIGH CAFÉ, THE EMPORIUM—GENERAL MERCHANDISE FOR ALL* were companion business firms still in operation, along with any number of small, hole-in-the-wall saloons and shops. On the New Mexico side, it was the *GOLD DOLLAR HOTEL* with its connecting liquor, gambling, and dancing facilities that dominated all other establishments. Ranged along with it were the competitors of the firms facing them in a row from the opposite bank: *J. GRUNSFELD—— THE HOME STORE, MISS EVE'S LADIES & CHILDRENS READY-TO-WEAR, GORDON'S GUN AND SADDLE SHOP, ESSLINGER'S GENT'S CLOTHING & BOOTS.* All were familiar if fading signs to him. There were many persons moving along the board sidewalks and loafing on the landings of the business concerns. Several were familiar to Ryker, but he was careful to return their glances with only a slight nod and did not slow the chestnut's walk, but simply continued on until he came to the Gold Dollar Hotel. There, he veered from the street into an alley that came in at right angles and led to the hotel's stable a short distance behind it.

Reaching the broad, squat structure, he came out of the saddle stiffly, glad to be on solid ground after so many hours. Giving instructions to the hostler as to the gelding's care, he slung his saddlebags over his shoulder and made his way to the hostelry's back entrance.

Pulling open the door, he stepped into the narrow hallway. It was cool inside the building, shielded from the heat by two-foot thick adobe walls, and he felt a glow of anticipation when he visualized a night's sleep in the comfort of the hotel's interior. Moving down the hall, he entered the lobby and crossed to the desk, ignoring the noisy clamor in the adjoining saloon, which was connected to the receiving part of the Gold Dollar Hotel by a wide archway. Thick, green portières hung in the opening but, as far as Jake knew, the heavy drapes had never been drawn.

"Need a room," he said to the waiting clerk.

The elderly man with a beet-red face and wearing an eye-shade bobbed his head. "Sure thing, Mister Ryker," he said, and pushed a register and a stub of pencil to the front of the counter.

Jake studied the clerk briefly, guessed he was being remembered from his last stopover, and taking up the pencil, signed in.

"Be Number Five," the clerk said, reaching for a key. "Top of the stairs, to the left."

Jake turned to the narrow flight of steps. Something crashed to the floor in the saloon and a woman's laugh pealed out above the shouts and cursing of a man and the muffled rumble of general conversation. Still ignoring the confusion, Jake continued mounting the steps slowly, wondering perhaps if he wouldn't have been better off to camp out on the flat. With the crowd that was packing Taladega that night, a man might find it hard to get any sleep.

"Knowed you'd show up!"

Jake Ryker halted, arrested by the familiar voice. He turned half around, threw his glance back into the lobby. It was Nat Clover.

"Got me a room here, too," the squat man said, grinning broadly. "Soon's you stash your gear, come on down. I'll be waiting in the saloon."

VIII

Ryker muttered under his breath. It had been his hope to encounter no one he knew, that he could pass through the settlement unnoticed. He shrugged, decided then that it didn't really matter. As long as no one knew the details of his trip, nothing could go wrong; to act suspiciously would be a mistake. It would be best simply to go about things as usual.

"Figured you'd be about halfway to Fort Worth by now," he drawled, leaning against the wall.

"Ain't in no big rush, and it'll sure still be there when I show up. You eat yet?"

Ryker watched the layers of smoke drifting from the saloon into the lobby and on toward the open doorway. "Nope. About the second thing I aim to do."

"Second? What's first . . . find yourself a woman?"

"No, wash off some of the dust. Go ahead. I'll meet you soon's I've cleaned up."

"Good enough. I'll be looking for you."

Ryker resumed the short climb, gained the upper hallway, and sought out his room. The quarters provided by the Gold Dollar were a notch better than average, being clean, cool, and with furnishings that were fairly new. Fresh water was in the china pitcher on the washstand, and, after stepping out of his clothes, he slopped a measure into the accompanying bowl and scrubbed himself down.

He felt better, and buckling the money belt again around his lean middle, he snapped the loose dust from the shirt he'd been wearing, drew it on. He was carrying only one complete change of clothing and figured it was best to wait another few days before switching.

Dressed, he made his way to the saloon. Halting in the archway, he glanced about, nodded to several familiar faces, and then, spotting Clover at the blackjack table, crossed to join him.

"Luck's sure running fine," Nat said, grinning. "Ought to try your'n."

Ryker had a few dollars in his pockets he'd brought along for expenses above the sum he was carrying for the cattle deal— and he did feel right. Nodding to the dealer, he entered the game. The cards fell favorably, and in less than a quarter hour, he had won five times straight and accumulated a winning of $25. The thought came to his mind then; with luck running for him, it might be wise to take a couple of hundred out of the cattle money, build it up to where he'd have some extra for expenses, or perhaps he'd do well enough to increase his capital and be in a position to buy more stock from Justin. Such would be a big boost for Tom and the Circle R, he knew, toying with the thought. Showing up with fifty or a hundred more steers than expected would really open some eyes. And he was feeling right.

Jake Ryker shrugged. He'd be a damned fool to take a chance. Sometimes a man's luck changed so swiftly that he was broke before he knew it. Besides, he was beat from the long ride, and he was hungry.

Turning away, he said to Clover: "Think I'll get a bite to eat.

You stay put while you're running hot. I'll meet up with you later."

"About time I was quitting, too," the scar-faced rider said, knuckling his bloodshot eyes. "Cards ain't falling like they was, and I'm ready for eating. Where'll we go, the Ace-High?"

"Still the best, I reckon. Cleanest for sure."

They crossed the gambling area, scarcely noting the adjoining room where a half a dozen garishly dressed women were performing lethargically on a small stage for an audience of two or three dozen men, and, avoiding the lobby, entered the street. The Ace-High Café lay on the Texas side, down a half a dozen doors.

Shouldering their way through the crowd milling aimlessly about in the shadowy light of store window lamps, they reached the café. The place was enjoying a good patronage, but they found an empty table near the back and sat down. The waitress, a young Mexican girl with coal-black hair and very white teeth appeared at once and took their orders. She returned to the kitchen, walking with an exaggerated swinging of her well-curved hips.

"See you made up your mind to go to Fort Worth, after all. Knowed when I mentioned it, there'd be no roping you down," Clover said as they settled back to await their meal. There had been little opportunity for general conversation back at the Gold Dollar's blackjack table.

"Not exactly where I'm headed," Ryker replied. "Only going far as the Brazos . . . Ben City."

"Ben City. Sort of recollect something special about it. What's there?"

"Only been there once myself. Not much more than a wide place in the road."

"Then why the hell do you want to fritter good time on a . . . ?"

"Little business I'm taking care of for my brother."

Nat Clover's mouth parted into a grin. "Sure! Recollect now what I'd heard about this Ben City. It's where that fellow Park Justin runs a big ranch. Your business wouldn't be with him, would it?"

Ryker's gaze was reaching through the dust-filmed window-pane of the café to the steadily increasing crowd in the street. Almost everyone, it seemed, had waited until sundown and the evening's resultant coolness to do his shopping.

"Yeah, that's it," Clover said, getting no answer to his question. "Know all about this here Justin. He don't raise cattle to sell to the market, gets rid of them to other ranchers. That way he don't have to fool with drives and such. They say he does right well at it. You making a deal with him for some beef?"

"Could be," Ryker said, realizing he had to make some sort of answer and get the subject dropped. "As soon you'd keep it quiet."

"Why? Nothing wrong with buying cattle from Park Justin is there?"

"No, but I've got me a sort of ticklish deal. Just don't want word getting out. Things going wrong could cause it all to blow up in my face, and leave me and my brother busted flat."

Nat Clover was silent for a time, then nodded sagely. "Sure, I savvy. You need any help? Be a pleasure to throw in with you, side you like I done in the old days. And I'm owing you a mighty big favor."

"No need. Obliged, anyway, and you sure don't owe me anything," Ryker replied, and paused, relieved to see the waitress coming through the kitchen's entrance with a platter of food in each hand. "Here's our grub. Sure ready for it."

They ate slowly, with relish, two trail-riding men who partook far too often of their own efforts over a campfire and knew how genuinely to appreciate the tasty handiwork of an expert in the kitchen.

Finished, they rose, paid their checks and, leaving a suitable tip for the girl with the semaphore hips, returned to the street.

Off to their right in front of the Emporium a fight between two cowpunchers was under way. Both were heaving back and forth, sweating, muttering curses, wrestling, and flailing about with their fists while two dozen or more onlookers yelled advice and encouragement. Standing on the boardwalk a short distance away and watching with little interest was a man wearing the star of the Texas side's town marshal. Farther down the row of buildings shots sounded in quick succession. The reports drew only passing notice from the crowd, none at all from the lawman.

"Figure to go back to the blackjack game?" Clover asked, probing at his broad teeth with a split match. Two men with a young girl between them moved by. The girl was very drunk, head wobbling, eyes rolling wildly. One of her companions said something to her as they drew abreast. She laughed uncontrollably. "Got me the feeling this is my night to buck the tiger," Nat continued, watching the three melt into the shifting crowd.

"Was having fair luck myself," Ryker said. "Feel more like some poker, however."

"Always find a good game in the Lone Star."

Ryker nodded. "Won't hurt to have a look."

Pressing on, they reached the tall building, mounted the gallery, and pushed through the scarred batwings into the saloon. Once there, they lowered their heads and bulled a course for the adjoining room, which was devoted entirely and exclusively to gambling.

"Hell of a lot of people around here, even for a Saturday night," Ryker said, wiping at the sweat on his face as he glanced around at the table. Practically every chair in the place was filled. The crowds around the faro and chuck-a-luck games were three deep.

"Bunch of drovers here, somebody said. Seven or eight different outfits, all close by, all on their way home from Wichita and Dodge. You never did say for sure if you was dickering with Justin for beef."

"Brother's been talking to him," Ryker said, still striving to avoid a direct answer. He knew Nat Clover probably as well as he did any man and figured him for one who could be trusted, but the less he or anyone else knew about the impending purchase, the better. Having $2,000 in cash was enough to tempt any man, even an honest one. "Couple of chairs over there at that corner table? Want to sit in?"

"I'm willing," Clover said, and led the way to the vacant seats.

An hour later, with Nat picked clean and wandering glumly about the room looking over shoulders, pausing now and then to talk with someone he knew, and Ryker down to his last double eagle, they abandoned the games.

"Figure to pull out early," Ryker said as they wound their way toward the door. "Going to treat myself to a drink, then turn in. You stand a shot?"

"Sure could," Nat said, and then throwing a look over his shoulder at the men still at the table, added: "That god-damn' dealer . . . I ain't so sure but what he was reaching up his sleeve."

Ryker shook his head. "Wondered myself, considering the kind of cards he kept drawing. Watched close. Never saw anything that looked out of line. Expect he was just a better hand at cards than us."

They reached the connecting doorway that opened into the saloon, shoved up to the long counter. Leaning against it they ordered whiskey. Ryker paid, slid the change into his pocket. Taking up his glass, he wheeled lazily, hooked his elbows on the rim of the mahogany bar, and gazed out over the crowd in the stuffy, smoke-filled room.

"I'm still puzzling about that sharp," Nat Clover muttered at his shoulder. "Seems mighty funny to me, him getting such good cards."

Ryker, a frown on his sun- and wind-darkened face, was only half listening. Two men had ducked through the swinging doors just as he had turned around. There was something familiar in the look of them, something that stirred a vague warning inside him. He thought about it for several moments, brushed it from his mind. He guessed he was letting the worry of carrying $2,000 make him edgy. Taladega was a rough town but he had nothing to fear as long as he stayed clear of bawdy houses and the back-alley saloons. Tossing off the last of the liquor, he bucked his head at Clover. "I'm turning in. Expect you'll be staying over tomorrow."

The squat rider finished his drink. "Yeah, couple more days anyway. Got to see if I can raise me some cash now. Stripped clean. That god-damn' fancy dealing Cajun."

"Short myself, but I've got a few extra dollars you're welcome to."

Clover stared at Ryker for a long breath, his features expressionless. "Obliged," he said finally, "but I can get by. Can use my face for a little credit, enough to get on my feet. Appreciate your offering it to me."

"Welcome to it," Ryker said, and pushed away from the counter. He extended his hand. "If I don't see you later. . . ."

Nat shrugged, ignoring the gesture. "Might as well tramp on over to the Gold Dollar with you. I was doing pretty good there."

Again in the street, they angled through the throng and spinning dust for the opposite side. The crowd had increased, it seemed to Ryker, and he guessed the rumor Clover had heard concerning visiting drovers had been true. They gained the

51

sidewalk, stepped up onto it, began to thread a path for the hotel's entrance. Abreast the narrow passageway separating the hostelry from its adjacent neighbor on the north, motion in the darkness caught Ryker's attention, brought him to a halt.

"Ryker!" a husky voice called from the darkness.

Instinctively Ryker stepped to one side, hand sweeping down for the pistol on his hip. Behind him he heard Nat Clover's voice.

"What the hell! Who's hiding in there?"

A gun blasted from the deep shadows, deafening in such narrow, confined quarters. Ryker fired at the flare of orange he saw dead ahead, heard the bullet that had been intended for him thud dully into the wall close by.

"Who is it?" Clover asked again, dropping to a crouch.

"Don't know," Ryker rasped. "Somebody aiming to hold us up, I reckon. Keep down."

In that next instant a pistol flashed once more in the blackness between the buildings. Jake Ryker staggered under a shocking blow to the head. Reflex triggered his own weapon, clutched tightly in his hand, and then he fell forward into a pit of silent darkness.

IX

Vaguely Ryker could hear shouts in the street, laughter, a rumbling of confusion as he slowly opened his eyes. Pain throbbed persistently in his head, and there was a paper dryness in his throat that made breathing difficult, recalling the time he found himself afoot in Arizona's Chiricahua desert country with no water.

"See you're still among the living. . . ."

At the sound of the unfamiliar voice, the last of the cobwebby screen blocking his mind drifted away. He turned to a round-faced man with sweat shining on his cheeks, steel-rimmed spectacles circling his eyes, and a fringe of cottony hair ringing his head.

"I'm Doc Carmer. You got yourself a devil of a rap on the noggin."

Ryker looked down. He was lying on a couch in a room that smelled strongly of antiseptics. He stiffened as it all came to him in a quick, flooding rush. He was in a doctor's office. Somebody had lugged him there after the bushwhacking alongside the hotel. A bullet had struck him a glancing blow, laid him out cold. Apprehension gripped him. His hands dropped to his waist, probed for the money belt. It was gone.

"Your gun?" Carmer asked. "Didn't figure you'd be needing it, lying there cold as a cucumber." He jerked his thumb toward a peg rack nailed to the wall. "It's hanging right there."

Ryker struggled to a sitting position, swung his legs over the edge of the leather couch. The swirling nausea the effort created was as nothing compared to the sense of despair that filled him as he realized his loss. Hunched there on the smooth cowhide, he reached up, touched the side of his head, felt the bandage Carmer had wrapped about it.

"Best thing you can do is stay quiet."

"Can't," Jake Ryker said groggily. The two thousand dollars was gone. He groaned, thinking of what its loss meant to Tom and Callie—to him. He raised his gaze to the medical man. "That all you took off me . . . my gun?"

Carmer nodded, frowned. "You miss something else?"

"I was wearing a money belt under my shirt."

"Never bothered to look there. Just got that belt and holster off so's you could lie flat after the marshal and Ed Grimsby brought you in."

Ryker's thoughts came to a halt. "What about the man with me . . . Nat Clover?"

"Clover?" Carmer shook his head. "Nobody with you, leastwise the marshal didn't say anything about it. They sure didn't carry anybody else in. Do you know who it was that jumped you?"

Clover had been crouched right behind him. It was strange that he, too, had not been hurt, or at least accompanied him to the doctor's office. Unless. . . . "No," he replied to Carmer's question, "but I'm getting a hunch. Which marshal was it?"

"Emerson. We're on the New Mexico side."

Jake Ryker got to his feet unsteadily. Carmer laid a hand on his shoulder. "Now, I'm not sure you're in any condition to. . . ."

"Maybe not, but I've got to get to the bottom of this quick," Ryker said, brushing the man's hand away and moving toward the peg rack. Reaching for his belt, he buckled it on, checked the pistol, and then dug into his pocket for the coins that should be there. He swore helplessly, withdrew his hand. Whoever it was that had lain in wait for him in the dark had stripped him. *Nat Clover.* Ryker stood perfectly still as his thoughts swung again to the squat, scar-faced man. It wasn't possible. Yet Clover had questioned him considerably, had undoubtedly guessed he was carrying a fair amount of cash to make a cattle deal—and Clover hadn't been with him when the lawman and some passer-by had carried him into Carmer's office. He thought he knew Nat Clover well, but he guessed a man could change, could fool his friends. And Nat was broke. A possible explanation came to him. "You hear the marshal say whether there was anybody else there . . . dead?" he asked hopefully.

"There was only you, unconscious from that bullet. I'd know. I'm the coroner here, too."

Ryker reckoned that settled it. He had all the proof he needed. Clover had been with him, yet there was no sign of him when the shooting and robbery were all over. It was hard to believe, but a man was a fool to deny facts. Ryker started to nod, thought better of it. He smiled wryly at Carmer. "Got to owe you, Doc. They cleaned me out."

Carmer shrugged. "You're not the only member of the club. Two-thirds of the county's on my cuff. There's always room for one more. I still don't think you ought to go gallivanting around given the shape you're in. Legs are liable to cave in under you if you get all worked up and overdo it. It'd show more sense to stay right there on that couch for the rest of the night."

"Expect you're right," Ryker admitted, "but it can't be done. Have to get back that money belt. More important than you might figure . . . than my head, for sure. First thing's to find out what happened to that partner of mine who was siding me."

"Emerson'll be the one to talk to. He got there just after the shooting started and found you."

Ryker drew on his hat carefully, cocking it to one side so as to not apply undue pressure on the throbbing wound above his temple. "Obliged to you for the doctoring," he said, moving for the door. "You'll get your fee soon as I can put my hands on some money."

"The universal cry of the general public," Carmer murmured, smiling wearily. "Take care . . . and good luck in finding your money."

Ryker stepped out into the dust-filled night. The crowd had decreased but little and he guessed he'd been out for no more than an hour. Grim, still somewhat unsteady, he turned left, pointed for the lawman's office that, he recalled, was near the end of the street. Halfway, he met Emerson, heading back for the center of town.

"Marshal, I'd like to ask you some questions. I'm. . . ."

"Recognize you," the lawman said, coming to a stop. "You're the bird that got himself rapped good by a slug next to the hotel."

"That's me. Name's Jake Ryker. Can you tell me what happened to my partner?"

"Partner? Didn't know you had one. Found only you, laying there, bleeding like a gut-shot dog."

That dull suspicion that had been building within Jake Ryker changed abruptly to absolute conviction. A coldness settled over him. Nat was one man he would have bet on. Features stiff, he faced the lawman again. "You the first one to find me?"

"Was. Had been standing a few doors down. Heard the shooting."

"And by the time you got there, whoever it was that shot me was gone . . . along with my partner?"

"Reckon so. I got there, fairly fast, but there was a lot of folks milling about, and I wasn't so sure where the shots come from. Whoever they were, they'd gone."

"They? Something make you figure there was more than one?"

"No way of telling. Just a way of saying it. Maybe come daylight we might puzzle it out, but I misdoubt it. Lots of trash and such blowed in there. Wouldn't be no tracks." Emerson paused, watched a half a dozen belted and spurred cowpunchers weave in from the opposite side of the street, slanting for one of the lesser saloons. He brought his small, dark eyes back to Ryker. "Hell, getting robbed ain't nothing special around here. Comes along pretty often, man getting hisself knocked flat on his ass and his money took. You ought to figure yourself lucky you ain't dead. There's plenty of them end up that way."

"Not just a matter of a few dollars. I was wearing a money belt, aimed to buy some cattle. Was quite a bit of cash in it."

Emerson pursed his lips, fingered his mustache. "Didn't know about that." He frowned. "Can tell you this much. I was the first man on the spot, like I already said. Nobody'd touched you yet. I looked to see if you was dead or alive. You was breathing so I hollered at Ed Grimsby. He was standing at the end of the passageway, holding folks back. Told him to give me a hand. You ask Doc Carmer about the belt?"

"Said the only thing he took off me was my gun."

"That'll be the truth. Doc ain't the lying kind. And I sure'n hell never glommed onto it. This partner of yours you mentioned . . . you real sure about him? Seems kind of funny, him disappearing the way he has."

"It's got me to wondering," Ryker replied.

"You see him talking to anybody before you two come walking by that alley?"

Ryker's thoughts cut back to the Lone Star. Nat had wandered about the room, had spoken to several men he evidently knew. "I remember now that he did. Over in the Lone Star's gambling parlor. He'd gone broke, was just stalling around, waiting for me."

Emerson nodded sagely. "Things're starting to make sense. The way I see it, he ought've been there beside you, either hurt or dead, or else still shooting at whoever it was that laid for you, but there wasn't no sign of him. That how you see it?"

Ryker, features expressionless, only nodded. He stared off into the crowded, noisy street with its restless throng and hovering clouds of dust. "How long ago did this happen? I was out, so I've got no idea of time."

"It's been a couple hours, more or less. Mostly less, I'd say. You want to give me a description of that partner of yours? Maybe I can spot him?"

"He'd be long gone by now," Ryker said heavily. "Obliged to you just the same." He was yet finding it hard to believe that Nat Clover would turn on him, sell him out, but the evidence, however circumstantial, was undeniable. "I'll do my own looking . . . and settling up."

Wheeling, he started through the crowd for the Gold Dollar. Halfway there a thought came to him, and, circling the hotel, he crossed to the stable in the rear. The hostler came forward to meet him at once, one cheek bulging with tobacco.

"You know Nat Clover?" Ryker said without ceremony.

The old man rubbed at the back of his neck. "Clover?" he repeated. "Seems I ought . . . what's he look like?"

"Little on the short side. Heavy. Got a scar on his face."

"Him, oh, sure. Rides a spotted Indian pony."

"That's the man. Has he been here tonight?"

"You bet he was. Come in a couple hours back. Was in a powerful hurry. Had me saddle his horse, then took off like the heel flies was after him."

A tautness filled Jake Ryker. "Anybody with him?"

The old man spat a brown stream at the base of the livery stable wall. "Nope. All by hisself."

Ryker studied the oldster's lined features. "You see which way he went?"

"Sure did. Took the Trail."

The Taladega Trail was a road that ran straight south to Mexico. Jake Ryker swore silently. It had been all set up. Nat would meet the man or men who'd been in on the hold-up with him at the edge of town after it was all over. Then, all would line out fast for the border.

"I'll be needing my horse," he said abruptly. "In a hurry myself . . . it's the chestnut with the diamond brand on his hip."

"Know which one. Was me that rubbed him down, done the feeding. . . ."

"I'll be back for him soon's I get my saddlebags."

"Aiming to pull out for good?"

Half turned away, Ryker gave that a thought. He had no cash with which to pay off, and if the hostler and the hotel clerk believed him to be leaving, he could run into delay and difficulties. "Just aiming to catch up with my fri- . . . with Clover," he said, and hurried on.

There was no one at the hotel's desk when he entered the lobby. Climbing the stairs, he picked up his bags, made sure all his belongings were inside, and returned to the lower floor. The clerk was still nowhere to be seen. Taking up the pencil he found lying beside the register, he located a scrap of paper and wrote: *Will settle later. J. Ryker.* He placed it between the pages of the book where it would be found.

That done, he returned to the stable. The hostler had the gelding ready, and Ryker swung immediately to the saddle. Wheeling the big horse about, he hesitated, gazed down at the elderly man. "You're dead sure Clover took the Trail south?"

"Sure as I'm standing here. Was right here in the yard and seen him do it."

"It was dark. He might've turned west."

"Dang it, he didn't! Don't take much light to see a man on a spotted horse riding straight away and keeping on going straight. There's a bright moon out there once a man gets out of all this dust."

"For a fact," Ryker said. "Hadn't noticed."

He rode off the hard pack. The moon should prove to be a big help.

X

The cool night air served as a tonic and stimulant. Riding across the flat on a course paralleling the road, the dull ache in Ryker's head became less noticeable and his mind clearer. The hostler had been right; away from the settlement and its scuffling, restless occupants, the moon was strong and a silver radiance flooded the country, turned it almost to daylight. He twisted about, looked back to Taladega. A pale glare hung over the town like a canopy. From the distance it lent a beautiful effect, but he realized it was no more than heavy layers of suspended dust against which lamps threw their yellow glow.

Morose, he turned his attention to the country stretched before him. He was purposely avoiding the road, not wanting to betray his presence by the hoof beats of the chestnut on its hard-baked surface. It was slower going in the loose sand but he felt the time lost was more than offset by the silence he could thus preserve. There was still a nagging reluctance within him to believe Nat Clover had been a part of the robbery. But the indications were there, and it all boiled down to a single point— only Nat had any idea that he was carrying a large sum of money on his person—and even that had been a logical assumption on the scar-faced man's part. Nat, by sheer coincidence, had known of Park Justin, had jumped to the correct conclusion that a cattle deal was in the making, and since Justin dealt on a strictly cash basis, it necessarily followed that anyone buying a herd from him would be carrying money. Thus, who else could it have been but Nat? If a man needed further proof he had but to consider Clover's unexplained disappearance in the passageway, and then his hasty departure from the settlement. There could be no question.

A gust of anger whipped through Jake Ryker. He would have been a hell of a lot better off if he'd let Ford and the rest of the Circle R cowhands string Clover up to that cottonwood. He'd still have Tom's $2,000 buckled around his belly and not be riding off into the night on what was probably a hopeless attempt to recover it. Hopeless, hell, he couldn't look at it that way. He had to get that money back somehow. Otherwise, Tom and Callie and the Circle R were busted flat—and he would have proved just what they always thought of him, that he was a shiftless, worthless saddle bum, completely irresponsible and basically dishonest. That's what Callie would certainly think. She'd make up her mind about him quickly, and then with that acid-tipped tongue of hers declare that he'd probably cached the money somewhere where he'd later recover it, while he came up with a cock-and-bull yarn about getting robbed—right in the middle of a town. That's what Callie Ryker would want to believe, and being who she was, that's what she actually would believe.

Well, she was going to be disappointed. She'd not get the chance to think that of him. He'd find Nat Clover and the man or men who were mixed up in the ambush with him, and get back the money if he had to chase them clear across Mexico. But he'd have to do it fast. And he realized he was lucky he was able to do anything about it at all. He was lucky to be alive when you came right down to it. That bullet had come within a fraction of putting him in the graveyard.

Staring off across the moonlit country, all soft and gentle-looking under the pale shine, he gingerly probed the portion of his head under Carmer's bandage. There was a rawness to it. He swore angrily as he flinched. That damned Clover, if he. . . . Something—motion—off to the left of the trail a short distance down the way brought him up sharply. Reining in the chestnut, he raised himself in the stirrups and endeavored to make out what it was that had alerted his senses—an animal of some kind, a wolf or a coyote, maybe. It seemed larger, however. Could be a stray from some nearby herd of cattle. He wouldn't accept any of those explanations for one reason—he was unsure. Roweling the gelding lightly, he sent him forward at a slow walk. Pistol in hand, he kept his eyes riveted to the dim, dark shape off to the side.

It was a horse. Ryker, puzzled by the appearance of the animal, evidently abandoned so far from the settlement, pressed on quietly. Abruptly he pulled the chestnut to a halt again. It was Nat Clover's spotted pony.

Directly opposite the horse Ryker dismounted. Tying the chestnut to a clump of *chamiso*, he moved toward the road carefully, not sure of what it all meant; it could be a trap of some sort. He reached the shoulder of the road, hunched in behind a thick stand of brush. The pinto was ten yards away. Head down, reins dragging, the horse still carried its gear. There was no sign of Clover.

Suspicion plucking at him, Ryker dropped back, continued along the road to a point where, hidden from the pinto, he crossed over. Then, doubling back up the opposite shoulder, he approached the pony from its off side. He saw Nat's body. The scar-faced man was in a shallow ravine a few steps from his horse. When he had fallen from the saddle, the leathers had dropped, also, and the well-trained animal, ground-reined, had come to an immediate halt. What the hell was going on?

Ryker, squatted on his heels, worked at the problem. Had Clover's friends turned on him, deciding not to share the contents of the belt? The question disturbed him but he did not move in for a closer look and possible explanation just yet; it could be a ruse, a trap. Thus, he continued to watch and wait in the shadowy brush, listening, testing the breeze for the smell of tobacco smoke or other distinctive odors that would indicate other men lurking nearby. Nothing. Finally convinced there was no one around, Ryker moved out of hiding and, still cautious and quiet in his actions, stepped to where Clover lay.

Nat had been taken from behind. There were two bullet wounds in his back. Ryker rolled the man over, stared at the slack features, noting the dark bruise over the right eye. Nat had never known what hit him, he guessed; the bullets had been fired from either side and at close range with unavoidable accuracy; his own .45 was still in its holster.

Jake Ryker felt no stir of pity for the scar-faced man. He'd chosen to run with wolves, therefore he had to expect the treatment of wolves. Crossing to the pinto, he pulled off the saddle and bridle, turned the animal loose. He would be better off shifting for himself unencumbered by tack. Dropping then to his knees beside the worn hull, Ryker examined the contents of the saddlebags. Finding nothing of interest to him, he returned to Clover's body, went through the dead man's pockets. He failed to turn up anything that would be of help there, either.

Rising, Ryker returned to the waiting chestnut and mounted. One thing was certain—he was on the right trail. Clover and the others had headed south out of Taladega, unquestionably making for the border. Thinking about it, he reckoned he'd run into a bit of good luck; Nat's partners, now rid of him, could be just taking it easy. They believed him dead back in the settlement, and with Clover now also permanently out of the picture, they would feel the need to vanish quickly had been removed. Clucking the gelding into motion, Ryker pushed on, still avoiding the hard surface of the trail, having his thoughts and wondering about Nat Clover, while his eyes searched ahead continually for indications of riders.

Nat's killing disturbed him. There was no reason for it other than the fact that his partners did not wish to share the money in the belt with him. But the fact that he, and not someone else, was the leader, the instigator of the hold-up would tend to make that reasoning illogical. Nat would have picked men he could control. Too, Clover had departed the Gold Dollar's stable alone and in a big hurry. Why hadn't they all ridden out together? Such would be more reasonable and understandable. Clover and those with him, slipping out of the passageway before anyone else had time to appear and leaving the town as a single party made sense. Nat's departure some time later did not. The matter became more confusing as Jake rolled it about in his mind. There were just too many things that didn't jibe, too many parts in the puzzle that didn't fit.

Time wore on and the long, lonely miles of a hushed, barren land, turned eerily beautiful by the moon and stars, moved endlessly by. The pain in his head began to increase, whetted no doubt by the jogging of the chestnut, the sense of loss and frustration that possessed him, and the strain of pushing a body that needed rest and care. It would be hard to trace the money if he lost the riders, he realized, as he had no idea of who they were or what they looked like—assuming there was more than one, which he was now inclined to believe; the two holes in Clover's back made by bullets coming from different angles tended to prove that.

While Nat was a member of the party and with the others, he would have had no difficulty in tracking them down, since it was possible to recognize and if necessary describe Nat. But that was out now, and, facing that, he admitted how difficult his job would be unless he could overtake the outlaws before they could give him the slip. Ryker's jaw came to a grim set. He couldn't, wouldn't let that happen. He had to catch up with them before they shook him off the trail—or the money would be lost forever. Searching for men he did not know and had no idea of their appearances or names would be a hopeless task no matter how determined he might be.

All such dark thoughts and considerations washed suddenly from his mind. On the brow of a hill he pulled the chestnut to a quick stop. Satisfaction stirred through him, filled him with a harsh grimness and relief. Not a hundred yards away a small campfire flared in the shadow of a butte. Two men were hunched nearby. They were sorting something on the ground before them.

XI

Jake Ryker dropped softly to the ground. Again tethering the chestnut, he went to all fours and, keeping in a shallow, brush-lined wash, crept in close to the two men. Their words reached him before he was near enough to see them clearly.

"Was pure damn' luck us nailing that jasper that was following us. . . ."

Ryker, flat on the cool ground, stiffened. The voice had a familiar tone. He racked his memory for some clue, some recollection of the past; it came to him suddenly. It was Lenny Gault.

"Well, he sure won't be following nobody else. You can bet your aces on that."

Chuck Virden had made the answer—and they were speaking of Nat Clover. A stab of conscience caused Jake Ryker to stir. It hadn't been the way he'd figured at all; Nat had evidently been chasing the pair, hoping to recover the money belt for him. The scar-faced rider had not double-crossed him, had instead been trying to help. That bruise on his head—that probably explained why he had been slow in leaving the settlement in pursuit; he had been injured, too.

Anger shook Jake Ryker as it all became clearer to him. Gault and Virden had then heard Clover coming, had pulled off the road to hide. When Nat passed, they closed in from either side, shot him in the back. Ryker's fingers moved to the butt of his pistol in a spasm of anger. Then, jaw clamped tight, he wormed his way in to where he could see the hunched men.

They were counting the money taken from the belt, were dividing it into equal piles. Gault, handling the worn bills, laughed. "Know what's funny about this? Us squaring up with that son-of-a-bitching Ryker for Ed and Tolly and getting paid for it."

Chuck grinned, nodded. "Had him fooled for sure. Expect he figured them sod-busters back in Lordsburg still had us cornered."

They'd been on his trail all the way, Ryker realized, had probably been a half a day behind him. He may have shaken them while he was at the Circle R, but, if so, it had been only briefly, for they were in Taladega while he was there. He knew now that these were the two men he'd caught a glimpse of as they ducked through the doorway at the Lone Star. From there they had gone to the alleyway beside the hotel and lain in wait for him.

"Mighty glad you spotted that belt when you was going through his pockets. Undertaker'd 'a' got it for sure."

"Sort of makes up for us finding nothing on that bird siding him."

"Made up!" Virden laughed again. "I'd say it more'n made up."

Ryker had the complete picture now. The pair had followed him to Taladega, watching for a chance to avenge the deaths of Ed Virden and the man they'd called Tolly. Their moment had come when Nat and he were passing the narrow alleyway next to the Gold Dollar. They had thought him dead, probably had figured Nat Clover was, also. Then they had rifled their pockets. Finding the money belt had been an accident.

"This is sure going to set us up good," Lenny Gault said, wetting a thumb and resuming the apportioning. "Why, down in Mexi-. . . ."

"It's going to hang both of you bastards!" Jake Ryker snarled, and rose to his full height from the shadows.

A startled oath burst from Gault's lips. Virden froze momentarily, then made a desperate stab for the pistol on his hip. In that same fraction of time Gault lunged, scooped up a double handful of fire and ashes, flung them straight at Ryker's face. Ryker instinctively threw up an arm to protect his eyes, fired pointblank at Chuck Virden. The outlaw jolted, went over backward as the heavy bullet smashed into him.

Feeling the burn of the live coals in several places, choking on the powdery ash, Ryker rocked to one side, dropped to his knees as he sought to locate Lenny Gault. An instant later Ryker saw him. Gault was still near the scattered fire frantically trying to collect the money now strewn before him and draw his weapon at the same time. Ryker threw a bullet into the ground in front of the outlaw. His eyes still smarted and stung and he was having trouble seeing clearly. But the slug drove Gault back. He dropped the bills he'd gathered, managed to trigger off a shot. Ryker snapped a reply at the dim, weaving shape, missed. An instant later Gault spun, flung himself back into the deep shadows of the brush a stride behind him. Ryker, again knuckling his eyes, fired once more, his only target a vague, fleeting shape. Gault cursed in the dark as luck rode the bullet and found its mark.

Ryker, vision now improving, avoided the flare of the dying fire, crossed to his left, and raced forward for another shot. The sudden, hard tattoo of a horse moving away fast reached him. He pulled up short, anger and tension beating at him furiously.

"Run for it, you son-of-a-bitch!" he shouted in an exasperated voice. "But you'll not get away from me!"

Spinning, he ran back to the fire. Casting only a side glance at Chuck Virden's still figure, he slid his pistol into its holster and, dropping to a crouch, gathered in the bills and gold pieces, crammed them back into the money belt. Then, rising, he started for the chestnut at a hard run, taking time only to cram the money belt inside his shirt. Later he'd buckle it on properly; at the moment catching Gault, making him pay for Nat Clover's death was more important.

Reaching the gelding, he yanked the leathers free and vaulted onto the saddle. Roweling the big chestnut savagely, he sent him plunging ahead into the night. Gault was hit; he knew that, but just how badly he did not know. The outlaw had chosen to run, however, and not shoot it out. That made it appear he was in a bad way. Ryker wasn't in too good a condition himself, he thought as the gelding pounded on through the moonlight-filled night. Dizziness was bothering him again. He supposed it was the result of exertion and strain. Carmer had warned him not to overdo anything.

The burns he'd sustained were minor, a place here and there

on his forearms and neck where live coals and sparks had settled when Gault tossed the fire at him. It was the ash powder that had reached his eyes that troubled him most. But they would clear up in time. Leaning forward, he brushed at them, endeavoring to wipe away the mistiness that persisted in gathering, and peered ahead. He wasn't sure, but he thought he could make out the dim outline of a rider. Urging the chestnut to faster speed, he drew his pistol, tossed away the spent cartridges, thumbed in fresh loads.

He saw Gault a few minutes later. The outlaw, a blurred shape, was bent low over his saddle. His horse was running erratically, almost wildly, either tiring or endeavoring to respond to heavy, faltering hands. Once more Ryker called on the chestnut for speed. The big red eased ahead, began to close the gap that separated him from the animal Gault rode. Ryker saw Gault straighten partly, half turn, throw a glance over his shoulder. Immediately the outlaw swerved his mount off the road, struck out across open country.

Ryker veered the gelding from the hard-packed surface of the trail, and followed closely. Gault's horse was in trouble, seemed to be breaking under the hard drive. All the signs were there. The chestnut needed only to keep pressing.

Suddenly Lenny Gault's mount went down. The outlaw hit hard in a flurry of dust and sand, came unsteadily to his feet. Ryker, caught by the suddenness of it all, swerved the gelding to one side. He saw the bright orange flash of the pistol in Gault's hand, felt the searing burn of a bullet cutting across the upper part of his arm. Deadly cool, he fired at the dim, weaving shape of the outlaw, fired again. Gault staggered, went to his knees, and then fell forward.

Ryker brought the plunging chestnut to a stop, a strange, wheeling sensation spinning through his brain. Motionless on the saddle of the heaving horse, one hand still clutching his weapon, the other the leather-covered horn, he stared at the outlaw through misty eyes. After a bit the whirling ceased and his vision cleared somewhat. He urged the chestnut in nearer to the man, halted. There was no need to dismount and examine Lenny Gault, even if he could muster the strength and the will. The outlaw was dead.

Reaching deep for a breath, he shook himself. It was over with. He had avenged Nat Clover, had recovered the money belt with its cash. He became aware then of the stinging on his arm, of a warm stickiness along his elbow. Unaccountably temper flared through him.

"Dammit to hell!" he shouted into the night as frustration and anger swept him. What kind of luck was plaguing him? Why was everything going wrong? He'd started out on a simple mission of buying a herd of cattle. He'd been bushwhacked, nearly killed, shot, half blinded, and lost a good friend and in the process forced to gun down two men. What the hell would happen next?

One thing was sure. Tom and Callie could have the ranch. Their way of life. He'd stick to his, and he'd pick it up just as soon as he could get the herd back to the Circle R and hire on a man to run things. He'd had enough. Muttering, he looked down at his arm. The wound was a raw, red splotch in the fleshy part above the elbow. Gault's bullet had carved a deep groove in its burning passage. It was bleeding freely. Still caught up in a strange light-headedness, Ryker dug out his handkerchief, wrapped it about the wound, and with teeth and fingers managed to pull the corners into a fairly tight knot. The effort sent his brain to spinning more furiously, and he settled back, waited for it to subside, then urged the gelding into forward motion. Best he go back to Taladega—see Doc Carmer again—get fixed up.

★ ★ ★ ★ ★

The chestnut was not moving. Jake Ryker became aware of that, aware also that a broad sheet of pearl filled the sky to the east, and that sunrise was not far off. He looked about, dazed. Nothing appeared familiar. The gelding must have wandered for hours on its own. Ryker raised a hand, brushed back his hat. A short distance ahead he saw a narrow, sandy wash beyond which a slight grade led to a stand of trees. The faint sparkle of a stream cut across the slope at the edge of the grove. That's what he needed, what would help—water. He'd get down, give his head a good, cool soaking. It should rid him of the dizziness.

The chestnut, smelling the stream, moved out eagerly without being urged by the spurs. He crossed the arroyo, ascended the slope, and pointed for the trees. At once two riders broke out of the deep shadows, fanned out, barred his way. Ryker hauled back on the gelding's reins, brought him to a stop.

"Now, what the hell do you want?" he demanded as a fresh surge of frustration and anger rolled though him.

XII

His mind clearing fast, Ryker's hand drifted to the butt of his pistol. His eyes narrowed. He took in the pair—a thin-faced, dark man and a husky, hard-jawed blond man. A cold resoluteness filled Jake; nobody was going to get the money belt again—not without one hell of a fight. He put his question to them again. "What's on your mind?"

"Reckon the first thing," a voice from behind him drawled, "will be for you to take your paw off that shooting iron unless you want me to blow it off."

Ryker stiffened, allowed his fingers to slide away. He cast a look over his shoulder. A third man had come from the brush, a small, wiry rider who looked as if he might be part Mexican or perhaps Indian. He was holding a cocked rifle in his hands. Ryker cursed himself for his carelessness. He knew better than to leave himself wide open like that, but somehow he wasn't thinking as straight as he should.

The narrow-faced one grinned crookedly, bobbed his head. "That's better."

"All right, it's better," Ryker snapped. "What's this all about?"

Again the man's mouth split into a smile. "Just you listen to him, boys. It's like maybe he don't know."

The speaker moved around to join the others, directing his horse with pressure from his knees while he kept the long gun leveled at Jake Ryker. The blond man shoved his hat to the back of his head, shrugged. "He ain't that dumb."

"Reckon I am," Ryker said blandly, "leastwise to what you're yapping about." His head was functioning normally now, and he was conscious of only a dull ache. "Happens I'm riding across country. That a crime or something in this part of Texas?"

"All depends," the narrow-faced man said. "Pull his fangs, Charlie."

The blond man moved in behind Ryker, halted close by. Reaching forward, he lifted Ryker's weapon from its holster, pulled away, frowning.

"He's been in some kind of a ruckus, Bud. Got wrappings on his head and his arm's been bleeding."

"I sure am sorry," the rider replied dryly. "Get at it, Frank. Shake out that there rope of your'n."

Frank unhooked his reata from the saddle horn. Charlie frowned again, rubbed at his ear. "You ain't aiming to string him up, are you?"

"Sure what we ought to do," Bud said. "Teague's been told to keep off Medford range, and it'd be smart to put some teeth in the old man's warnings, let that Rocking T bunch know we're plumb tired of being hoorawed and kicked around."

71

Ryker, motionless on the saddle, mouth set to a thin line, listened in silence. This was no hold-up. He'd blundered, instead, into some sort of range trouble. When the man called Bud had finished, he shook his head. "You've got me wrong, friend. I don't know anybody named Teague or Medford, and I've never heard of the Rocking T."

"Yeah, I'll bet," Bud said scornfully. "How about that loop, Frank?"

"It's the truth," Ryker insisted. "I'm from over New Mexico way, the Circle R Ranch. My brother's name is Tom Ryker. Could be you've heard of him?"

"Nope, never heard of him, same as you ain't never heard of nobody I've mentioned. What's more I don't believe a god-damn' word you've spoke."

Ryker's shoulders came back slowly. Somewhere in the fields below the trees a meadowlark was pealing out its song. "Don't like being called a liar," he said quietly.

Bud laughed. "You ain't going to like a lot of things that'll be happening to you in a couple of minutes. We're owing you Rocking T yahoos aplenty, and now you're going to get a little payment on account. See what it's like to be on the getting end of all this hoorawing you been dishing out."

"I'll tell you again, I've got nothing to do with the Rocking T outfit. . . ."

"Drop that rope around him, Frank."

The half-breed shaped a loop. Charlie held up a hand, stayed the rider. "Maybe we'd best take him to see Medford first, let him decide."

"Hell, the old man's run plumb out of guts. He'd just turn him loose."

"Could be that's what we ought to do, too. Maybe he ain't one of Teague's crew. Sure ain't never seen him around here before."

"That ain't no surprise. Cowhands come and go real regular-like on the Rocking T."

"Sure, but I still figure we. . . ."

"Now, mister," Bud shouted, suddenly out of patience, "if you want to trot over and tell the old man what we're doing, you go right ahead! Me and Frank's got a better idea. Come on, get that lasso around him!"

Frank swung in quickly, dropped a loop around Ryker's middle, jerked it tight before Jake could throw it off.

"We dragging him, that what you're planning?" Frank asked, throwing his weight against the line to keep it taut.

Bud bobbed his head. "Just what I got in mind. Maybe if we scatter a little Rocking T hide across Medford range, Teague's bunch won't be so anxious to jump any of us next time we meet up."

Ryker's fingers wrapped about the reata encircling his waist, loosened its choking grasp. Instantly Frank spurred away. Ryker came off the saddle with a jerk. He struck the ground on his right shoulder, groaned at the solid impact. His senses reeled briefly as pain shot through him, but taking a tight grip on himself, he managed to recover balance and come upright. Legs spraddled, eyes blazing, he faced the three riders. "This'll be something you'll regret. . . ."

"Sure we will," Bud cut in with a laugh. "But I reckon it won't be half as much as you'll be doing. We're up to our ears with you Rocking T waddies running around taking pot shots at us, acting like you owned the whole god-damn' country. I'm aiming to give you a swallow of your own medicine."

Ryker's anger settled into a cold stream. He wasn't being robbed of the cash he carried, and that was one thing he could be thankful for, but he was not looking forward to being dragged across the flats as an object lesson to others he had no knowledge of or connection with. "Telling you again, you're making a mistake. I don't work for this Teague you keep talking about. Better play it smart, take me to Medford, if he's your boss, like Charlie there says, before it's too late."

"Too late for what?" Bud demanded, leaning forward. A sly grin pulled down the corners of his mouth.

Ryker could feel the warm stickiness above his elbow again. The fall from the saddle had started the wound in his arm to bleeding again. "You and me will have some settling up to do when this is over. I won't be letting it pass."

"Doubt if you'll be in shape to do much of anything, 'cepting patch your hide. Get going, Frank!"

The lean cowhand looped the rope around his forearm, dug spurs into the buckskin he was riding. The horse leaped away, and Bud and the blond Charlie swung in beside him, both yelling. Desperate, Jake Ryker threw himself to the nearest tree, placed it between himself and the departing riders. The rope went taut against the cottonwood's unbending trunk. Bracing himself with stiffened knees and the heels of his boots digging into the soil, Ryker laid his weight against the tough strands of the lariat. The rope snapped to a rigid line. Frank, having neglected to anchor his end to the saddle but winding it around his arm instead, catapulted backward off the buckskin, slammed hard to the ground.

Pain roaring through him, breathless from the shock and wrench of the rope, its sharp jerk only partly absorbed by the tree, Ryker lunged forward, fell upon the stunned rider. His hand darted out and closed upon the pistol in its holster. Bud and Charlie, taken by surprise at the swift change, hauled up short. The narrow-faced rider swore loudly as anger swept him.

"You damned fool!" he roared at Frank. "Ain't you got sense enough to throw a dally around your horn instead of trying to hold a rope with your hand?"

"Never mind him," Ryker said coldly. "Just keep your hands

where I can see them." He shifted his attention to Charlie. "You. Climb down, walk over here. Try dropping your arms and you're dead."

The blond came off his horse hurriedly, crossed to where Jake stood.

"Back up to me."

Charlie complied obediently. Ryker recovered his own pistol from the cowpuncher's waistband, relieved the man of his weapon.

"Now, you!" he called then to Bud.

Muttering under his breath, the rider dismounted. Jake put him through the same procedure. Afterward he pointed at Frank, now stirring feebly. "Load him on his horse."

Bud and Charlie wrestled the man to his feet, got him onto the buckskin, and turned. The blond man's eyes were wary.

"What's next? You taking us to Teague's so's your bunch can work us over good?"

"No, you're taking me to this Medford you keep talking about," Ryker answered, backing slowly to the chestnut. He had the inclination to step up to Bud, clout him soundly alongside the head as an object lesson, but his own wounds were throbbing. It could wait.

Charlie frowned. "Medford?"

Keeping his gun on the three men, Ryker swung up to the saddle, eased himself into the tree. "Mount up and head out. I'll be three jumps behind you all the time with my iron pointing at your backbones. And the way I'm feeling right now, you'd best not worry me."

"But . . . Medford. . . ."

"Move!" Ryker snapped impatiently, and drew back the hammer of his .45.

XIII

They rode due south for a time, finally broke over a low ridge, came out at once into a much greener country where thick grass grew and more trees were in evidence. For a while they followed out a broad swale, and then once again topped a hogback, where they looked down upon a large lake shimmering like blue-tinted crystal in the bright sunlight. Despite the ache in his head, the throbbing soreness of his arm, Jake Ryker stirred in admiration. Medford, whoever he was, had a fine range. He'd seen little as good anywhere, in fact. He began to notice cattle, many small herds of four or five hundred animals, an occasional group of less, all drifting leisurely along or else grazing on the lush forage.

Questions came to Jake Ryker's mind that he would like to ask of the men riding sullenly in front of him, but he held his tongue. He was in no mood for friendly conversation, and, considering that he had turned the trick on them and was driving them home under the sights of his pistol, he doubted very much they would be in a talkative frame of mind, either. But whatever the nature of the trouble Medford was having with the man the cowpunchers called Teague, the rancher certainly had every reason to fight for his land. He could only wish the Circle R was as fine.

Beyond the swale where the lake lay, they came out onto a broad plain that seemed to have neither high nor low areas. Grass was again plentiful, and the purple heads of the slender stalks nodded and shifted in the light breeze constantly, changing the mesa into a restless ocean. Many trees were to be seen, and well off to their right Ryker caught sight of a tall line of darker green growth in front of which were several structures. That would be Medford's ranch.

He sighed deeply, brushed at the sweat on his face. It would be a relief to climb off the gelding, get some medical attention for his irritating if not serious wounds, and grab a little food and rest. Too, it would be good to shed himself of Bud and his two companions.

They rode into the deserted yard, pulled up to a hitch rack placed beneath a spreading hackberry near the end of the house. It was a place dedicated strictly to business, Ryker noted, glancing around. Medford had no womenfolk on the premises, he guessed. There were no frills, no light touches to break the monotonous scene. Everything was of definite need and of practical use.

"Where'll Medford be?" he asked, swinging his attention to the three cowpunchers, halted and still in the saddle, awaiting his direction.

"Who the hell knows?" Bud demanded sourly. "Might try yelling."

"Can do better than that," Ryker said curtly, and pointing his pistol skyward, pressed off a shot.

At the blast of the weapon, the riders jumped. A voice sang out from inside the barn, and a dog came rushing up from behind the corrals, barking furiously. The kitchen shack's screen door flung open, banging against the wall of the clapboard building.

"That him?" Ryker asked, eyeing the elderly man who had appeared.

"Naw, he's the cook," Charlie answered. "That there's the boss coming up from the barn."

Ryker turned about. "Sit easy," he said quietly as Frank made a move to leave the saddle. "I want the lot of you where I can watch you."

Bud swore. "Hell, we ain't figuring to run."

"You sure as hell better not try," Ryker said mildly. "But with no more brains than you've showed, I'm not taking any chances."

Medford was a loose-jointed, thin man of sixty or so with almost no hair. He moved across the yard at a shambling gait, head pitched forward, small dark eyes sparking hotly. He halted at the end of the rack, took in his three hired hands along with Ryker and his drawn pistol all in one swift glance.

"What the devil's going on here?"

"Caught him trespassing," Bud began hurriedly, and then halted as a half smile broke the rancher's lips.

"You caught him? Appears to me it's the other way around." He faced Ryker. "Who're you, mister?"

"We figured him for one of Teague's bunch," Charlie explained.

Ryker shrugged. "Happens I'm not. Name's Jake Ryker. I'm from New Mexico. Brother and me have got a spread on the Pecos . . . the Circle R."

"He was on your range," Bud insisted doggedly, "and he sure looks like one of them Rocking T gunnies."

Ryker shrugged again. "Your hired hands are plenty hard to convince. Truth is, I've never heard of Teague . . . or of you, either, until I run into these three."

Medford plucked at his stringy mustache, eyes touching the bandage on Ryker's head, the bloodstained handkerchief wrapped about his arm. "I'll be begging your pardon for them, Mister Ryker. They was just looking out for me, and we're all a mite jumpy. Could say they was just doing what they figured was needful."

"Dragging a man across the flats, that's needful? I come close to parting with some hide."

"Glad you stopped it, and it looks like Frank there got the worst of whatever they started. Is it all right if they head over to the bunkhouse where he can get fixed up?"

Jake Ryker's shoulders stirred indifferently. He pulled the pistols he'd collected from the three cowpunchers from his saddlebags, handed them over.

"I was aiming to have a few words with Bud, but I reckon I can forget it."

"Be obliged if you will. Like I said, they was only thinking of me. Expect you'd better come on into the house. Seems you could use a little fixing yourself. They do that?"

Ryker shook his head, came off the chestnut. "Some trouble I had back on the trail." He paused there, his thoughts going to Nat Clover, to Gault and Chuck Virden. He wished there had been something he could do about their bodies. Leaving them there for the vultures and the coyotes was wrong, but he'd had no choice. Maybe he could do something about further trouble, however. He'd had his fill of it. Turning to Medford, he said: "One thing I'd like to mention while it's in my mind. I'm heading east for the Brazos country, Park Justin's place. Looks like I'll be on your range for a spell. If all of your hands are as touchy as these birds, I'd like a letter or something from you telling them I'm not against you."

Medford smiled faintly, nodded to Bud and the others who immediately pulled away from the rack and angled across the yard for the long, low-roofed building that evidently was the crew's quarters.

"Can sure fix that," the rancher said, leading the way toward the main house. "And you'll need it, I can tell you that. It's like a war was going on around here. How about a cup of coffee? Cook'll have some hotted up on the stove."

"Would taste mighty good," Ryker said, sinking into one of the several chairs scattered about on the porch. Out of the saddle, and with the lessening of tension, he was feeling somewhat better. Laying his hat aside, he watched Medford limp to the edge of the gallery, look toward the kitchen.

"Angus! Bring some coffee! Two cups," he yelled. Wheeling,

he returned to where Ryker was seated, drew back a chair for himself.

"What's all the fireworks about?" Ryker asked, when the older man was settled.

At that moment, Angus, the man Ryker had seen earlier in the doorway of the cook shack, came into the open. He crossed the yard to the porch, carrying the cups and a gray enamel pot. Setting them all on a table, he stared curiously at Ryker for a moment, then retraced his steps to his kitchen.

"Way those hands of yours talked, this Teague must be a real hell-raiser."

"Ain't no guessing about that," Medford said wearily, filling the cups with steaming, black liquid. Putting the pot to one side, he sank back glumly, small, dark eyes on the floor. "Teague's out to ruin me, bust me flat. And the way it's shaping up, he's going to do it."

Ryker brushed sweat from his face and neck. "Range war?" he asked, twirling the cup slowly between his fingers to cool it.

"Worse'n that. He wants my whole damned place."

"Got real big ideas."

"Plenty big. Bill Teague wants to own the county. Damned near does, excepting for my spread and a panhandle of brakes to the south of me."

Ryker took a swallow of the coffee, felt it jolt him. He stared wonderingly at the dark fluid. Medford chuckled. "Reckon I forgot to tell you. Angus uses a fair amount of whiskey in his coffee-making. Puts hair on it, he always says. We've sort of got used to it around here."

Jake took another pull at the cup. It was hot coffee royal with the emphasis on the royal. He nodded appreciatively. "Does a man good," he said. Then: "Teague sure can't make you sell out if you don't want to."

"Maybe not, but he can drive me to the wall."

80

"How? You've got plenty of beef, all of it in prime shape."

"That's just it. I've got me a fine, big herd that's not doing me a whit of good because I can't sell off a single head. Got to just stand by and let them eat up good grass, get fat for nothing."

Curiously at ease now, Ryker finished off his cup, reached for the pot. "Don't savvy what you're getting at. Market for beef's plenty good, I hear."

The rancher drained his cup, refilled it, wagged his head. "It ain't that I don't want to sell my beef, or that I haven't tried," he said, settling back in his chair. "But . . . well, it's this way. Like I said, Teague's out to get my spread. The Box M is the only thing left around here he don't own, and it's setting right smack dab in the middle of everything that's his."

"Then he's bought up everything around you?"

"Right. Bought if he had to, but just plain took, mostly. My ranch is sort of the key to it all, and with the lake that's on my west range. . . ."

"Saw it. A body of water like that is a mighty fine sight in this part of the country."

"The Box M is something Teague's wanting in the worst way," Medford went on. "Tried to buy me out several times. It never was a real good offer, and never was too bad, either. It's just that I ain't selling . . . not to him or nobody else. Hell, it took me a long time to build up to what I got and I'm not looking to turn it loose."

"I can understand. Money doesn't always count."

Medford smiled. "Ain't every man feels that way about it. I can see you do. Anyway, when Bill learned he wasn't going to yak me into a deal, he started forcing my hand . . . or trying to. Keeps hoorawing my hired help. I got less'n a dozen riders left. All the rest's been drove off by, scared by his bunch of hardcases. About ten men, that's all I've got, and me running better'n five thousand head of beef!"

"Five thousand," Jake echoed, startled by the figures. "How can you . . . ?"

"Might as well be fifty," Medford cut in bitterly, "for all the good they're doing me. I'm flat broke. Can't even meet wages."

"With all that stock and you're broke?"

"Can't sell a head. Teague's got me bottled up. No way of getting a herd to market. Tried this spring, three times. All it got me was about a hundred steers slaughtered and some of my cowhands shot up."

Jake Ryker considered the rancher's words in silence. He found it hard to believe that such a thing could happen. "Seems there ought to be a way."

"You don't know Bill Teague. He'll stop at nothing. Besides carrying all the politicians in the county around in his hip pocket, he's got the hired help . . . guns . . . to do what he wants. Expect there's thirty, maybe forty men riding for him. Fixes it so's he can keep a tight ring around me day and night."

"Didn't see anybody when I came in other'n those three men of yours."

"Some of Teague's bunch spotted you. You can be sure of that. Where'd you ride in from?"

"Came down the Taladega Trail, then cut across country. Not too sure just where it was."

"Be northwest of here. They seen you. Didn't give you no trouble since they figured you was just some pilgrim headed east. Where'd you say you was going?"

"The Brazos. Park Justin's ranch. Know him?"

"Heard of him, never met him. Got hisself a big outfit, I'm told."

"Never met the man, either," Ryker said, downing the last of his second cup of coffee. He felt much improved, but the need for sleep was beginning to tell on him now.

Medford took up the enameled pot, glanced at Ryker. Ryker shook his head, watched the rancher pour his third helping.

"Figured to be big once myself," the rancher said absently. "Reckon all men get the notion somewheres along the line, but most of them get it knocked out of them like me. Teague's got me crowded up to where I'm caught between a hole and a high place, and can't move. Got a mortgage note to meet and hired hands to pay, along with regular expenses always hanging over my head. If it turns out I can't meet any of them, I'm done for."

"Shame. You've got a fine place."

Medford's thin shoulders sagged helplessly. "Man can sure do a heap of hard work then have it end up meaning pure nothing. Like pouring sand into a rat hole . . . gets a fellow nowheres. Heard you say you and your brother had a ranch on the Pecos. You sell out?"

"No. We're sort of partners, but he does the ranching."

Medford paused, cup halfway to his lips. "I see. Somehow I got the idea you was headed for Justin's to hire on."

"No, aimed to buy some cattle."

Medford drew himself up slowly. His eyes were bright as he set the cup back onto the dusty table. "Buy cattle!" he echoed. "Hell almighty, Ryker, I can sell you cattle, all you want! Don't know what you figured to pay Justin for beef, but I'll let you have all you want for eight dollars a head."

XIV

"Eight dollars . . . ," Ryker murmured thoughtfully.

Medford pulled forward, came half out of his chair. His weathered face was eager, reflected the hope that now coursed through him. "All right then . . . seven dollars." The rancher was grasping frantically at straws that would save him from sinking into ruin.

Methodically Jake Ryker did some calculating. At $7 a head

he could buy almost three hundred steers, a third more than he and Tom had planned on. If pushed, Medford would probably make a deal on that basis, but he'd not press the rancher to do so; he was never one to take advantage of a man when he was in a tight. Regardless, the extra cattle would be a big boost for the Circle R.

There was another advantage to consider, too. He'd be spared the long, dangerous drive from the Brazos, thus cutting down the chances of loss and putting him back on the Pecos a lot sooner than he'd figured. If he could get back at all. That sobering thought clouded the bright vision from his mind. That was the catch—the whole problem. Bill Teague and his small army of hardcases had Medford pinned down. What made Ryker think they'd let him drive three hundred steers off Box M range?

"What d'you say?" Medford asked tensely.

"A plenty good offer, but. . . ."

"How much was you aiming to spend?"

"Two thousand. . . ."

"Two thousand," Medford repeated, sucking in his breath. "All right, tell you what. I'll give three hundred head, your pick or mine, range count or book tally, whichever. I'm ready for any kind of a deal you name."

Three hundred head for the same money Tom had intended to lay out for two hundred, and a drive that would be weeks shorter. It wouldn't matter to Park Justin, Ryker was certain. A man doing as much business as he wouldn't miss the sale; likely he'd forgotten all about Tom Ryker and the Circle R by now.

"It a deal?" Medford asked anxiously.

Jake Ryker shrugged. Best to play it safe. There was too much at stake, and if things went wrong, Callie and Tom would believe only that he had been careless and irresponsible and let them down. They'd never consider what the rewards of it would have been if he had come through.

"Like to take you up on it, but I don't see as I'd have any better luck driving a herd off your range than you've had."

Medford seemed to collapse. His shoulders went down and he settled back in his chair in defeat. "Well, maybe not. Could be Teague wouldn't bother you, them being your cattle and such. You'll be carrying a bill of sale, saying so."

"He'd know I bought them from you, and it'd be all the same to him . . . you selling cattle. Good offer, though. One I'd sure jump at if it was only me concerned. The way it is, however, I've got to play it safe."

Medford began to toy with the tips of his mustache. "Sure could use that two thousand," he mused. "Just ought to be a way somehow. You're looking to buy cattle, and I'm needing to sell. Got to be a answer somewheres."

Rising, the rancher moved to the edge of the gallery, stood there staring out into the sun-baked yard. Ryker, turned restless and fighting sleep, rose to his feet. Getting three hundred steers for what he intended to pay for two hundred would have really put the ranch on top, but there was no use hashing it over; he'd be a fool to gamble with the cards stacked the way they were.

"Real sorry," he said, stepping up beside Medford. "Wish there was some way. You mind if I drop over to your bunkhouse, grab myself about forty winks? Like to do some doctoring to my hurts, too, if it's all right with you."

"Sure . . . sure, go ahead," Medford answered, and then glanced up at the sudden rap of a horse entering the hard pack at a lope. "Hold on a minute," he said, as if struck with second thought. Beckoning to the rider, he yelled: "Max! Come over here for a minute!"

The rider bucked his head in acknowledgment of the summons. Pulling up to a corral, he dismounted, crossed to the house in quick, short strides. A thin, tall, mustached man, he was somewhere in his forties.

The rancher turned to Ryker. "Jake Ryker, like for you to meet my foreman, Max Cameron."

Cameron nodded in a brisk, curt way, offered his hand. His eyes were small and coal-black. "Pleased to meet you, Mister Ryker."

Ryker said: "Same goes for me."

"Jake Ryker's from over in New Mexico. Got a place on the Pecos. On his way to buy beef from that fellow, Justin. I'm trying to sell him some of my stock, only there's the problem of getting them by Teague and his bunch. You got any ideas on how he might move out three hundred head?"

Cameron folded his arms across his chest, studied the distant plain.

"Don't see how I'd have any better luck than you've had," Ryker said. "Being mine wouldn't help none since they'd know the steers came from here. Couldn't fool Teague on that."

"Expect you're right," the foreman said, toying with his mustache. "Let's see now, you'd aim to drive them west. One thing, Teague'd never figure us to start a herd in that direction because there ain't nothing that way . . . no market, I mean. We always have to take the trails to the north and east."

"What's that got to do . . . ?"

"Not saying for certain," Cameron continued, "but seems to me the odds would be plenty good. Teague's boys don't pay no mind to the panhandle. You just might get through."

Medford's eyes had recovered their bright glow of hope. "Why, sure. There's a danged good chance of it. Better'n a good chance, I'd say . . . just about a sure-fire cinch maybe."

Ryker listened, also hopeful, but yet chary. The possibility of losing the cattle, once purchased, was a deep worry in his mind. "Can't afford to take a risk," he said. "Have to tell you plain out that getting that herd taken away from me would put the Circle R out of business fast."

"Won't be much of a risk . . . and a man's got to take a few chances now and then if he expects to get ahead in this world. Stay poorer'n a church mouse if he don't."

Ryker shrugged. "I'm not afraid to gamble. Done plenty of it one way or another in my time. But this is different." He could have told of the bad luck that had befallen Tom and the shaky condition the ranch was in, and of his own position in the matter, but such was family business and none of theirs.

Cameron turned to face him. "I'm telling you straight, the odds will be better than good."

"Take something better than that, something stronger."

Medford sank back into his chair, weary, beaten. He stared at Cameron hopelessly. "Well, it was a thought. I can't blame Ryker for being careful. Two thousand's a lot of money."

Cameron drew out his handkerchief, mopped at his face. "Think maybe I've got a plan that'll work," he said, not giving up.

Ryker considered the man narrowly. "It'll have to be a good one," he said flatly. "Else save your breath."

"What is it, Max?" Medford asked, this time not responding to the prod of hope.

"How many steers did you say we're talking about?"

"Three hundred."

The lean foreman bobbed his head. "That's good. Not a big bunch." Moving to the table, he pushed the empty cups and granite pot into a corner. Digging into a pocket, he produced a pencil and a folded piece of paper. Turning up a clean side of the sheet, he flattened the creases and said: "Here, let me show you what I'm thinking." Drawing a small circle on the paper, Cameron said: "Here's where we are now. About five miles to the south of us is the panhandle. Lot of rocks and brush and arroyos, not much else. There's one big wash that cuts across the whole works. Peters out this side of the New Mexico border, say ten, maybe twelve miles."

"Sure," Medford said, face drawn into a tight frown. "Apache Wash. You saying he could take the cattle through there?"

"At night," Cameron said, nodding.

Medford rose to this feet. "Down the wash at night to where it ends, then cross over to the border. By God, it'll work!"

Max Cameron smiled quietly, confidently. "I can just about guarantee that if he makes it to the end of the arroyo, he's in the clear."

"And moving the stock at night, when nobody'll notice, ought to make that part for sure."

"Right. We could set things up for him. I'll have the crew drift three hundred head into that hollow north of the wash tomorrow morning, let them graze and bed down there in case any of Teague's crew just happen to be watching. They'd not get leery, just figure we were changing a part of the main herd, moving it on to different grass like we're always doing. Then, come midnight, Ryker could head them out. Moon's pretty bright this time of the month. Don't figure the stock'd give any trouble."

"Why, it'd be no chore a-tall!" the rancher exclaimed. "Sure, the way I see it."

Jake Ryker rolled the proposed plan about in his mind. It sounded practical, and the odds did seem to favor getting through. He'd evidently be on the lower end of Medford's range, a portion that bordered on brakes and that the rancher did not ordinarily use, since it led to no particular point. It seemed to him Max Cameron's reasoning was sound. The Rocking T outfit wasn't likely to be paying any attention to that section of the Box M. "If you do that . . . drive the steers to where Apache Wash begins . . . how far will it be to the New Mexico border?"

Cameron stroked his mustache again. "Well, I'd reckon it at

thirty miles from where you'd start to the point where you'd cross out of Texas into New Mexico."

"But you'd reach the end of the wash in about eighteen or twenty miles," Medford put in hurriedly. "You get there, you're safe. You wouldn't have to worry about nobody. Teague's bunch never rides that far south. Not his property for one thing, mainly because he don't want it, and there ain't nobody in that part of the country for another."

"Something else," Cameron said, adding to the reassurances his boss was outlining, "if somebody spied the dust after it's daylight, they wouldn't think nothing about it. By that time you'd be a far piece from here and they'd just figure it was dust devils blowing across the mesa."

Jake Ryker rubbed at his chin, his mouth, weighed the problem: its advantages against the risks that he'd be taking. It was well worth the gamble, he decided abruptly. "All right," he said. "If you'll get me three hundred head down into that swale, like you said, you've got a deal."

XV

"That's good, that's good!" Medford exclaimed, thrusting out his hand. "You're showing sense. Ain't but once in a lifetime a man comes across the kind of bargain I'm giving you."

Quietly Ryker took the rancher's hand, sealed the deal. Now that the decision was made, he felt better. It would be risky, he was not overlooking that, but so was any trail drive. He could lose cattle, the whole herd, in fact, on a long drive such as he would face if he bought cattle from Park Justin—violent storms, raiders, wolves—a half a dozen or more similar possibilities. It seemed to him he'd be taking no greater chance slipping through Bill Teague's blockade of the Box M than he would be assuming on a two-hundred-and-fifty-mile march, and the pay-off would be much greater—a hundred fine, fat steers, to be exact. But he had to make it through. If he failed—Ryker shook his head thoughtfully as he realized what Callie and Tom would say and believe should he fail. It wouldn't be easy. He'd need to be on guard every moment of the time until he was across the line into New Mexico—even for a while after that. "Expecting you to keep this quiet," he said then, turning to Medford and his foreman. "Get some of your crew to move the stock into that swale, the way you planned. Let everybody, including your own hired hands, think it's just a regular. . . ."

"I'll handle it," Cameron cut in coolly. "They won't ask questions. If they do, they won't get answers . . . none that'll tip them off to what you're doing, anyway."

Medford rubbed his palms together, frowned. "Are we able to spare a couple of men to help him make the drive?"

"Best I don't use any of your riders," Ryker said before Cameron could reply. "Be less chance of word leaking out, but mostly, if I'm spotted by any of the Rocking T crowd, I might have a better chance of talking my way through them if they don't see any of your men."

Medford nodded. "You're right. They could just leave you alone. But you sure can't drive three hundred head by yourself."

"Don't figure to try. Is there a town near here?"

"Closest is ten miles or so southeast. Place they call Polvareda."

"Teague's bunch hang out there?"

"Not much. Nothing to the dump. Cowhands usually do their drinking and womanizing in Rock City, twenty miles north. Bigger town."

"Polvareda'll do fine," Ryker said.

"Best I tell you it's a Mex settlement."

"That's all right."

"You speak the lingo?"

"Pretty good. Cook my pa had . . . and my brother's still got

. . . brought me up on it. Can usually get by with no trouble. We all understood now? Herd'll be in that hollow at the head of the wash and ready for me to move it out tomorrow at midnight?"

"Three hundred . . . they'll be there," Cameron said.

The rancher nodded his affirmative, brushed at his sweating face. "The two thousand, you're aiming to pay in cash, I take it?"

"In cash," Ryker said. "When I take over the herd, I'll have the money ready. I'd like that bill of sale then."

The rancher bobbed his head. "It'll be waiting for you." He paused, smiled apologetically. "It ain't that I'm mistrusting you, son, just want to keep things on a pure business basis. Now, about tonight, you're welcome to bunk in with me."

Ryker said: "Obliged to you. Expect I'll take you up on the offer, but could be I'll be getting back late from this Polvareda. One thing I forgot to mention. I'll be needing two or three pack horses."

"Something I got plenty of, too," Medford said. "I'll throw them in on the deal for ten dollars each. Can scrape up enough grub to get you to the next town, too, if you like. Know you'll be wanting to travel light but there's a few things you'll have to have."

"Be a help. Once I get the herd over the line there won't be such a push."

"Just you leave it to me," the rancher said. "You go scare yourself up a crew. I'll look after everything else, grub, horses, water . . . the whole passel."

Ryker hesitated. He had only a few dollars of his own, and as far as he knew the belt contained an even two thousand cash, and no more.

"Little problem of money to pay for all that. . . ."

Medford dismissed the objection with an airy wave of his

hand. "Owe me! I'm beholden to you for buying some of my beef. No reason why I can't show it by trusting you for a few dollars."

Ryker grinned. Doing business with Medford was a real pleasure; there was no limit to his accommodation. "You'll get your money soon as I'm back on the ranch," he said. "Now, if it's all right with you, I'll go over to your bunkhouse, clean myself up a bit. Could be I'll grab a couple hours sleep. Then I'll ride over to Polvareda."

"Place is yours," Medford said. "Anything you need, just holler."

Jake Ryker, much improved after cleaning up, eating, submitting to the cook's medical ministrations, and a nap, mounted the chestnut around midafternoon and struck out along the road that bore into the southeast. Within a short time, he rounded a low butte and sank into a broad valley through which a stream cut a crooked, shining path. Not long after that, he arrived at a cluster of trees growing in one of the creek's wider bends and there saw the scatter of two dozen or so squat adobe huts and buildings that made up the settlement of Polvareda.

The single street—actually a lengthy patio along which the structures were arranged—was silent and deserted when he turned into it. In a sweeping glance, Ryker took in the plain huts, the one saloon with the sign *CANTINA* canted above the door, the tiny Catholic church and its adjacent fenced-in cemetery, the single store that served as a supply point for all the inhabitants' needs.

Ignoring the two or three mongrel dogs that came forth finally from the shade alongside the houses to challenge his appearance, he pulled to a halt underneath a spreading cottonwood that grew in the center of the village. There was the smell of cooking chili on the still air, and that stirred a recollection of his childhood, when old Cocinero kept a quantity of the biting peppers continually cooking on his stove and filling the yard with their fragrance. The dogs tired, slunk off into the weeds. The place appeared to have been abandoned, but Ryker knew that was far from the truth; he was being observed by many pairs of eyes, some curious, some suspicious, others fearful. Americans—*gringos*—weren't particularly welcome in such villages. The best course to follow was to take it slow and easy. Sooner or later someone would come into the open. Patience, he'd learned from Cocinero, was a prized facet of the Mexican personality, almost a way of life, in fact.

Response came more quickly than he had anticipated. A boy, between twelve and fourteen years of age, wearing worn but clean cotton shirt and pants, eased through the doorway of the hut immediately opposite the big cottonwood, watched him silently.

Ryker swung off the chestnut, smiled at the youngster. *"¡Hola, muchacho! ¿Qué tal?"* he said, mustering his Spanish.

The boy remained impassive to the greeting for several moments. Finally he sauntered disinterestedly into the street, brown face tipped down shyly.

"I am in search of riders who can drive cattle," Ryker said. "Do you know of any?"

The boy looked up, frowned. After a bit, he said: "There are some. I do not know if they wish to work."

"I will pay in gold."

The boy's dark eyes brightened. "This work, it is near the village?"

"Partly. Also in New Mexico. A man would be gone from his house for a time of seven days perhaps. I will pay twenty dollars gold for each."

The young Mexican drew to sharp attention at that. His features became serious. "There are those who may accept such work. I for one."

Jake smiled. "You are but a boy. . . ."

"But strong. Often I have done the labor of a man."

"There could be danger."

The boy shrugged. "When is there not? I have no fear."

"It may well be. These men of whom you speak, where will I find them?"

"I can take you to them, but first I must know for myself. Is there work for me, also?"

Ryker mopped at the sweat on his face, grinned. He was being neatly blackmailed and knew it. He nodded. "Your name?"

"Miguel Calderón."

"Very well, Miguel Calderón. If your mother and father will permit it, you have a job."

"It is my mother we must speak of. My father is dead by the church."

"I understand. We will talk with her, but first take me to where I can speak with these men."

Miguel wheeled and led the way to a small building behind the general store.

"Aquí está el ayuntamiento," he said, pointing.

The word was not familiar to Ryker. He rubbed at his jaw. *"No comprendo."*

"The house where there are meetings," the boy explained.

A town hall, Ryker realized. "Is there a meeting now?"

"The men gather there each day to talk and drink wine when there is no work in the fields or other places to be found. Some will be there. Blas Armijo . . . he is one with much experience where there are cattle . . . you will find him. He is always there. My mother says he drinks too much wine."

One *vaquero.* That was fortunate, assuming he was sober, could remain so, and was willing to work. Ryker felt the boy's sharp, brown eyes drilling into him.

"Will you not enter?"

"If it is permitted."

"I shall go with you. That will make it all right."

Miguel crossed over to the deep inset door, opened it, and stepped inside. Ryker followed more slowly, hearing the bantering greeting the boy's appearance evoked.

"A man of tender years," a voice called jokingly. "Does he seek to tip the skin of wine with us?"

"Perhaps he desires something of greater strength," another remarked.

Miguel squared his slight shoulders. "I come with a friend . . . one who wishes to pay gold for a short time of work in New Mexico."

There was a faint scuffling sound in the murky depths of the room. A door was opened in a back wall and a band of daylight broke across the darkness. Ryker could see a half dozen men squatting about, backs to the mud brick walls. Most were too old for the job he had to offer.

Spurs jingled. A moment later a lean, middle-aged Mexican dressed in the full regalia of a *vaquero* moved up to the entrance. "You are welcome here," he said to Ryker, and bowed slightly.

Ryker entered, halted. There was a table at the opposite end of the dirt-floored room. A few benches were placed here and there. All were being ignored for the more informal habit of squatting on the heels. The *vaquero*—Blas Armijo the boy had called him—handed Ryker the skin of wine, again inclined his head. "We are honored to have your share our wine."

Ryker could detect the faint thread of irony in the man's tone, the tinge of patronizing mockery. He ignored it. "The honor is mine," he said, and tipped the vessel to his lips. The wine had a tart, fruity taste, burned somewhat on its downward passage. Passing the liquor back to Armijo, he said—"Many thanks."—and waited. The matter of business would come in due time. It had been mentioned. It would be impolite for him to bring it up again.

"You have come from New Mexico?" asked an elderly man, puffing on a limp, brown cigarette.

"From the Pecos River country."

"Once I was through there," the old one mused. "It was in the days when I often journeyed to Santa Fe. Ah, Santa Fe, it does well?"

Ryker had not visited the ancient capital in years but little ever changed there, he knew. "It does well," he assured the man.

Armijo leaned against the door's thick frame, struck a match to a slim cigar. "This work of which you speak, it has to do with cattle?"

Ryker nodded. "Yes. I have a small herd of three hundred I wish to drive to the ranch of my brother and me in New Mexico. It will require three men of experience . . . and Miguel here, who I have already hired."

There was a moment of quiet laughter during which the boy shifted self-consciously.

"For the work I will pay twenty dollars in gold. Food will also be furnished."

"It is fair," the *vaquero* said. "When will this drive begin and from where will it start?"

"I wish those who agree to meet me at the arroyo to the south of the Medford Ranch. At sundown."

"The place is well known to us all. It is called the Arroyo of the Apaches. Once there was a fierce battle with the Indians there."

Ryker nodded to the elderly speaker. Medford and Cameron had mentioned the name; he had neglected to state it. He said nothing of that, however, simply bowed slightly to the old man and said: "Thank you, uncle." He turned his attention again on

Blas Armijo. "It is settled? I can expect three men at the arroyo at sundown tomorrow?"

"It is agreed," the *vaquero* replied. "I myself shall be there with two others of reliable character."

XVI

Ryker backed into the open, beckoned for the *vaquero* to follow. Armijo complied quickly, with Miguel trailing behind.

"There is something?" Armijo asked.

Ryker said: "A matter of importance to me. It will be wise to say nothing of this to others. Also, it will be a favor if you will caution the men inside not to speak of it."

Blas Armijo's brows lifted. He leaned against the weather-washed adobe wall of the building, a spur making a clear, bell-like tinkling as he cocked one booted foot against its base. "There is a secret that must be kept?"

"From certain persons. You know of the trouble that lies between the rancher Medford and another of the name Bill Teague?"

The *vaquero*'s eyes glittered. "Who does not know of Bill Teague and his men. Also of the trouble. Such is not of a secret nature."

"True. The secret concerns me in that the cattle that are to be driven were purchased by me from Medford. Should Teague or his men learn of this fact, they will attempt to halt us and there will be trouble."

Armijo sucked at his slender cigar in thoughtful silence. Finally he stirred: "We have no wish to involve ourselves in the trouble of these two men. Teague is one who is no friend of the Mexican people. Nor are his riders. And since we are but a small village and few in number, it is wise for us not to have them as enemies."

"I hope to avoid trouble. The plan I shall follow is such that we will not encounter any of the man's riders unless ill luck befalls us."

Again Blas Armijo's features were solemn in thought. "An encounter would then be only in the nature of an accident? There is small chance that will occur?"

"A very small one, greatly lessened if word of the drive is not spread. We shall take a route that Teague's men do not frequent, most of which will be traveled at night. I have faith there will be no incidents."

"Very well," the *vaquero* said in his stiff, formal way. "The others will be warned. We have no love for this Teague and those who work for him. It will be an honor and privilege to partake of a venture that reduces him in stature."

Ryker extended his hand. "I thus have your word that caution will be used and that you, with two good men, will be at the Arroyo of the Apaches tomorrow at sunset to begin the drive?"

"It is true," Armijo assured him, closing his slim fingers around those of Ryker.

"Good. It is settled. Until later."

"Go with God," the *vaquero* murmured, and turned to reënter the building.

Ryker dropped his hand on Miguel's shoulder. "We must now speak with your mother, young one."

The boy looked up at him, worry in his eyes. "You will say little to her of this man, Teague?"

"How can it be avoided? She must be made aware of the possibility of trouble."

"But if she believes the work to be dangerous, she will oppose my going."

"Perhaps, but it is always wise to be honest, especially with one's elders."

Miguel's shoulders drooped. "Very well," he said disconsolately, "but I shall go whether she wishes it or not."

Silently he led the way through the late afternoon sunlight to the hut where he lived. Jake Ryker trailed him through the low doorway, noting the caged mockingbird near a window as he stepped into the cool interior created by the thick walls, noting also the few furnishings and the utter cleanliness of everything.

"Mama!" the boy called, halting in the last of the three rooms strung end to end—parlor, bedroom, and kitchen, identical to the shotgun shanties of many homesteaders.

"Here. . . ."

Her reply came from the yard. Ryker followed the boy into the open where a woman somewhere near his own age was removing wash from a clothesline stretched between two trees. She was light-skinned for her race, but she had the shining black hair and large, doe-soft brown eyes that distinguished her kind.

When her gaze fell upon Ryker, she straightened, the stiffness of fear coming into her manner. Dropping the cloth she was holding into the reed basket at her feet, she straightened her black cotton skirt, tugged briefly at the collar of the white shirtwaist she was wearing, and stepped forward. "There is trouble, Miguel?"

"No, no Mama!" the boy replied indignantly. "This gentleman wishes to give me work. He will tell you of it."

Relief came into the woman's features. She moved nearer. Late afternoon sunlight caught at the coil of jet strands on the nape of her neck, glinted softly.

"I am María Calderón," she said, smiling, and offered her hand.

"My name is Jake Ryker," he introduced himself and gave her firm, work-worn hand the single pumping motion customary with the Mexican people. "It is a pleasure to know Miguel's mother. He is a fine boy."

"Thank you. This work you have for him?"

"I am driving a herd of cattle from a place near here to the ranch of my brother and myself in New Mexico. . . ."

"He will be taken from here?" María broke in, her features filling with alarm.

"Yes. The work will require a few days of absence. A week perhaps."

"I shall be paid twenty dollars in gold, Mama!" the boy said excitedly. "So much money!"

"It is a small fortune," María agreed, not taking her eyes off Ryker. "Why do you wish for him to accompany you? He is hardly of an age for such a. . . ."

"I can do a man's work," Miguel protested, seeking to head off her objection. "Have I not done so before? This will not be hard for me, this riding of a horse and driving of cattle."

The woman continued to study Jake Ryker, awaiting his answer to her question. He smiled. "It is that he asked and is one of considerable persistence. I had promised."

María nodded, smiled, also. "Of this I am aware." Her manner relented. "I suppose there is no harm in it . . . a cattle drive. Are there others from Polvareda who are to work with you?"

"Blas Armijo. He is also to find two more men. There will be four of us, and Miguel."

At the mention of the *vaquero*'s name María Calderón's nose crinkled slightly in disapproval, but she made no comment.

"I must tell you there is a possibility of trouble, but only a small possibility. I shall watch the boy carefully and protect him from harm if it is in my power to do so. This can also be expected of Blas Armijo, I am sure."

Again María frowned. "I . . . I do not know. He is so young, and I have nothing else . . . no one."

"I am the man of the household," Miguel stated soberly. "It is right that I do the things that are expected of me."

"Of course."

"Can we not use the twenty dollars in gold?"

María smiled then, showing her strong, white teeth. "Very well, it shall be. As you have said, it is only right." She turned to Ryker. "I thank you for what you do."

"For nothing," Ryker said. "I am pleased to help, but he will work just as the others. He will receive no favors except if there be trouble."

"That is as it should be. He will take his place with the men, then he must be treated the same as the men. When is it you leave?"

"Tomorrow night. From the place they call Arroyo of the Apaches."

María Calderón nodded slowly. "My grandfather was slain there in a terrible battle with the Indians," she murmured. "Could such have evil portent for Miguel?"

"I think not," Ryker replied, and glanced to the boy. "I will have a horse there awaiting you. Is it possible for you to ride with one of the others to the place?"

"Blas will take me with him behind his saddle," Miguel said confidently.

"Good. Then I shall see you at the proper time. Now, I must go."

María Calderón's face clouded immediately. "You will not stay for the evening meal with us? It is late, and I note that you have been injured."

Only a woman would have commented on the presence of his bandages, Ryker thought. None of the men, although the white strips of cloth on his head and arm were unavoidably notice-able, had said anything. It was their way, for to inquire would have been considered probing and therefore impolite. But a woman's way was different, one of genuine concern and heartfelt sympathy.

"The injuries are nothing," he assured her, "and while I would be honored to take the meal with you and Miguel, I must return at once. There is much that I have yet to do. There will be another time, perhaps?"

"Our house is your house," María said. "You are welcome at all times. *Vaya con Dios.*"

"*Gracias y adiós,*" he replied, echoing the gentle farewell.

Returning to the chestnut, he swung onto the saddle and cut around, headed back for Medford's. He was hungry but he had not wanted to impose on María Calderón's hospitality, knowing well that for them food was not always easy to come by. To have offered to help would have been an unpardonable insult, accordingly to decline was the only course open to him. If he hurried, he probably would make it to Medford's in time to eat with the crew. And he could get back to talking in plain English again. He was weary of the prim, formal manner in which he'd been required to speak, of the polite fencing, of being careful to observe all the amenities so dear to the Mexican people. He respected their customs and their courteous mannerisms, even admired them, but that hour or so in Polvareda had called for more Spanish than he'd spoken in years, and the effort had drained him bone dry.

XVII

There were three hundred and five head in the herd, Medford tossing in the five extra when they turned up in the tallying, for good luck, which he said he was sure Jake Ryker would have. Ryker, fingering the bill of sale he had received at the conclusion of the transaction, watched the rancher and Max Cameron ride off, taking with them the cowhands who had brought in the cattle. The full realization of the responsibility that he now shouldered drove home to him at that point, and for several long, lonely moments he stood there, staring at the departing horsemen.

He had given over the $2,000 Tom had entrusted to him, and he had a fine herd of cattle to show for the money. He should have no qualms. In times past he had handled larger sums of cash, managed herds of greater number. But this was different. He supposed it was the fact that Tom and Callie were depending upon him—that they had done so reluctantly and with little faith in his ability to come through. A bit of impatience stirred him. Hell, money was only money, cattle only cattle, and while he didn't expect it, anybody could have bad luck, run into trouble. Only he couldn't let that happen. He had to get the herd to the Circle R, come tornado or taxes—and then he'd be through.

He wasn't cut out for this sort of life: all the strain and worry and sweating out the possibility of losing money, of mothering a bunch of steers and keeping them alive for his sake and that of his kin. Where someone else was concerned it was different; they recognized his ability and never doubted his integrity, and he was free to come and go as he pleased. He'd do what he'd decided earlier, find a good man for a foreman, and then take off. But first he had to get the herd to the Circle R. It was all up to him now. He could not fall back on Medford or Cameron for help, and there was no turning back and canceling out the deal to recover the $2,000. It was the same as having walked out onto quicksand. He could do nothing but go on, try to reach the opposite side.

Tucking the ownership paper in his pocket, he glanced to the horizon in the west. The sun was gone, and now a flare of gold was spraying into the steel blue of the sky, touching the bellies of the scattered clouds and setting them afire. It would be dark in another hour. He'd start the herd moving then. No sense holding off until midnight. The herd had loafed, grazed, and watered in the swale all that day. They wouldn't be difficult to handle, and two or three more hours on the trail during the night could spell the difference in avoiding trouble or encountering it.

Touching the chestnut with his spurs, Ryker moved forward, swinging along the west side of the bedded-down cattle. Blas Armijo and the two men he'd recruited to help, Oreste and Tiofilo Luna, brothers, and young Miguel were already on the job, drifting quietly about the fringes of the herd. The *vaquero* was keening softly in a low voice, and twice Ryker had seen him reach into the ornately decorated leather pocket of his big Mexican saddle, procure a bottle, and have a swallow of its contents. So far the liquor seemed to be having no effect on him; until it did, he'd say nothing to the man about it.

Miguel, overwhelmed by the pony and gear Ryker had provided, was being careful to do all things right, listening attentively to the instructions Armijo gave him and carrying them out with the alacrity and enthusiasm of youth. Each time Ryker caught his eye, the boy responded with a wide grin.

Medford had made it easy. When the final moment came for passing over the cash in exchange for the herd and the bill of sale covering it, the rancher had produced also three pack mules loaded with trail grub and water as well as a quantity of grain for the horses to keep them in good condition for the trip. Ryker had gone to some pains personally, however, in selecting a mount and gear for Miguel, insisting that the rancher add it to what he owed for the mules and the supplies. A boy trying to take the place of a father deserved encouragement and reward, he felt.

Coming to the far end of the herd, Jake crossed over to where Blas sat, one leg hooked around the horn of his hull, smoking one of the thin, black cigars of which he seemed to have an inexhaustible supply. "Soon as it's full dark, we'll move them out," he said.

The *vaquero* nodded. "I have note there is a leader steer," he said, also using English. "Oreste has taken him to the front. The others will follow."

That was good news. Ryker raised himself in the stirrups, looked to the forward line of cattle. He located the long-horned, old brindle standing, spraddle-legged and somewhat belligerently apart from the rest. "Fine. Once we get him headed down the wash, we shouldn't have too much trouble. Oreste and Tiofilo . . . have they driven cattle before?"

"There have been times," Armijo said, lapsing into his more easily managed native tongue. "They are good men. They will do as directed." He paused, turned his eyes to where Miguel was walking his pony slowly along the edge of the herd. "The young one, he will be a man, eh?"

"A good one," Ryker said, "but no harm must come to him." He roweled the gelding into motion. "I will give the signal when it is time. Also, it is best that all things be done quietly once the drive has begun."

"Agreed."

Ryker rode on. The *vaquero* was armed, he saw, and was relieved to know that. If something developed, there would be at least two guns among them. Neither Oreste nor his brother, or, of course, Miguel had a weapon. He glanced again at the west. The gold flare had paled to a thin yellow and the cottony clouds no longer were tipped with color. Long fingers of shadow were beginning to creep across the land, and in the deeper recesses of the wash where flash floods had in times past gouged great handfuls of the red soil, pockets of blackness had formed. A pearl-like haze was settling over the country. Overhead, a gaggle of crows were cutting their way through the sky, headed, no doubt, for the trees around Medford's and the easy pickings they would find around the corrals and barn. Somewhere in the stillness a cock quail gave his sharp, quick call.

Things would be starting to stir in the saloons and gambling halls of the big trail towns—Abilene, Wichita, Fort Worth, Dodge, and all the others. They would have the big hanging lamps lit, and the soft, yellow glow would be seeking out the corners of the rooms, tinting the skins of the drovers and cowhands and gamblers and like frequenters who came within range of their flare, and shining on the bangles of the saloon girls' dresses. The good smell of smoke would be everywhere, blending subtly with the stale, but still friendly odor of spilled whiskey and beer and the plain, everyday stink of sweat and dust. An undercurrent of excitement would be threading the crowds, further heightened, perhaps, by the sudden tenseness of a threatened gunfight over the turn of a card, a misspoken word, or possibly the smile of a woman. And there were those nights on the trail. A man was a king then, alone but never lonesome, hunched over a fire on some high plain, or deep in a quiet, warm valley while hardtack and bacon heated and sizzled over the flames to the accompaniment of gently bubbling coffee.

In that way of life a man wanted for little, needed but little: a good horse, strong tack, a few trail conveniences—spider, coffee can, and cup—and a few dollars now and then to buy grub and an occasional drink or play a few hands of poker. True, it was a road that led nowhere if calculated on the basis of worldly possessions and accomplishments, but the importance of that was a matter of opinion; one involving the question of values and just what constituted the greatest worth. For himself, Jake Ryker was sure he knew what was more important to him—simply being a man among men, free to come and go as he willed in a life uncomplicated by possessions and firm attachments, while he reveled in the appreciation and enjoyment of simply being alive in a world of matchless grandeur and beauty. That was where he and Tom differed so vastly. To the older Ryker security was what counted most, a consideration Jake never wasted a moment's worry over. It had always been that way, and that bridgeless gap between them was one that would never close. Jake knew that, and while he regretted it for the sake of blood ties, it caused him no loss of sleep. He was glad of one thing, however—the extra hundred steers he was bringing back to the Circle R should cause Tom and Callie to feel their future was a much better one.

He swung away from the herd, loped the chestnut to the crest of a nearby hill. Halting, he swept the darkening country with a probing gaze. There was no sign of riders anywhere. Only the scurrying about of a family of gophers in a ravine to his left broke the absolute, inert quality of the surroundings. So far they had not drawn any attention from Bill Teague's men.

He cut back, dropped off the short slope, and angled toward Blas Armijo, still taking his ease on the slim-legged bay horse he rode.

"Move 'em out," he called in a low voice.

The *vaquero* bobbed his head, flipped his stump of a cigar away, and dropped his leg into place. Roweling his mount with the big star spurs he wore, he wheeled off, slanting for the front of the herd. Ryker heard him sing out in a guarded voice to the Luna brothers, and turned away, doubling back for the rear of the herd. Looking over his shoulder, he saw the men riding in among the cattle, flaying about with their rawhide lariats. Ryker, with Miguel suddenly close by, followed the same procedure, and shortly, with the first shine of the moon silvering the landscape, the steers were up and moving sluggishly down the wash.

An hour later, with the old brindle in charge, the herd had strung out into a compact, narrow oblong that flowed steadily within the banks of Apache Wash. It was accomplished much more easily than anticipated, and Ryker guessed he could thank

Medford and Max Cameron for that; the cattle had rested for almost a full day and were far from tired. As a result, their customary reluctance to travel after sundown was greatly minimized.

Leaving the Lunas to ride drag, Miguel and the *vaquero* at flank positions, and relying upon the lead steer to follow the course of the arroyo, Ryker pulled away from the herd, began a constant circling of it at a distance, while he maintained a watch for riders appearing in the night. The dust lifted by the plodding hoofs turned dark and heavy, began to hang like a threatening cloud over the wash. By day it certainly would have been noticed from a considerable distance; in the light of the stars and moon it would go unseen except at close range. He owed Max Cameron his appreciation for that idea, too, that of a night drive through the arroyo.

The herd moved on steadily, and as the hours passed the miles melted away. Apache Wash, Ryker recalled, was somewhere in the neighborhood of twenty miles long, a bit less possibly. He couldn't hope to cover the entire distance before sunrise, of course, but at the pace they were traveling, they would not fall too far short. All they need do was reach the end of the arroyo safely and they'd have half the job done insofar as Bill Teague's riders were concerned, Medford and his foreman had assured him.

The wash deepened, narrowed, became a brush-cluttered gorge. A short time later it widened again, lifted toward the level of the surrounding plain. Loose sand slowed the pace; rock-studded ground increased it. The sky to the east began to gray, the earth formations and growths that were mysterious, unfamiliar silhouettes in the night took shape, lost their enigma. Ryker veered into the herd, sought out Blas Armijo.

The *vaquero* met him with a broad grin. "It goes well, this cattle drive, eh?"

Ryker nodded. "Couldn't ask for anything better. Going to be daylight soon. Any idea how far it is yet to the end of the arroyo?"

Armijo shrugged. "Five miles, perhaps less."

They'd fall that much short of making it out of Apache Wash by sunup. It couldn't be helped. He'd hoped to be nearer than that but a herd travels just so fast, and he had to admit they had done better than usual.

"We do not stop?" the *vaquero* asked. "There is a place of wideness not far. Possibly one hour from now."

Jake Ryker frowned. "I want to cover as much ground as we can before we pull up and camp. The nearer we are to the New Mexico border, the better I'll feel."

Blas glanced around, dark eyes sweeping the gradually lightening country. "There has been no one to follow?"

"Haven't spotted anybody. If Teague's bunch are onto us, they're keeping out of sight."

"That cannot be so. There is little place on this prairie land to hide except in this wash, and we are there." The *vaquero* produced one of his cigars, offered it to Jake. When the tall redhead declined, he bit off the tapered end, spat it aside, and thumbed a match into a small flame. Puffing the weed into life, he jerked his head in the direction of the herd. "They will go two, maybe three hours more. Then they will wish to stop. There will be no driving them for they will be tired and stubborn. And there is no water for their thirst."

"I know that, but the worst of it will be behind us. From what Medford told me, there's water on the other side of the border."

"Yes, a small place of water provided by a windmill. It will take much time and labor to water the cattle there."

"Only place we'll hit before we reach the Pecos, unless you know of another."

"I do not."

"Then we'll have to make it do. But that's something we'll worry about when the time comes."

A hollow, flat crack echoed through the dust haze. Armijo, holding his cigar by thumb and forefinger, suddenly released it. A look of puzzlement crossed his swarthy features. Ryker stared at the man, and then, as a red stain began to spread down the front of the *vaquero*'s shirt, he realized that Blas Armijo had been shot, that the sound he had heard was the report of a rifle.

"*Señor. . . .*" the *vaquero* murmured, raising a hand. "*Yo. . . .*"

Abruptly he fell forward, toppled from his saddle. More rifle shots began to pop through the racket of the suddenly running herd. A bullet sang off Ryker's hull, another plucked at his arm. Galvanized into sudden action, he wheeled away, dragging out his pistol as he spurred for a rise to his left.

He could see no one through the hovering clouds of yellow dust, could only guess that the raiders, whoever they were, had come in from that side of the arroyo. Cursing, he broke out into the clear, looked frantically around for Miguel, for the Luna brothers and the attackers. Two men were bearing down upon him at a fast gallop. One carried a handgun, the other a rifle. Likely he had been the marksman who had sighted in on Blas Armijo and picked him off. Anger rising in him, Jake Ryker raised his weapon, snapped a bullet at the oncoming pair, and veered back into the pall. Miguel should be on the opposite side of the running herd. He would be fairly safe there unless more raiders were moving in from that quarter. Grimly Ryker crouched low over the saddle as the chestnut legged it for the farther side of the wash. Were these Teague's men, or had he run into a bunch of rustlers out to grab a small herd for themselves? It didn't matter; they meant to get what they came after and were not adverse to killing everybody who stood in their way.

Again he was out of the boiling dust. He saw two riders wheel off to his left, white-clad figures flat on their saddles as they raced to gain the safety of the distant brush. The Luna brothers. They were getting out of it fast. Unarmed, they had no other choice. Miguel! Where the hell was Miguel? Motion to one side caused him to swerve the chestnut. He tried to pierce the wall of shifting brown with squinting eyes. A horse broke into view, two more. Raiders! The pair he'd seen earlier, and another. He threw two quick shots at them, spurred the gelding again into the sheltering curtain of dust, hearing the vicious chatter of rifles, the higher pitched crackle of pistols.

Miguel must have made a run for it, too, just as the Lunas had. He hoped so. There was nothing the boy could do but get himself hurt, Ryker realized. It was best he face the outlaws alone, for the only thing that counted now was a gun. But Miguel. . . . Worry and uneasiness plagued him. He must be sure the boy was safe first. He had to find him, had to be certain of it. Roweling the chestnut, he sent the big horse plunging ahead. One thing, if the cattle continued to run, his chances for saving them were good. But that really didn't matter. It was Miguel that counted. The hell with the cattle. Miguel. . . .

Abruptly two riders loomed up in the murk. Ryker reflexed a shot even as he saw the pale flash of their weapons. In the next fleeting fragment of time the gelding veered hard to the right. Jake Ryker saw the broad, spreading horns of a confused steer directly in front of him, clawed at the saddle horn to save himself from falling. Ryker's fingers wrenched free of the saddle horn. He felt himself pitch forward and down. He struck hard. Pain surged through him, but the instinct to survive kept him conscious, drove him back to his feet. The herd was all around him, it seemed, bawling, heaving, wild-eyed steers cutting back and forth in the dust. Something hit him from behind. He went down again, endeavored to rise, and then, as force from a different angle smashed into him with a sickening impact, he lost all awareness.

XVIII

It was cool and dark when Ryker once more opened his eyes. Somewhere nearby a dog was barking and the air was clear and sweet and filled with the smell of simmering beans larded with pork. He shook off the haze that drifted loosely about in his brain, winced as the movement brought on a momentary onslaught of stabbing pain. He waited for several long minutes, then struggled to gain a sitting position. The best he could do was come to an elbow. He was in a small, familiar room. A caged mockingbird in the deep-set window opposite his bunk-like bed eyed him mistrustingly, and that, too, evoked a stir of remembrance. It came to him then. He was in the home of María and Miguel Calderón.

Fighting to organize his thoughts, he lay back, began to puzzle it out. There had been the raid—rustlers, or maybe they'd been Teague's men. Regardless, Blas Armijo had been killed, the Luna brothers had fled the scene, and he had been thrown from his horse while searching for Miguel. Relief registered on his mind. Evidently the boy was all right. Only Miguel could have brought him to the Calderón house after he'd been knocked out. But the herd was lost—gone.

A bitter oath slipped from his lips as that fact broke through to him. Maybe, if he could get on his feet, go back to Apache Wash, there'd still be a chance. Again he tried to rise. Curiously he had no strength, and movement rewarded him only with pain. He relaxed, lifted a hand, and touched the tightness that encircled his head. Either he'd taken another hard rap there or else the old wound had reopened, for a fresh bandage had been applied. He noted then the strip of new, clean white about his arm. Evidently María had dressed both his injuries. There had been nothing she could do for the soreness that claimed his body, however. Every muscle and bone of his being was making itself known. He swore again in a low, breathless way. It didn't matter. He had to get on his feet. He'd weather the pain somehow. The important thing was the herd.

"You are awake."

María Calderón's voice greeted him from the doorway leading into the kitchen. Turning her head, she called into the yard: "Miguelito, he is awake!"

Ryker lay back, watched the woman come into the room, hearing at the same time the quick rush of footsteps across the hard-packed floor. A moment later the boy was standing in the room, smiling at him through the dimness.

"You are well!" he exclaimed happily.

"Not well," María corrected. "It is only that he has returned from the unconsciousness given to him by the fall. Another day, perhaps two. . . ."

"No!" The word sprang angrily from Ryker's lips. "I must find my cattle, recover them."

"That cannot be done so soon," María replied in her calm, quiet way. "If you will arise, you will learn that it is true."

Jake Ryker mustered his strength once more, sought to draw himself upright, failed. Frustration ripped through him again. There was no use trying to fool himself. He didn't have it in him.

"Now perhaps patience will come to you," the woman said. "Do you hunger?"

Ryker moved his head slightly, very carefully, replying that he did not. He reached out for Miguel's hand, wrapped it in his own. A quietness had moved into him now that he had accepted the situation. "You were not injured, young friend?"

"No. I am well."

"Good. But the herd . . . it is gone?" He knew the answer

without asking, but he was hoping against the inevitable. The boy nodded solemnly.

Jake Ryker was silent for a long minute, eye on the mockingbird. Then: "Did you see all that happened there in the arroyo? Part is known to me. Blas Armijo was shot and is dead. The Luna brothers escaped to the brush. I was riding with the herd, seeking you when my horse was frightened by a steer that turned upon him. I remember falling but little of what took place after."

"I was safe," Miguel said. "Oreste called to me to hide by a small tree that was near when the shooting started. I saw the bandits ride among the herd. There were four of them, I think. Perhaps five."

"Were any known to you?"

"I do not think so. Possibly I have seen them, but there was none I can call by name."

"What of the Lunas? Did they return to the village?"

"No, it is thought they are hiding among the trees of the sand hills because they fear to return to their homes."

Ryker mulled that over. It could mean the brothers knew the identity of the raiders. It would pay to find them, ask questions. "It was you who brought me to your home?" he said then, coming back to the boy.

"Yes. It was near where I hid that you fell from your horse. I waited until the bandits were gone and went then to where you lay. There was much blood."

"Miguel did well," María said, a note of pride in her voice. "The wound in your head was bleeding. Also that in your arm. And you had many cuts and scratches. He stopped the flowing with his handkerchief. What is of a mystery to me is how he was able to put you on your horse . . . one so small."

"I am strong for my size," the boy declared. "Also, it was with his own help. When I explain to him that he must rise to the saddle, the effort was made, although I truly do not think he was awake entirely. Thus, with my help, it was done."

Ryker could recall nothing of climbing back onto the chestnut, or of the ride back to Polvareda. He had managed it all instinctively, he supposed. "I am in your debt, my young friend," he said, again grasping the boy's hand. "To you also, *Señora* Calderón." He glanced down at the clean clothing he wore, the change he had carried in his saddlebags. "It appears you not only took me in but also were kind enough to clean and dress me."

False modesty was no part of María Calderón. She shrugged, said matter-of-factly: "The clothing was torn in many places, covered also with blood and dust . . . as were you. It was necessary to remove the rags and bathe you, after which the clothing found with your saddle was used."

"That was a great kindness. I hope no trouble will befall you from the outlaws because of me."

María looked down. "It is to be hoped they will not search here for you."

Alarm shot through Ryker. "They search for me?"

"Yes."

"Then it is best I leave your house, find a different place to hide."

"Wait, hear it all. The men who went to recover the body of Blas Armijo encountered two of the bandits. They asked of you. It was hoped by them apparently that you were dead, also, since that is what they wished. The men replied they knew nothing and the outlaws went away. It is not known if the information satisfied them or not."

Ryker frowned. "Likely they will come here for there will be those in the village who saw Miguel bring me to your house."

"Nothing will be said by them if questioned. There is no love among them for the *gringos*. Too long have they . . . we felt the point of their cruel ways."

There was a bitterness to María's words, and looking closely at the woman, Ryker saw anger in her dark eyes.

"There are few in Polvareda who do not owe the one who worked for the ranchers a debt of hate," she continued. "Each would look forward to a means for repaying in kind the treatment they have received."

"I am sorry for what has happened to you," Ryker said. "But all of my people . . . all Americans . . . are not as those of whom you speak. Most respect the Mexicans and the Spaniards. There are bad apples in all barrels."

"This I know," María said, sighing. "It is that there are times when I am carried away by strong thoughts . . . by things I remember."

"Life will change for you, become good. You are deserving of it," Ryker said, and added: "Do you think it would be possible to find Oreste and Tiofilo?"

María shrugged. "Perhaps. I think they will send word to their families, advise them of their hide-out. You wish to speak with them?"

"Yes. It is of importance. I believe they may know the raiders by name. It might bring about the recovery of my cattle. Unless I am able to do that, the loss will come as a great blow to my brother and his wife. And to me."

"I shall make inquiry," María said, glancing through the doorway into the dark. "If. . . ."

"You must not do this," Miguel broke in anxiously. "If they search for our friend, it is possible they will find you. When it is late, I will go and look for the cattle."

"You . . . ," Ryker began protestingly.

"It will be a simple task. I shall return to where the attack was made. The cattle continued down the arroyo when last I saw them. It is probable they are still in the arroyo. Would it not be better to find them than to seek information from the Lunas?"

"That is true, but there is risk."

"There will be small danger. I have learned to move in the shadows and the brush with the silence of the coyote. I shall not be heard or seen."

Ryker glanced at María. It had grown so dark in the room he could scarcely make out her features. "This is agreeable with you?"

The woman was silent only briefly. "It is all right. You will take care, Miguelito?"

The boy's small shoulders squared. "I am not a child, Mama, and only a child would take a foolish risk. This was explained to me by Blas Armijo." He moved to the edge of the bed, an erect, sober young figure. "Trust this to me, my friend. When I return, I shall have the information you wish. Until later."

"Until later," Ryker replied, and watched the boy slip from the room and disappear into the night.

XIX

The singing of the mockingbird somewhere in the yard aroused Ryker. He lay motionlessly on the narrow bed for several minutes, listening to the clear, trilling intimations of the bird while his mind gradually began to function. María had given him, besides doses of other kitchen-concocted remedies, something that had induced sleep. He had scarcely moved during the night. Now, as a result of such unbroken slumber, he was much stronger if slightly drugged. Rolling to one side, he dropped his legs over the edge of the bed, and sat up. His brain spun sickeningly and he paused, irritably allowing the discomfort to pass. One thing, the myriad of aches that had belabored his battered frame were gone, and that was some relief.

He heard voices. They were coming from the yard. He started

to rise, go there, but at that moment María entered the room. She gave him a quick, smiling glance, wheeled and returned to the kitchen to reappear shortly with a cup of steaming, thick chocolate.

The favored hot drink of the Mexican people was no novelty to him. Old Cocinero had brewed it regularly; still did, he supposed, although the cowhands as a rule preferred black coffee. Jake accepted the cup gratefully, nodded his thanks to her, and took a deep swallow.

"You are much better," she commented, folding her hands together under the apron she was wearing.

He managed a grin. "You have good medicine. I am the same as well."

"There will still be a weakness. Another day, perhaps."

"I cannot wait another day," Ryker said, draining the cup and passing it back to her. "Has Miguel come?"

"Oh, yes, by midnight. He found the cattle."

Jake Ryker straightened abruptly, then settled back slowly as pain smashed through his head. Reaching up, he brushed the sweat that had gathered on his brow, swore under his breath.

María smiled sympathetically, creating the picture of a wise, dusky-skinned Madonna. "I have food prepared. After you have eaten, doubtless you will feel much better."

"Likely, but first I must hear of my cattle. Where is Miguel? I would speak with him."

María shook her head. "He watches your herd and will return late in the day. He has told me the things you wish to know."

"Good. Tell me."

"After you have taken food," she replied firmly, and went into the kitchen.

When the meal, one of corn, slices of stewed chicken, tortillas, and more chocolate, was over, Ryker waited impatiently for María to clear away the dishes and return. When she did, he was on his feet, moving nervously but slowly about.

"Where did they take the cattle?" he asked before she could seat herself on the bench placed near the window.

"A short distance from where the attack was made, so Miguel said. In a place where the Arroyo of the Apaches is wide. The men believe you have been killed, and there is no necessity to drive the herd farther."

"They saw the Luna brothers ride away. . . ."

"They fear nothing from them. They make a joke of their flight. Miguel heard one of the bandits say that both were so filled with dread that likely they have gone to Mexico."

"They will learn they are mistaken in many things," Ryker murmured grimly. "How many bandits are there? Was it mentioned by Miguel?"

"Four, although he said there was talk of another man to come. Also they expect to meet with yet a different man from Abilene for the purpose of selling him your cattle."

That was it then—rustlers and nothing more. He had successfully slipped by Teague's riders only to come up against a gang of rustlers. "This buyer, was it said when he would come?"

"No time was said. Likely it will be tomorrow, or perhaps the day that follows."

Taking into consideration the distances involved, that would be his guess, too. It didn't leave much time to make plans and act. Ryker plucked at his chin. What the hell could he do? He just couldn't stand by and let the outlaws get away with the herd, cattle that meant life or death for the Circle R. Should he return to Medford's, seek the rancher's help? He'd not get it, he realized in the next breath. Not that the man wouldn't sympathize with his problem, but he had his hands full trying to hold his place together under the pressure of Bill Teague's steady aggression. He could forget trying to recruit aid from the men in Polvareda. There'd be few, if any, guns around, and he doubted if there were any more experienced hands such as Blas Armijo available. Too, the villagers, aware of the *vaquero*'s death and that the Luna brothers had fled for their lives, would want no part of his troubles. He had the day to come up with something, some plan. One day in which to recover his strength fully, get back on his feet, and have a program worked out that would enable him to recover the stock. One day. The way it shaped up, he reckoned there was little else he could do but wait out the sun. He would have to stall until dark to have his look at the place where the cattle were being held; he should hold off for Miguel, to see if there had been any changes. Too, he doubted if he'd be up to a hard ride in the heat right then, regardless of how much he would like to act.

Moving to the bed, he sat down. María, who had remained silent on the bench during the time he was pacing back and forth, rose and went into the kitchen where she began making preparations for the day. There was no stove in the room, only a corner fireplace in which pots could be suspended or a grill of iron bars placed above the flames. Everything was meticulously clean. Even the dirt floor, which was a dustless surface made so by countless sprinklings of water and painstaking sweeping. It was as hard as if made of oak planks.

The little nag of worry that had come to his mind earlier concerning the safety of María and Miguel should it become known they had befriended him again rose in Jake Ryker's mind. But he knew the matter should not be broached directly to the woman.

"It is a good home you and Miguel have," he said, rising and starting again to prowl.

"It belonged to the family of my husband. It was given to us on the day of our marriage," María replied, coming back into the room. She gazed wistfully about. "There was much happiness here until. . . ."

Ryker, halted by the window, nodded understandingly when she hesitated. "Until your husband was lost. How did that happen?"

"He was slain by a man."

"By an American?"

"By a *gringo*. An incident near the store. One of little importance in itself. Words were passed concerning the Mexican people. My husband refused the insult and made a reply."

"An act of courage."

"Yes, but the man drew his pistol and killed him."

"Was your husband armed?"

"No. Long ago we learned it is unwise to carry weapons. Only those like Blas Armijo have done so."

"It was murder. Is there no lawman close by?"

María's short laugh was dry with scorn. "The law is not for my people, only for the Americans and the *gringos.*"

Ryker looked at her curiously. "You speak of the Americans and the *gringos* as if they're different. Is not a *gringo* an American?"

"There is difference," she answered with a shrug. "Both are Americans, just as you are an American. But you are not a *gringo.* That is a word reserved for those who have no understanding or respect for our ways or our persons. They are those who would treat us as if we were of less importance than the lowliest dog. Those we call Americans, as yourself, look upon us as equals, as a people having rights and entitled to be accorded and judged as Americans would their own race."

It was a long speech and it had brought color to María Calderón's cheeks—an angry flush. She looked away.

"I see," Ryker murmured. "Many times I have wondered about the term. I now understand. I am sorry about your husband. Words are of small solace, I know, and I fear I may have brought new troubles upon you."

María again moved her shoulders. "If it comes, it will come. There is little that can be done to avoid trouble, even less to meet it. We do not live, we exist from day to day. When there is happiness, it is possible to do so without thought. But when. . . ." Her voice trailed off as she rose abruptly and went into the kitchen. "It is best that you sleep," she called back. "By the coming of night your strength will be with you. Then you can do what must be done."

Ryker nodded, stretched out on the padded bunk. "True, it is best, but if the boy comes, will you call me?"

"I shall do so," María promised, and busied herself at her chores.

XX

Near the end of the day Miguel Calderón rode in. He had been gone since early morning, had spent the hours hiding in the brush watching over the herd and the rustlers. There had been no change. Ryker, fit once more thanks to María's periodic medications and his own vitality, had awaited the boy's return anxiously. Now, with the evening meal over, his patience was again being taxed as he stalled out the minutes until darkness settled over the land. It was a good two-hour ride to where the cattle were, the boy had informed him, but since it was across open country, they would have to use extreme care in approaching.

Miguel was right, Ryker saw, when a while later they cut out of the wash, circled west, and came to a halt on a low butte from which they could see the herd. Only a thin screen of *chamiso* and plume prevented their being seen by the rustlers. The raiders had brought the cattle to a halt where the arroyo had flattened out into a shallow swale. There was little there for the herd to graze on, and it was immediately evident to Jake Ryker that the men would have difficulty holding the steers for any length of time. With no water and only scattered clumps of bunch grass the stock would have to be moved in the next day or so.

"There are four bandits," Miguel said, pointing to the small campfires, placed one at each side of the hollow. "They do not rest but ride back and forth. I believe they fear for something."

Ryker did not doubt it. The rustlers probably realized they had a powder keg with a lit fuse on their hands. "It is something they must do," he said. "Unless the cattle are kept quiet, they will stampede. They are in a bad mood."

As he spoke, he was watching the riders nearest the embankment. They had paused by the fire, dismounted. One was gathering more of the dry wood strewn about and replenishing the dwindling flames. Ryker wished it were possible to work in closer, listen to what was being said. He might then get some idea of their plans and come up with a thought of his own as to how he could recover the stolen beef.

"Another man comes."

Miguel's low warning brought Ryker around. He turned his head, saw a rider loping in from the east. There was something familiar in the way he sat his saddle, and Ryker had the feeling he had met the man before. But in the darkness, only partly relieved by a moon harried by scudding clouds, and because of the distance that separated them, he could distinguish nothing clearly.

The newcomer pulled up to the fire where the outlaws had paused. Without dismounting, he conversed with the pair for several minutes and then, wheeling around, doubled back over the trail he had just traveled. He had brought a message of some sort to the rustlers, Ryker concluded. Probably word as to when the buyer from Abilene could be expected. Ryker rubbed at his jaw uneasily. Whatever he planned to do must be done soon, and with the cattle growing more restless and unmanageable with each passing hour, they would become increasingly difficult to handle.

Again he considered the idea of riding to the Box M and asking Medford for help—and once more dismissed the suggestion, knowing the rancher would be compelled to refuse because of his own problems. Too, it would be a fatal mistake; Teague's men, keeping close watch over Medford and his crew, would see Box M riders pulling out and follow. Thus they would be led to the herd, and it would be for Jake Ryker just a matter of jumping from the kettle into the fire. But with no help how could he expect to recover three hundred thirsting, hungering steers primed for a stampede at the slightest provocation?

That was it! The answer to his self-imposed question came in a single flash, like a beam of sunlight breaking suddenly through an overcast sky. Touching Miguel's arm, he drew back, returned to where they had tethered the horses.

"Do you know, young friend, is there a town near here on the New Mexico side of the border?"

Miguel pursed his lips, drew his brows together. "Yes, a place that is called Llano. I have not been there, however."

"Do you know where it lies from here?"

The boy stared off into the pale night. "I am not certain, but I believe it is to the north. I have heard the men speak of it. You will go there?"

"Not for help. There would be no point in it. I could not ask others to assume my trouble and thus endanger their lives. Already Blas Armijo is dead, and the Luna brothers live in fear for their lives because of me. And you. . . ."

"I do not fear."

"I know, and I shall not permit it to come to you and your mother. As well we return to your house now. I have a plan to consider deeply."

They mounted, cut off through the scattered brush to where

they were again in the more easily crossed arroyo.

"This plan," Miguel said in a tentative voice, "does it include me?"

"I am afraid not. The danger of your getting hurt will be too great."

"No harm has come to me yet. May I ask what is this plan?"

"A simple one. I shall stampede the cattle in the direction of New Mexico. From what I was told the border is but a space of ten miles, even less. If I am able to get the cattle to run that far, there is a good possibility I can recover them. This will be more true if there is a town where a lawman can be found."

"I see," Miguel said gravely. "I do not know if there is a sheriff in Llano or not. It is a larger village than Polvareda, so I have heard. Perhaps my mother will provide the answer."

Ryker hoped María Calderón would be able to tell him the location of the town as well. Driving the cattle straight for it would be almost as important as finding a lawman to whom he could show his papers for the herd and ask protection from the rustlers.

"It will be difficult for you alone to cause a stampede," Miguel continued in that serious, old-man way of his. "There are four bandits, five if the one we saw this night returns. Must you not deal with them before you can get the cattle to run away?"

Ryker nodded. "It is a problem I must solve," he admitted.

"In that case I can be of help."

Jake smiled at the boy in the half dark. "I am sorry, young friend, but I must decline the offer. As I have said, this time the danger will be far too great."

"And as I have said, also, no harm has come to me before, for I have taken care."

"This will be different. There will be shooting."

"Was there not shooting before?"

"Yes, and a good man was killed. I cannot permit you to be

exposed to it."

The boy fell silent for a time, then: "Will you again leave the question of this to my mother?"

Jake Ryker swore softly. Winning an argument from Miguel was a difficult task. There was always a stubborn logic to his way of thinking that was not easy to get around. "Very well, it shall be your mother's decision. I shall tell her of what I plan, also of a new thought that has come to me concerning the two of you. Then we will see what she decides."

XXI

A stillness lay between Ryker and Miguel as they rode into Polvareda. They entered by a back way, following a path that took them through fields of maize, small gardens of chiles and ripening squash and melons, along a line of sun-grayed sheds and brush. Ryker felt it was a necessary precaution since there was still the possibility the outlaws, having failed to find his body, could be keeping a watch on the village.

Dismounting, Miguel took the reins of the horses and said—"I shall care for the animals."—and led them off to the lean-to that had been erected by him beneath a tree in the rear where it could not be easily noted.

Ryker, feeling a bit shaky from the long ride, nodded, made his way to the house. María was waiting in the doorway and motioned him to a chair at a table where she had hot chocolate and tasty *galletas* ready.

"You are not well," she said, accusing him with her tone. "It was too soon for you to have made such a journey."

"I am all right," he replied, impatient with himself. He took a deep swallow of the thick, sweet drink, wishing again it was black coffee, or a good belt of straight whiskey. But it helped, and he sighed, leaned back in the chair.

"You have seen your cattle?"

He nodded, feeling the place in his arm where Lenny Gault's bullet had cut its path. The wound it had etched ached dully. "They are in the Arroyo of the Apaches as Miguel has said. Four men guard them. While we watched, a fifth outlaw came with a message. I believe it was regarding the buyer they are expecting."

María refilled his cup from the earthenware pot. "You will he able to recover the herd?"

"I must try," he said simply, and glanced to Miguel, just entering the doorway.

The boy took his place at the table solemnly, greeting his mother with only his eyes, and took up his cup of chocolate. Barely sipping it, he looked at Ryker. "You have asked her?"

Jake Ryker shook his head. "I wished you to be here so that you might hear all that was said."

He lowered his eyes. "Thank you."

María's attention sharpened. "What is it I am to be asked that is so important?"

Ryker folded his arms across his chest. "I have a plan to recover my cattle. Tomorrow morning I shall attempt it. But first there is another matter I must speak of." He paused, glanced around the small room. "This house . . . would it be difficult for you to leave it?"

María frowned. "I . . . I am not certain of your meaning. In truth, leaving this house has never entered my mind."

"You spoke once of being happy here as if it were no longer possible."

The woman shrugged. "Happiness of one sort. There is another that comes of being a mother with a fine son. I have him with me and there is happiness in that."

"I understand."

The boy was staring at him intently. "What is it you would say?"

Ryker shifted on his chair. He wished he could speak in English rather than in the stiffly precise Spanish tongue; it would be much easier to express what he had in his mind. "I do not think it is good that you remain here. I fear the outlaws will find that you have helped me after I have gone and take revenge. Therefore, I ask you to come with me to the ranch of my brother and me, and make it your home."

Miguel's eyes brightened. María at once became thoughtful. "Why?"

"The reason has been given, the important one. I fear for you. Also, Miguel is deserving of more than he can receive here in Polvareda. I would give him the opportunity to work, to become a man. I would help him . . . and you."

She studied him coolly. "What would I do at this ranch of yours?"

He knew what she was thinking and shook his head. "Your person would be inviolate," he replied, stumbling for the proper word. "No harm would ever befall you. I have not said this but my brother has been injured. He can no longer walk. If I wish it, he and his wife will move into the town and the ranch will be in my charge. It is no great ranch, only a small one with a few men, mostly elderly."

"I would thus be cook and housekeeper for you?"

"Something of that nature. There is now a cook, however, a Mexican we call Cocinero. You could help him if you wished, or decline. It would not matter."

"I see."

"It would be a good life for you and the boy. I will tell you that it was in my mind not to stay there once I had returned with the cattle. Now I find that I have different feelings, ones I cannot exactly explain to myself." Jake Ryker paused, seemingly puzzled and not a little surprised at what he was saying. "Since I have met you and Miguel, there is a change. My acquaintance with you has opened my eyes to . . . to the belief that in this life there are more worthwhile matters than the waywardness that I felt was freedom." Again he was stumbling for proper words, and a fine beading of sweat had appeared on his forehead. "Miguel would learn the business of cattle raising. Perhaps one day he could have a ranch of his own. If that was not his desire, there would always be a job for him with me."

María nodded slowly. "What of your brother and his wife? Would they agree to this arrangement?"

"It would not be for them to say since they will be living in the town. However, they would welcome you."

It was likely Tom would approve of the idea; probably Callie would not. It didn't matter. He would see to their comfort and guarantee that they would never want for anything.

"This is what I have often dreamed of."

Miguel's voice came to Ryker. He glanced up. The boy was staring at his mother, eyes aglow. "We would live in a fine house as we have often hoped, be proud and honored."

María smiled softly. "I know, Miguelito, but it is hard to leave this house of your father's, the people who are our friends."

"We could make new friends, better friends . . . ones who would not fail us as they did my father."

Ryker pushed back his chair. "I shall go outside if you wish to discuss the matter."

"There is no need," María replied. "It is what Miguel wishes, therefore it is what I also wish. There is this small problem."

"Problem?"

"In this house, humble as it is, there are a few things that I will wish to keep. They are family possessions that one day should be the property of Miguel's wife, when that comes to pass."

"It will be possible to take them."

"How can it be done? On a saddle . . . ?"

"Is there someone in the village who will lend or perhaps sell to me a wagon and horse?"

"Procopio Mondragón . . . he has a small carriage that can be drawn by one horse," Miguel said quickly. "He no longer has use for either. The vehicle is what you call a . . . a board."

"Buckboard?"

"Yes, that is the name."

"It will do fine. Then it is agreed? In the morning we will see this Procopio Mondragón, buy or borrow from him the horse and buckboard. You will load up the things you wish to keep. You will take food and water for at least three days' journey. I shall furnish you with a map showing you how my ranch is to be found."

"You will not accompany us?"

"No, I shall be with the cattle."

"But if you do not return, what of your brother and his wife? We shall be strangers."

"They will welcome you as if I were there . . . which I shall be. I will give you a letter telling them of what I had planned. Regardless, you will have a home."

María shrugged. "I do not know. It would not be the same."

"For Miguel it would and for you, also. My brother requires great care on the part of his wife. You would be of aid and comfort to her."

"I would not wish us to be a burden because of a kindness given."

"You would not be. Then it is arranged?"

"It is agreed."

"Good. I shall make my plans for recovering the herd and go to the wash after I see that you and Miguel are on the way."

María stared thoughtfully at her folded hands. "This has occurred to me. How can you, one man, take the cattle from four, perhaps five outlaws?"

"By allowing the cattle to do it for me. Do you have a blanket or a large piece of cloth that I may have?"

"A blanket, yes. How can it help?"

"The steers are hungry and thirst badly. In the morning I plan to go where they are being held. I shall avoid the rustlers and at any opportunity stampede the animals. Using the blanket and my pistol, it will not be a difficult task with the cattle in such nervous condition. I shall come at them from the east side, thus forcing them to run to the west and the New Mexico border."

María's lips had parted into a small, admiring smile. "I understand. But will not these bandits try to prevent you from frightening the herd?"

"It will be necessary to slip by them unnoticed until the stampede has begun," he admitted.

"And that will be possible only with my help," Miguel said. "I shall go with him, Mama."

María Calderón's mouth tightened at the boy's pronouncement. A paleness came into her cheeks. "Are you not to come with me in the wagon? Is that not the plan?"

"He is our good friend, this man called Ryker," Miguel said stubbornly. "It would be wrong to let him face so difficult a task unaided. My father would have said so. Blas Armijo would also have said so. You will start with the wagon. After the cattle have begun the running and are safe in New Mexico, I shall hurry and join you."

María, her features grave, shifted her eyes to Ryker. "This is your wish?"

"I cannot deny that his help would be welcome to me, but I will not ask him to give it unless you permit him to do so. There is small doubt that there will be considerable danger."

Face sober, the boy watched his mother. Only his pleading eyes betrayed the hope that surged within him.

"He is all I have, all that remains of love of a fine man. . . ."

"That I have realized. Miguel and I agreed that it would be your decision. If you do not wish it to be, the matter will end. Either way, it does not alter our other plans."

María rose, walked slowly to the doorway, and gazed off into the silvery night. Something disturbed the chickens in their nearby pen of woven willow reeds. There was a brief flurry of clucking, then quiet. "He is truly not a man, only a small boy. . . ."

"With a man's good sense of responsibility and duty to you."

"This I know. Very well, to refuse would be great hurt to him. He shall go with you, but I shall also come. It is possible I can help with the cattle in some way. Also, there is the matter of cooking during the journey. Those tasks will be my lot."

Ryker's shoulders stiffened. "That is not wise."

A stubbornness came into María Calderón's features. Her lips set themselves firmly, formed a tight bow. "Only in this way shall I agree."

Jake Ryker shrugged, turned to the boy. "I am sorry, young friend, but I cannot permit. . . ."

"There is no place for a woman, Mama!" Miguel cried, ignoring Ryker. "This you must understand!"

"I shall not be in the way but remain in the distance, if that pleases you. Then, when it is all over, I would join you."

The boy turned to Ryker. In the yellow, flickering flare of the candles placed on the table, his face reflected worry and uncertainty. Ryker smiled, dropped a hand on his shoulder.

"It is all right," he said, and turned his attention to María. "You will keep far from us and the herd until we are safely in New Mexico. Then we will meet. This is thoroughly understood?"

"It is understood," María replied, also smiling.

XXII

It was María who went to deal with old Procopio Mondragón. Deciding to prepare for the trip immediately, and fearing to have Ryker in the open where he might be seen by one of the outlaws should they be keeping an eye on the village, she assumed the task of acquiring the horse and buckboard that was to furnish transportation for her and her belongings to New Mexico. She did well, bargaining away those pieces of household furniture and other items she did not wish to keep, along with the chickens, two pigs, and a small hoard of preserved fruit and vegetables that she had set aside for the winter months. When she had finished, it was necessary for Ryker to hand over only five silver dollars of his dwindling funds to the elderly Mexican.

They slept but little in the few remaining hours of the night and were up long before first light. María prepared a final breakfast, extending her cooking activities at that time to include food that was to be carried for use during the remainder of the day. Then, as the sun broke over the foothills to the east, the tiny cavalcade moved out, careful to keep the trees and brush between them and the settlement so as not to be observed. They traveled together for the first few miles, eventually separating, María continuing due west, Ryker and the boy slanting off toward the south.

Looking back over his shoulder at the buckboard with its solitary passenger as it disappeared beyond a rise, Miguel turned an anxious face to Ryker. "She will be safe, is that not true?"

Ryker nodded. "Your mother is a very wise woman, young friend. She knows well what she does. We need have no fear for her."

The boy looked at him with steady intent. "Do you not also believe that my mother is very beautiful?"

Jake Ryker rubbed at his stubble of beard. He'd not shaved for several days now and the bristles were beginning to be a bother. "There is no doubt of that."

"A wise and beautiful woman," Miguel murmured, settling back. "A man who would take her for his wife would indeed be most fortunate."

Ryker cast a wondering glance at the boy, but Miguel's eyes were off in the distance, blandly innocent. He grinned wryly, swore under his breath. Here was another time when Miguel was older than he looked.

The morning was clear, already warm as they rode steadily on. They followed a route somewhat east of Apache Wash, planning to come in, as Ryker had determined earlier, on the flank of the herd. If the stampede succeeded and the cattle reacted as expected, the herd should take flight in the opposite direction, a course that would carry them out of Texas and into New Mexico.

Ryker looked again at Miguel. The boy's features were smooth, a light brown in the strong light. A dreaminess filled his eyes, and Ryker knew he was living and enjoying those first moments of being a man in a man's world. He would be a credit to his mother and to the Circle R.

"We are near," the boy said a time later, slowing his pony and pointing off to his right. "The brush that looks to be a fence grows along the rim of the arroyo."

Ryker pulled up. They were still a considerable distance from the herd, he thought, but he could not be sure. He'd been through there only once, and then at night.

"The herd, is it near, also?"

"A distance yet, I believe. Perhaps a mile."

Ryker accepted the boy's judgment without question. Swinging the chestnut to the left and down into a narrow gully, he resumed the wide circuit. When they had covered what he considered the necessary length, he once again halted, checked now by the faint bawling of cattle. He nodded in satisfaction. They were directly opposite the herd. He could see nothing of the steers, however, nor of the men, hopefully still no more than four in number. The ground rose in a fair swell before them and clumps of brush and sun-scoured weeds blocked the openness of the country. He motioned to the boy.

"We will move toward the cattle. It is necessary you keep the *chamiso* in front of you at all times so that you will not be seen by the outlaws. Since we cannot see them, it is not possible to know of their exact positions."

Miguel said: "I understand. The embankment is high on this side of the arroyo. It will protect us. Is that not smoke?"

Ryker looked quickly to where Miguel indicated, somewhat to their right and above the wash. A thin streamer of black was twisting lazily up into the empty sky.

"That'll be them, sure'n hell," he muttered in English, and then bucked his head at the boy. "They have made a fire for cooking. We are in a good place."

He touched the gelding with his rowels, sent him moving on. Immediately he slowed, beckoned to Miguel. "Keep to my left hand," he directed, and resumed the slow, careful advance. If shooting developed unexpectedly, he wanted to be in between the boy and the rustlers. Miguel moved into position, not questioning the order, likely giving it no thought. They pressed on, taking advantage of the scarce brush, the scattered junipers, the minor gullies and washes that broke the flatness of the land.

The sounds of the cattle grew louder, and from the timbre and frenzied quality of the bawling, Ryker realized the animals were in a bad frame of mind, needed but little to send them into a wild flight. He would have no difficulty in starting the stampede; the problem would be getting in near enough to the steers without being seen by the outlaws. If he began the stampede attempt while still at a distance, the cattle could break and head into the wrong direction—or, worse yet, split into several bunches, each having its own idea of where to go.

The chestnut broke out of a low swale, climbed a short grade, and halted as Ryker pulled him in sharply. They had reached the edge of the Arroyo of the Apaches. The cattle were a quarter mile ahead on the farther side of the flat and sandy stretch of open ground. A few hundred yards to the right Ryker saw the rustlers. There were still four of them. This was small consolation, however. The instant he and Miguel left the embankment and started across the flat for the herd, they would be seen. Rifles would open up and they would both go down before they were well started.

Wheeling the gelding about, Ryker dropped back into the swale. Dismounting, he tied the gelding to a scrub, motioned for the boy to do likewise. Keeping low, he returned to the edge of the arroyo.

Miguel, at his side, eyes on the herd, murmured quietly: "It is a far distance to the cattle."

"Much too far," Ryker agreed. "And it is not possible to race a bullet and win even on the fastest horse."

"That is true. Also there are no places in which to hide. Would it not be wise to circle and approach from the other side? Or perhaps, from below?"

"I am afraid to do so. The cattle will take fright easily. If we do not go at them from this side, it is hard to guess what they will do. My plan to recover the steers depends upon driving them into New Mexico."

"This I know. But if it is not possible. . . ."

"Got to make it possible, dammit all!" Ryker declared, lapsing into more vigorous English. "I've come this far. By God, I'm not quitting now!"

"¿Perdón?"

Ryker glanced at the boy, shrugged. "It was nothing. I said only that a way must be found. If the bandits could be attracted to something, persuaded to leave only long enough for us to go forward with the blanket and start the stampede, we would have. . . ." Jake Ryker's words faded into silence. A frown crossed his face as he saw motion at the edge of the arroyo some distance beyond the outlaws, crouched now about their fire, drinking coffee. A buckboard with a solitary occupant. Ryker strained for a better look while fear toyed with him. It couldn't be María. She was supposed to cross the wash miles to the north. Yet, it looked like her. If so, how could she have gotten so far off course?

It had been no error on her part but a deliberate move. Ryker realized that even as he recognized her for certain. She had perceived the night before his need to draw the outlaw's attention to permit him and Miguel to work in close to the cattle. She was simply making it possible. He saw her stand up in the buckboard, survey the broad, sandy wash as if searching for a place to cross. The bright flash of a colored petticoat, the sharp contrast of her snow-white shirtwaist and black dress were distinct.

One of the outlaws came to his feet abruptly, face turned to her. He looked down, said something to his companions. They rose, also, and for a long minute all four stood and stared as if in disbelief. Then, suddenly, they tossed away their tin cups and wheeled to their horses. Leaping to the saddle, all raced off for the buckboard with its tempting woman occupant.

"It is your mother," Ryker said, drawing the boy's attention to the departing riders. "She makes it possible for us to start the stampede."

At once Miguel's face showed alarm. "Will they not harm her?"

"Not if we act quickly," Ryker said, leaping up from his crouch and wheeling. He hurried to where the horses waited. Miguel followed at his heels.

Mounting, Ryker pulled the blanket María had given him

from his saddlebags, ripped off a third of it, and tossed it to the boy. "Do not wave the cloth until we are near. I shall give the signal."

Miguel nodded, but his gaze was to the north—to the buckboard.

"Do not worry," Ryker reassured him. "When the outlaws see us, they will halt and return instantly. Your mother will be forgotten. Come, there is little time to lose!"

Jamming spurs into the chestnut's flanks, he sent the big horse lunging out of the swale, across the narrow ridge and into the wash.

XXIII

Ryker restrained the gelding, held him to an easy lope, fearing that too fast an approach would spook the cattle, cause them to break and run too soon. He threw a glance after the four men rushing toward María Calderón. They had not noticed Miguel and him as yet, being too intent on the woman. With a little more luck his timing should prove to be perfect.

A frown crossed his features. He'd congratulated himself too soon. Another rider had appeared on the flat, was loping steadily toward the wash. The fifth outlaw again. A grim smile pulled at Ryker's lips. Four to one odds weren't bad enough, it seemed— they had to go to five. But there was nothing to be done about it. Jaw set, he rode on, careful but without deviation.

The cattle were bawling noisily, shifting restlessly about in small bunches. He didn't know if the rustlers realized it or not, but chances were better than good that they'd be unable to hold the herd in the wash much longer—even if he wasn't about to start them off on a wild run. It could be that the buyer from Abilene and his drovers were due to arrive that morning and take over, and that could be the reason for their indifference. One thing sure, the Abilene cattle broker had made a long ride for nothing, regardless of how matters turned out.

Ryker looked ahead. The herd was near. Many of the steers had faced about and heads hung low, were watching Miguel and him with suspicious eyes. He slowed the chestnut. It would be unwise to press in too closely. Looking to the boy, he raised his arm as a signal. "Use your cloth but take care! Do not let your horse get in front of the steers!"

At once Miguel let out a piercing screech and, taking the oblong of cloth tucked under his arm, began to wave it back and forth. Ryker, unfurling his piece of the blanket in the same moment, shouted, drove spurs into the gelding, and sent him thundering toward the line of steers. The lead animals broke, flung themselves about, horns clacking loudly as they came in contact with the steers behind them. There was a quick boiling up of dust, a surge of sound, and then in a solid mass of flowing color the herd began to move toward the west bank of the broad wash.

The steers had turned fast and headed due west as Ryker had hoped. Now, if Miguel could keep them running in a straight line—he glanced toward the boy. The youngster was bent low on his pony, mouth wide as he yelled, while he continued to use the strip of blanket. Mindful of the warning Ryker had given him, he was staying back from the herd and a bit to the side. His mere presence there should keep the herd from swinging off.

The faint crack of pistols lifted above the drum of pounding hoofs. Ryker instantly swung his attention to the upper end of the wash. The outlaws were returning. He could barely see them through the thickening dust haze, strung out in an uneven line as they raced toward the herd. Their fifth member was midway into the wash, angling in to intercept and join them. Ryker raised himself slightly in his stirrups, strained to catch a glimpse of María. There was no sign of her, and worry began to tag at his mind. She should be crossing the arroyo unless the outlaws, out of spite. . . .

More gunshots echoed through the choking air. Ryker grinned tautly. The rustlers were only helping by using their weapons. The shooting served only to frighten the cattle further, causing them to increase their speed. But the rustlers weren't thinking of the cattle, he knew. Weapon in hand, he veered to the right, still hoping to see María and the buckboard. Gusts of dust swept against him and he reached for his bandanna, drew it up over his mouth and nose. In almost that identical instant one of the outlaws appeared directly ahead. He fired hastily.

The bullet went wide of its target, but the rustler swung off, pointing for the denser haze. Ryker threw a second shot at the man and cut back toward the tail of the hard-running herd. A solid wall of yellow now lay all about him, dry, choking, and blinding—but he was grateful for it. The pall was a curtain shutting off the outside world and the five men endeavoring to close in on him.

He swiped at the sweat caking dust on his face and clogging his eyes. The cattle were now out of the wash, were pounding across the long mesa that lay to the west. They showed no indication yet of slowing. Held for so many hours without water and ample forage, they were wild to run, to expend their nervousness and temper. Keeping a sharp watch on his rear where he figured the outlaws were most likely to appear, Ryker looked about, hopeful of a glimpse of Miguel. He saw him a moment later. The boy was holding his position, still shouting and waving his blanket. Satisfaction pushed through Ryker as he let the gelding fall back. It was going to be easier than he'd thought; the cattle were continuing in a straight line and the possibility the rustlers were giving up and moving off was growing. He'd seen no more of them. But María?

He spurred the chestnut on toward the center rear of the

herd where he planned to ride, slicing diagonally across its wake until he reached the flank. María should be somewhere on the flat to the north unless something had happened back in the wash. Relief flowed through him as he caught sight of her, when he emerged from the film of dust. She was driving the buckboard parallel to the cattle, keeping pace as best she could at a distance of only a hundred yards or so. She had tied what appeared to be her white petticoat to the back of the vehicle's seat; it was flapping vigorously as the buckboard bounced along at top speed.

The ease that had slipped over him upon seeing her safe changed then to anger. She had ignored his instructions to stay clear of the herd and take no risks. Muttering an oath, Jake Ryker spurred to catch up. She saw him coming, turned a dust-smeared face to him. "Pull away!" he shouted, motioning her off with his hand.

She shook her head, continuing her course alongside the running cattle. Her position there was the reason the herd was maintaining its direct line of flight, he knew. And with Miguel on the opposite flank and him crowding from the rear, the stampeding steers were doing exactly as he wished. But he didn't like the thought of her exposing herself to such danger. If the thundering cattle for some reason cut north, she would have a difficult time getting out of their path—if she could at all. "Too close!" he yelled, and again waved at her to move away.

María only smiled. She recognized the need for having someone flanking the herd on that side, accepted the responsibility. Ryker swore again. He had quite a pair on his hands— María Calderón and her son Miguel! But that didn't lessen the worry plaguing him. She must be made to realize, to understand. . . . He saw her raise her arm, point excitedly toward the rear of the herd. He looked quickly. Two riders were cutting through the dust for the opposite side.

"Miguel!" María screamed at him.

He caught the fear in her voice even as it welled through him, and instantly swung away, roweling the chestnut cruelly as he bore straight for the pair. They had evidently spotted the boy at his key position, were intending to drive him off and turn the herd. They hadn't given up on the cattle after all. Low on the gelding's outstretched neck, Ryker leveled his pistol at the dim figures coming in on the left. They were yet unaware of his presence, thanks to the swirling dust and the continuous thud of the running steers. They wouldn't be for long. Approaching on a course that would intercept them, they were bound to catch sight of him shortly and his advantage would be lost.

The outlaw slightly to the rear of his partner was the first to notice. He stiffened suddenly, surprised at Ryker's nearness. His arm swung up and he pressed off a shot. The report was a dry crack above the dull roar of the stampede. Ryker felt the breath of the bullet as it whipped by his head. He fired back as the first of the two looked over his shoulder, a dark-faced man whose whiskers were matted with sweat and dust. Ryker's bullet missed but his second shot found its mark. The outlaw jolted, clawed at his belly, and wheeled off into the murk.

His companion opened up instantly. Ryker winced as a leaden slug ripped across his thigh, leaving a streak of red. Another slapped against the horn of his saddle, screamed into space. Hunched low, steadying his right arm with his left hand while he allowed the chestnut to run free, he triggered his weapon again. The pistol bucked in his grasp. The rustler recoiled, sagged to one side as his horse rushed on.

Again Jake Ryker took deliberate aim. His bullet had gone true but evidently had struck no vital place. The man was still in the saddle, still slanting across to get at Miguel. He pressed the trigger once more, swore savagely as the hammer came down on an empty cartridge. Cursing, he let the chestnut slow as he thumbed cartridges from his belt. He should have taken greater care, been mindful of the number of times he'd gotten off a shot. Never before had he been guilty of such laxity. What the hell was wrong with him? In his anxiety to look after María and Miguel he'd left himself wide open for a bullet.

Reloading, he spurred the gelding into a fast lope again, brushing at his eyes to clear his vision while he searched the gloom for the outlaw. The man was no longer visible but he could not have gotten far. Abruptly Ryker saw him. He was directly ahead. Beyond him the indistinct, smaller figure of Miguel Calderón was a blur in the haze, still bent over his straining little pony, switching his piece of flannel back and forth. The boy was unaware of the outlaw's presence, was intent on the job of keeping the steers running hard and straight.

Ryker brought up his gun, threw a shot at the outlaw to distract him. Instantly the man glanced around. He veered off, evidently taken by surprise by Ryker's nearness. His own weapon came up, paused. Cool, Ryker once more steadied himself, squeezed off his pistol. The rustler folded to one side. His horse shied at the unexpected shift of weight on his back, cut sharply in the opposite direction. The outlaw fell to the ground, bounced limply like a rag doll, and lay still.

The firing attracted Miguel's attention. He twisted about, features smudged with dirt and sweat, choking and coughing from the spinning dust. Ryker lifted a reassuring hand to him, swung away to resume his place at the rear of the herd.

The steers were slowing down, but they should be drawing near the New Mexico border. Another two or three miles, Ryker reasoned, and all would be well. He'd let the stock run until they stopped of their own accord. That should guarantee they would be far out of Texas. One thing, there sure as hell had better be some water close. After a run like this, he'd have some dead beef on his hands unless. . . .

Three riders spurted suddenly from the bank of yellow to his left. Ryker's jaw sagged as he recognized the man in the lead—Max Cameron. The others were strangers. All fired at him simultaneously. He threw a bullet at the one nearest, saw him buckle even as he felt the chestnut under him falter, start down. Grimly he got off a second shot as he struck the ground, rolled clear of the gelding's flailing hoofs. Cameron—Medford's own foreman. He was the one back of the raid. It all came to Ryker in a flash. It had been Cameron who had laid out the plan for him, who had picked the route the herd would follow, then he'd had the rustlers waiting in ambush to take over when the herd reached a certain point.

Anger swept Jake Ryker as the full import of the double-cross registered on his mind. Likely Cameron worked regularly with the gang of rustlers, made it possible for them to help themselves to Medford cattle whenever they wished. But more, he was responsible for the death of Blas Armijo, for the near loss of the herd that wasn't really safe yet, and for all the grief and worry and pain. "God damn you!" Ryker yelled, and bounded to his feet. He went into a half crouch, fired from the hip. The outlaw riding in tight on Cameron's left, jerked, slid from his saddle. One booted foot caught in the stirrup and the suddenly frightened horse bolted, galloped off dragging the outlaw through the dust.

Cameron's bullet smashed into Ryker's leg, spun him half about, drove him to one knee. Ryker cursed, took dead aim at the oncoming man. The foreman had been the fifth man, the one he and Miguel had seen ride up the night before, the one who had joined the gang moments before the stampede started. Ryker had thought he looked familiar; now he knew why. He squeezed off the shot. Cameron stiffened, drew himself rigidly erect. An instant later the Box M foreman's shying horse was upon Ryker. It's foreleg caught him against the shoulder, knocked him back. Something struck his head, a loose, swinging stirrup, and then he went down hard.

XXIV

Dazed, Jake Ryker shook off the smothering cloud of breathless dark that sought to weigh him down, struggled back to his feet despite the searing pain in his leg from the outlaw's bullet. Dust was swirling about him in a blinding cloud. He could see nothing, no one. The hammering pound of the stampeding herd seemingly had grown fainter.

Hand gripping his pistol, he swiped at his eyes and lips with a forearm, staggered forward a step, halted. Max Cameron lay on the baked, churned earth before him. The outlaw's lifeless eyes stared upward as if endeavoring to penetrate the layers of drifting silt hanging over him. Beyond the foreman was a prone shape of another of the rustlers. He tried to remember, to figure. He'd accounted for all of the outlaws—he thought. But he wasn't sure. There could still be one, possibly two running loose, trying to turn the herd, recover it.

If so, there was nothing he could do about it. He was alone with the dead. His mind swung to María, to the boy, Miguel. He hoped they were unhurt, alive. And the cattle. The sound of their running was now a low rumble, fading into the distance. He grinned wearily, once more brushed at his mouth. That had worked out pretty well—if they continued to run. If not, then it had all been for nothing—the killings, the blood, the sweat and worry, perhaps even the lives of María and Miguel, and his own.

Holstering his pistol, he glanced around. It was as if he were a solitary survivor in a room, one with tan walls that lifted and fell, thickened and thinned, walls that were insubstantial yet solidly closing him off from the remaining world. But the pall was dissipating. A quietude was settling over the flat, and the diminishing drum of the racing cattle had ceased. He wished he had a horse. He turned, went to one knee as the wounded leg failed to respond, drew himself upright once more. Cameron's horse should be close, or else that of the outlaw lying near him. He had to find one, get into the saddle, see that María and Miguel were all right, that the cattle were safe—and get that hole in his leg plugged up before he bled himself out.

A grating sound came to him, brought him up short. It was the slicing noise iron-tired wheels made when cutting through loose sand.

"Ryker!"

A sigh went through him as a tight grin stretched the corners of his mouth. It was María Calderón's voice. "Here . . . over here!" he shouted back.

He hung motionlessly for a few seconds, striving to locate her position, masked from him by the restless wall of dust. Abruptly the horse and then the buckboard, with María standing erect and looking anxiously about, broke through.

"Ryker!" she called again, relief now in her tone as she caught sight of him.

He bucked his head, moved toward her. The wounded leg gave out once again. He went half down, recovered himself, and struggled on to meet her.

"Had me worried," he mumbled, forgetting to speak in Spanish. "You and the boy . . . was afraid. . . ."

She only smiled at him, and leaped to the ground. Taking him by the arm, she assisted him into the buckboard and onto the seat. Then, taking quick note of his wound, she ripped a strip of cloth from the petticoat yet hanging from the vehicle's backrest, quickly and expertly bound up the injury.

He reached out as she finished, caught her by the wrist. "Miguel? He has not been harmed?"

She shook her head. "He is with the cattle. They have reached the place of water. There is a village."

Ryker released her. His features knitted into a frown, he waited while she circled the buckboard and climbed up to sit beside him. "The cattle . . . they are all right, too?" There was a thread of doubt in his voice as if he found it hard to believe.

She unwound the reins, nodded. "They ran to where they reached the small lake of a wind pump. There they have stopped. A few are dead but not many." María paused, her smooth, dusty features serious. "Ryker . . . I . . . I. . . ." She hesitated again, a curious look in her eyes. "It is that I do not know your other name. Only Ryker."

"Jake . . . Jacob," he said.

"Jacob," she murmured, translating it into her own tongue. "Jacobo . . . it is a good name. Now it is possible for me to call you properly."

Ryker heaved a sigh of contentment, settled onto the seat as the buckboard rolled forward. It was finished. Except for the wound in his leg and a few steers lost, they had come through unscathed. A day or two's rest, and then the drive to the Circle R would be as nothing. He glanced at the woman beside him, smiled.

"Jake, Jacobo . . . you call me anything," he said in English. "Makes no difference what, long as you don't stop."

María turned to him, puzzled. "What is it you say?"

Ryker grinned again. He'd explain it later at a better time.

★ ★ ★ ★ ★

LAW COMES TO LAWLESS

★ ★ ★ ★ ★

I

John Glyde thought of the letter as he rode steadily westward toward Lawless. There had to be a catch to it. No town paid its marshal $100 a month and keep unless there was a special reason. But for that kind of money he would fight the devil himself. $600 was all he needed. Add that to the $900 he had already deposited with the banker in Pecos City, and he could take possession of the Widow Claypoole's ranch—a nice little spread that lay along the New Mexico-Texas border. Like every other footloose saddle warmer, John Glyde had dreamed of the day when he would have his own brand. He had worked tirelessly to bring it to pass.

But all had not progressed as planned. Times grew lean. Money was hard to come by and that day in El Paso, when a friend mentioned that a marshal's job could be had in the town of Lawless, a settlement in southwestern New Mexico Territory, he had acted quickly. He wrote to the mayor of the town, a man named Henry Strickland. A letter of reply came immediately. Terms were stated, needs outlined. Glyde was not long in accepting. The offer was a stroke of good fortune. Three days later he had quit his job as an outrider for a freight line that ran into Mexico; he had notified the Pecos City banker of his future whereabouts, and was in the saddle, astride his bay horse, headed for the town of Lawless.

He glanced upward. The sun was high and hot. Sweat oozed freely from his body. A few yards to his left a thinly clothed cottonwood thrust its bulk from the sandy floor of an arroyo. He pulled off the trail, halted beneath the tree. He swung down stiffly. After a few moments he unhooked his canteen from the saddle and removed the cap. Tipping the container, he took a long swallow. His own thirst satisfied, he then poured a quantity of the water into his hat and held it for the gelding.

Lawless could not be far now, he reckoned. Another two or three hours' ride, at most. He replaced the canteen, drew tobacco and papers from his shirt pocket, and rolled a slim cigarette. High overhead, in the steel blue and gray arch of the New Mexico sky, an eagle drifted in a lazy, circular fashion, and watched something on the flats far below. *Like a man,* he thought, *always on the hunt.*

When he and the bay had cooled off as much as could be expected, he arose, made ready, and stepped again to the saddle. He did not move out immediately, but sat and studied the unfurling land that seemed to run endlessly on before him. It was good country. Had he not already contracted to buy the Claypoole Ranch, he might have found a place here.

His directions straight in mind, he touched the bay with his spurs, sent him into a slow lope. He wondered again what he would find in Lawless, what the underlying cause of Henry Strickland's urgency might be. Was it a hell town? Was it another Dodge or Abilene? Or was it something else, a brewing range war or possibly a homesteader-cattleman feud? He was thinking of that when, a short time later, he rounded a turn in the brush-lined trail and the gelding suddenly reared.

Five riders, with leveled guns, blocked his way. He fought his startled horse to a standstill. Hands raised, he stared at the dark-faced men.

"What the hell's this all about?" he demanded. Anger whipped through him. "If you're looking to hold me up, you'll find pickings mighty slim."

One of the men, a wiry, bitter-faced individual of forty-five years or so, prodded his horse a few paces nearer. "Name's Wescott. Cole Wescott. Mean anything to you?"

Glyde shook his head. "Afraid not."

"Own the Spade Ranch. Biggest one around. You're the new marshal the town sent for, I take it. Glyde . . . that the name?"

"Right. You're not much in favor of the idea, I'd guess from this delegation."

"You'd be guessing right," Wescott said. "I mean to set you straight on that, first hand. Spade owns this country and that includes the town. I gave them the land it's built on and I can take it back mighty quick if I get the notion. But I don't want it that way. I need that town, same as it needs me and Spade, and I figure to keep it there just like it's always been without no hard-nosed lawman cluttering up things."

"Seems to me people there got some rights. . . ."

"Rights be damned!" the cattleman exploded. "Get this in your head, Glyde. That town's going to be run the way I say it should. That's the way it's been and that's the way it's going to stay. They want a marshal. All right, I've sent for one. If they're so set on having a lawman, I'll furnish one, not them. And he's going to be my dog. He's going to run things my way."

"Which sure won't mean much, far as law is concerned," Glyde commented dryly.

"Maybe," Wescott shot back, his thin lips drawing into a hard, gray line, "but it'll be Spade law, and that's all the kind they need."

"And to hell with the people who live there."

"Right. Like I've said, it's my town. It's there for me and the men who work for me. That's the way it's going to stay."

"Could be you're wrong," Glyde said softly. "There's such a thing as a town growing up, getting bigger than the man who started it."

"Lawless won't ever get that big. That's something you can lay odds on. I won't let it. I intend to hold my town, come fever or famine. The merchants and other yahoos squatting there can take it or leave it. I notice they're always ready to latch on to the dollars we spend with them."

There was a time of silence after that. Glyde watched the rancher with a level gaze that Wescott returned just as steadily. One of Spade's riders, a young, freckled-faced redhead, shifted on his saddle. "You the Glyde I heard about over in west Texas?"

"Sure he is, Otis," Wescott said before Glyde could reply. "He's what Strickland and the rest would hire, a fast gun. Probably figure a man like him won't run like that last one they talked into taking the job."

"Meaning you think I will?" Glyde drawled.

"If you're smart, mister, you will. Your fast gun don't mean a thing to me. Once I turn my crew loose in that town, everybody hightails it. They can be real mean when I tell them to."

This, then, was the catch in Henry Strickland's offer. This accounted for the good pay. A feud between the town and the man who had birthed it, who now refused to let it come of age. The merchants and citizens of Lawless wanted independence; they wanted to stand on their own and become a town of consequence. Wescott saw it otherwise. He would have it remain little more than a branch of his mighty Spade holdings—a convenience for himself, a playground for his crew during their off hours. It was not difficult to understand Cole Wescott's thinking. Supplies were always a necessity on a big ranch. And help was hard to keep unless there were attractions close by. It was three long days to the nearest town where a cowboy could find the diversions he periodically yearned for, and to keep Spade's crew content and working, Wescott must provide those attractions close to hand. A strict lawman would give rise to many problems.

"I take it this is a warning for me to keep riding," Glyde said.

"You're guessing right," Wescott answered. "I got my own lawman coming. No job open there now. Just you keep going."

John Glyde considered the words. A vision of his ranch, of the $600 he must have, flashed through his mind. And he recalled the letter he had received from Henry Strickland. The hopeful plea that he would accept the job as a marshal for Lawless was almost piteous; it was as though the town was in real need of help. He lifted his eyes to meet Wescott's hard, pushing gaze. "Reckon I'll just go on ahead and see things for myself."

The rancher stiffened in the saddle. Anger flared briefly through him. After a time he said: "Have it your way, but don't figure on pinning on that star!"

"You going to let him ride on into town, anyway?" one of the riders, a dark, slim man asked in surprise.

Wescott shrugged. "Why not, Cal? Figure I've made my point with Glyde. He's been around. He knows which end of a horse is the front. And he can't just turn back to El Paso without first grubbing up himself and his animal."

Glyde said nothing. The man called Cal spat, heaved about on his saddle. "Might not be so smart. . . ."

"I'll say what's smart and what ain't!" Wescott snapped. "I reckon I'm figuring this bucko right. You go right on into town, Glyde. Tell Strickland you're not interested in his job. If you want to go to work, come on out to Spade. I can always use a good man."

"Obliged," Glyde said, again in that paper dry tone, "but I don't think I'd be comfortable around the kind of boys you're hiring on."

Wescott's eyes sparked once more. "Suit yourself," he said. "Just remember what I've said. We'll be paying the town a visit tonight. I don't want to see you walking around with a badge on your vest. Could be the last walk you'd ever take."

155

Glyde's face betrayed anger for the first time. "Reckon I'd have a little something to say about that."

"Just a friendly warning, that's all," Wescott said with a wave of his hand. "Take it or leave it. Come on, boys."

Glyde watched them wheel about, lope off down the arroyo. He saw them reach its end and climb out onto the flat prairie land, and slowly dissolve into the haze of distance. Even then he did not move, but sat and stared moodily into the space that had swallowed Cole Wescott and his men. Finally he reached down, patted the gelding's neck. "Let's get along, old horse," he said. "Nobody's going to do me out of a good job."

II

Glyde rode the gelding down the center of the main street. He was not a devious man, and he cared little who saw him arrive. He sat straight in the saddle, hat pulled low, while the sun glinted dully off the exposed metal parts of the pistol at his hip.

Lawless was a short, double line of single story buildings, some showing evidence of recent repairs and painting. Back of them huddled a fan of nondescript shacks and a few passable houses that served as residences. It was plain; the settlement, or at least a part of it, was endeavoring to make itself more presentable. Glyde ignored the citizens who paused to stare curiously at him, and allowed his glance to run the dusty street. Strickland would have a place of business somewhere along the way, he reasoned. On the corner, to his left, stood a large, square building that bore the freshly lettered words: *THE BULL RIVER SALOON, Joe Moon, Prop.* on its high, false front. Beside it was Krieder's feed store and stable. That was followed by a succession of smaller stores and then, lastly, the ornate, pillared front of the Great Western Hotel. On the opposite side of the street he noted the front door of the Valley Trust Bank, gleaming under new, jet-black paint. Next to it, in small, cramped quarters, were a print shop, a dressmaker, and a lawyer's office. The American Café stood next in line, looking clean behind crisp, white curtains that covered the lower half of its windows. There were two vacant stores following the restaurant, and then the jail and marshal's office. Glyde scrutinized it closely. It was dusty and long unused. Beside it he located what he was searching for: *H. STRICKLAND, GEN'L. MCHDSE.*

He wheeled the bay in to the hitch rail that crossed its wide front, and swung down. Beyond, and to the side of Strickland's, he could see the wagon yard where customers might park their vehicles. Farther back, a small, white, clapboard church stood in lonely rejection. Lawless didn't appear to be such a bad town, he thought. He had seen worse. He looped the reins of the gelding around the bar, and moved up three steps onto the gallery. He threw a casual glance back down the street, along the way he had just come. The few citizens, who had noted his arrival, no longer were interested, and now went on about their business in the late afternoon sun.

Glyde pulled wide the screen door to Strickland's establishment and walked into the cluttered, odorous building. A slight, gray-haired man of fifty or more, with full mustache and sharp black eyes that peered from beneath startling white brows, detached himself from the rear of the store and came forward.

"Something for you, friend?"

Glyde halted in the center of the room. "Name's John Glyde. You Strickland?"

The merchant appeared surprised. His eyes widened, then he came up quickly and extended his hand. "That's me. Sure glad to see you, Glyde. Expected you yesterday. When you didn't show up, we figured you'd changed your mind and decided not to come."

Glyde took the man's hand. "I had a little business to tend to. Came fast as I could."

Beyond Strickland, a second man moved into view. The merchant saw the question in Glyde's eyes. He half turned and said: "Meet Damion Paull, John. He's the preacher around here."

Paull, a middle-aged, colorless man, dressed in shabby, blue serge, walked to Strickland's elbow. "Glad to know you, Mister Glyde," he said in a pallid voice.

Glyde acknowledged the introduction. Strickland, looking at Paull, said: "Go get the others, Damion."

The minister departed hurriedly, acting more like an obedient errand boy than one befitting his station. Henry Strickland said: "Be a few minutes until the rest of the committee gets here. How about a drink?"

Glyde nodded, and followed the merchant to the rear of the store. Strickland procured two glasses. He poured each half full of whiskey.

"Not much of a drinking man myself," he said, holding his glass aloft, "except on special occasions. Guess that's what this is."

Glyde downed the fiery liquid. The front door slammed. He turned, watched a balding, thin-faced man clad in conservative brown approach. His left arm, Glyde noted, was small and withered.

"Aaron Daunt," Strickland announced. "Runs the bank. This is John Glyde, Aaron. The man we sent for."

The banker shook hands gravely. "Pleasure to see you here."

The screen swung back again. "That's Sam Vorenberg," Strickland said. "Owns the hotel."

Vorenberg was a big man with a heavy, lined face and a ponderous tread. Metal pots on Strickland's shelves rattled faintly as he walked the depth of the store.

He took Glyde's hand, pumped it absently, and asked: "Where's the others?"

"Coming," Strickland answered.

"There's Lucy," Aaron Daunt said.

A tall, tastefully dressed young woman entered. She had chestnut-colored hair, a fair complexion that was set off by deep blue eyes and a soft, perfectly shaped mouth. As she glided toward the men, a slow smile on her lips, John Glyde felt something stir within him. It died instantly when Henry Strickland spoke.

"This is Missus Lucy Covington, Mister Glyde. She owns the American Café, down the street a bit."

"We had about given you up," she said, and offered her hand. "We thought you had perhaps heard more about the job and had a change of heart."

"No, ma'am," Glyde murmured. "Just a mite late getting started."

"You see anything of Joe and Dutch?" Strickland asked.

"They're coming," she replied, and sat down in the chair Daunt pushed toward her.

The minister and two more men came in at that moment. They halted in front of Strickland. The merchant waved at the man to his left, a huge, blond man, unquestionably of German descent. "Karl Krieder. Runs the feed store and livery stable. Everybody calls him Dutch."

"It is goot to see you," Krieder said in a slow, heavily accented voice.

"Joe Moon." Strickland turned to the other man. He was short, paunchy, and with a face to match his name. "Owns the Bull River Saloon. This is John Glyde, gentlemen."

The chore of introductions over, Strickland hunted up chairs for them to be seated. That accomplished, he said: "We're all mighty glad you're here, John. The job's still open and it's yours if you want it. But first I reckon you're entitled to know the situation."

Glyde said: "Got myself a fair idea of what's going on, but go ahead."

Strickland nodded; he stroked his mustache. "As you see, we're a small committee, but we're the ones who have the biggest stake in this town. We think we have a good future here, if we handle things right. There's a good chance of another stage route coming through, a north-south run that would do us a lot of good. We've already got the east-west line stopping over. Then, we think we might get the railroad when it decides to push on West. There's quite a bit of talk about it. Its coming through here would really boom things for us, put us on the map in a big way! But first we got to have a decent town to offer them. And that's our problem."

Glyde studied the merchant's earnest, intent face for a few moments. "Place looks pretty good to me."

"Well, we're doing what we can to make it *look* good, but that's not enough. It comes down to a matter of law and order."

John Glyde already knew the problem. He had it from Cole Wescott's point of view. But he did not interrupt the merchant. He wanted to hear the other side of it.

"North of here there's a rancher named Wescott. He owns the Spade outfit, largest spread in this part of the territory. Somewhere upward of two hundred thousand acres, I'd say. He started this town, donated the land for it, in fact. But he can't . . . or won't face up to things and see what's going on."

"Just not interested in the town stepping out on its own," Glyde said.

"Exactly. He figures Lawless is his own private property and everybody in it should do and think the way he wants them to. His crew feels the same. To them this town is their personal playground any time they ride in, which is about once a week."

"Do they spend much money with you?"

Joe Moon said: "Sure, when they feel like it. Other times they just take and forget all about the money end of it. The main thing is, if they paid for everything, it still wouldn't be enough to make it worthwhile for us. We need new business and more of it. And that sure won't come until we get the town tamed down. People just give us a wide berth because they figure this is Spade's town and they're scared to come in."

"The damage Wescott's crew does when it takes over far outweighs the business the merchants get from them," Aaron Daunt volunteered.

"That's for damn' sure!" Moon said feelingly, and then turned quickly to Lucy Covington. "I'm sorry, Lucy."

"It's all right," the girl said. "I agree with you completely. We can never have a good town until we break Cole Wescott's hold on it. Even the name frightens travelers away."

"Another of Wescott's little jokes," Strickland said. "He tacked the name Lawless onto it. Said he wanted it to be something people would remember."

"Have you tried bringing in a lawman before?"

"Twice," the merchant said. "The first man was shot in the back. That was a year or so ago. We hired a second, a younger man. Wescott and his bunch ran him out of town."

"When was that?"

"About two months back. Maybe a little more. When that happened we decided we'd find a man . . . well, a man with a reputation for not backing down. One who could take care of himself. That's why we were pleased when you wrote us. Some of us had heard about you and right away we figured you were the man we needed."

Vorenberg had been silent through it all. Now he said: "You ever a lawman?"

"Not exactly," Glyde answered. "Worked with the law. But don't worry about that part of it. I reckon I can handle the job. Your proposition was a hundred dollars each month with a place to live and my meals thrown in?"

Strickland said: "Right. You'll get your money every first. There's a room off the back of the jail where you can live and you take your meals at Missus Covington's."

"Use my stable for your horse," Krieder said, upping the offer even more, "and you're welcome. Also, I got a goot blacksmith."

"Fine," Glyde said. "I'd like to ask something else. You tell me this is all your committee? Nobody's missing?"

"This is all of it. Paull, there, actually doesn't belong, but he's with us. Why?"

"Just this. I met Cole Wescott as I rode in. South of town a few miles. He knew I was coming, even called me by name. I understand from your letter that you were keeping this quiet. The question is . . . how did Wescott know?"

Strickland frowned, glanced at the others. "We took special pains to keep our plans under cover. The seven of us, and of course you, are the only ones who are in on it. Somebody must have let it slip."

Each member of the committee, and the minister, Damion Paull, expressed denials. Strickland wagged his head. "There's been a leak somewhere. Lucy, you sure you didn't let it out, accidentally, of course? I saw Cole and a couple of his hands in your place a couple of days ago."

The girl's skin colored faintly. "Certainly not. There has been no mention of it by me to anyone."

"Well, Cole got wind of it somewhere, if he was waiting for Glyde at the edge of town. Did he give you any trouble, John?"

"None I couldn't handle. He told me not to take the job. Said he had his own man coming in to take over. He had four men with him and I couldn't do much arguing."

"That would be Otis Canady. And Cecil Burke and Hank Johnson and that Cal Wolff. Sort of keeps them with him when he's out, like bodyguards. Mean bunch."

"Looked it," Glyde agreed.

"You say Cole claimed he had a man coming in to take over the marshal's job?" Joe Moon asked.

"That's what he said. Didn't mention any name."

"He's threatened us with that before," Strickland muttered. "Could be just talk again."

There was a long minute of quiet. Glyde said: "One thing I want to get straight. If I take on this job, I expect a free hand to run it my way."

"Absolutely," Strickland said quickly while the others chimed in, agreeing. "There'll be no interference from us. We hire you to take over and put this town on its own. How you do it is your business."

"Good," Glyde said. "Reckon we got a deal."

Strickland turned to an iron safe standing against the wall. From its interior he took a Bible, a ring of keys, and a star. "Raise your right hand and swear," he directed, and administered the oath of office. That done, he pinned the badge on Glyde's left breast, and handed him the ring of keys. "It's all yours," he said, and stepped back. "Good luck."

Glyde grinned at the merchant, accepted further well wishes from the others. Lucy Covington paused long enough to say more. "I'm happy you've accepted the job. I feel as though we now may be making some progress."

"Thank you, ma'am. . . ."

"And don't call me ma'am! I'm not that old. Call me Lucy, like everyone else does."

"Yes, ma'am . . . I mean, Lucy. My other name's John."

"Fine, John. I'll see you at suppertime."

There was a general move toward the front door. Glyde suddenly remembered Cole Wescott's words.

"One thing more," he called. They halted, turned to face

him. "Might be a good idea to keep off the street tonight. And pass that word around. Wescott said he and his bunch would be in just to see if I was wearing this star. When they see I am, I expect there'll be a little trouble."

Strickland's face paled a shade. Vorenberg mopped at his florid face. Joe Moon finally spoke. "Well, reckon it had to start sooner or later. Might as well commence tonight as any time. Much obliged for the warning, Marshal."

John Glyde nodded, followed them on into the street. He picked up the gelding, led him to the adjoining building that housed his new office and the jail. An odd thought stuck in his mind. Strickland, and the others, had appreciated his warning on the possibility of trouble; they had expressed their willingness to let him have his way in whatever he elected to do. But there had been no offer of help.

III

It wasn't much of a jail. Once the building had served as a store of some sort for the scars of shelving still marked the walls. The room had been divided somewhere near the center with a wooden partition. The front half was the office area. It contained a battered desk with the usual, accompanying swivel chair. Long benches lined two of the walls and in the gun rack beside the single front window, a short-barreled shotgun, gray with dust, stood at solitary attention.

Glyde crossed over, threw back the door in the partition. It opened into the second half of the structure where bars had been erected to create two cells. They, too, were under a layer of thick dust and appeared to have gone unused for a great length of time. He walked the length of the cell room to another door at its rear. He opened it, saw his living quarters—a ten-by-twelve-foot wooden shack that stood a few paces away. He did not trouble to examine it. Likely it would be in the same, neglected state as the jail and marshal's office.

He returned to the forepart of the building and halted just inside the door. A boy, fifteen or possibly a year older, stood in the center of the room. He was thin to gauntness, with straw for hair, and a round, scrubbed face liberally sprinkled with freckles. But he had a cheerful grin and friendly eyes. He wore old, cast-off boots, badly run down, faded and patched Levi's, and a white shirt with red polka dots that had long since turned pink from many washings.

"How do, Marshal," he said.

Glyde smiled at him. "Howdy. Who are you?"

"People just call me Heber," the boy answered.

"Glad to know you, Heber. What can I do for you?"

The boy shook Glyde's hand solemnly. "Nothin' much, Marshal. Figured maybe I could do somethin' for you. This here place sure is in need of a sweepin' and dustin'."

"That's a fact. You live around close?"

Heber shook his head. "Mostly in Mister Krieder's stable, that's where I live. Lets me sleep there and I do his sweepin' and shovelin'."

"Where's your folks?"

"Ain't never had none. Leastwise, I don't remember none. Reckon this town's all the folks I got."

"Sorry to hear that," Glyde said. "People around here pretty good to you?"

"Sure are. But I don't ask for nothin' free," the boy added with pride. "I work for what they give me. Was wonderin' if you'd maybe have a chore or two I could do."

"You bet I have," Glyde answered. "First off, fetch me those saddlebags and that blanket roll off my horse. Better bring the rifle in, too. Then you can take my horse over to Krieder's. He's going to look after him for me. When you've done that, come on back and we'll start cleaning up this place."

"Yes, sir," Heber said with a broad smile, and darted through the doorway to do Glyde's bidding.

An hour and a half later they had finished. The jail and office were clean, and set to order. Glyde had gone through the desk, thrown away all useless papers and clutter and accumulated trash. Finding no shells for the shotgun, he sent Heber to Strickland's store for a box, placing it beside the weapon. His own rifle now stood beside it, ready for use, if necessary. What few personal possessions he owned had been carried into the room back of the jail, which was now ready for occupancy.

"You're a good man," he said to Heber as the boy started to leave. "A real hard worker." He reached into his pocket for a coin, handed it to him.

Heber stared at the piece of money. His eyes widened. "A dollar! That sure is a lot of pay, Marshal. More'n I ever got before for workin'."

"You earned it. What's more, you drop by every day and sweep out and sort of dust things off, and I'll make it permanent. A dollar a week. That suit you?"

"You bet!" Heber exclaimed, his face beaming. "I'll come by every mornin'."

"Fine. Now, what say we go over to the restaurant and get some supper?"

Heber's eyes fell. "Thanks, Marshal, but I can't. I always stay for Mister Krieder and look after the stable while he goes to eat. And he always brings me back a plate of vittles. But I'm obliged, just the same."

"It's all right. Some other time. See you in the morning."

"Yes, sir, Marshal. First thing. I'll be here."

Glyde watched the boy trot through the doorway, and head down the street for the Dutchman's. Youngsters, such as Heber, were no novelty along the frontier. Waifs cast up from a sea of shifting violence, they could be found in any town, alone, unattached, and eking out an existence by whatever means they found possible. Ordinarily they were not so fortunate as Heber. He was strong, healthy, and willing to work.

Glyde left the office, entered the street. He crossed over to the American Café, let himself inside. He settled down at a table near a window. The place was empty, but Lucy Covington, wearing a white apron, came from the back at once. She saw him, smiled. Bringing a glass of water, she placed it before him on the table.

"Your first meal with me, Marshal. What will it be? Steak and potatoes with biscuits and gravy?"

"Sounds good to me."

"Coffee while you wait?" she added.

He nodded, watched her walk back to the kitchen area where the cooking was done. He wondered about her husband, listened to see if she repeated his order to someone unseen, possibly Covington. He heard nothing, and when she returned, moments later, with his coffee, he asked his question.

"You and your husband run this place?"

She shook her head. "My husband is dead. Killed in the war, at Indian Bend."

He watched her pour the cup full of steaming, savory liquid. The late sun, almost down now, reached through the window and glinted off her hair. There were red shadows in it, he saw. And her eyes were bluer in the light. "Too bad," he said.

She shrugged. "It was a long time ago . . . or it seems so, anyway. And the years cover over memories." She paused, looked directly at him. "Have you a wife waiting somewhere?"

He said: "No, never got around to getting married. Never found enough time, I reckon."

"Or never the right woman," she amended his words. "Be a few minutes before your steak is done. If you want more coffee, call me."

John Glyde leaned back in his chair. He took a swallow from the cup. A pleasantness was upon him, seeping through him. He was not certain of its source. It could be getting settled on the new job, or it might be the excellent coffee, or possibly it was the presence of Lucy Covington. He was not sure which. But one thing was definite in his mind—he was going to enjoy eating at her restaurant. Already the smell of frying meat and potatoes, of biscuits baking in the oven, was turning him ravenous.

He tarried as long as possible at Lucy's place, then finally went back to his office. There he sank down in his chair to await the coming of Cole Wescott and his Spade crew. They would arrive late, he guessed, and, to while away time, he fell to cleaning and oiling his weapons.

Near 8:00 p.m., with the town quiet, and weighted down by the lack of sleep, he arose, locked the doors to the jail, and stretched out on one of the benches for a short nap. He had rested little since he left El Paso.

He had scarcely closed his eyes, it seemed, when a frantic pounding on the back door brought him leaping to his feet. He blew down the lamp, crossed swiftly to the rear of the building, and halted. He listened for a moment. He could hear the heavy, gusty breathing of someone just outside.

"Who is it?"

"Me . . . Dutch Krieder!" the thick voice of the stableman answered. "Open quick, Marshal!"

Glyde slid the bolt. He jerked the panel wide. From off toward the end of the street, in the direction of Joe Moon's saloon, a spatter of gunshots erupted.

"Ach, *Gott!*" Krieder groaned, stumbling into the dark room. "Already it iss too late maybe!"

"Too late for what?" Glyde demanded. "Who is it?"

"Poor boy, poor boy!" the stableman moaned, incoherently.

"It iss a bad thing. . . ."

Glyde wasted no more time. Whatever it was that had happened, Krieder was too distraught and confused to explain. He wheeled to his office, grasped the shotgun and a handful of shells. A vague feeling of guilt moved through him as he rushed into the street, slanted for the Bull River Saloon. He had been caught off guard by Cole Wescott and his crew, if that was the cause of the trouble.

Swearing softly to himself, he ran toward Moon's place. When he reached the corner, he saw a dozen or more men standing about in a circle. They seemed stunned, in a daze. They were looking at someone lying on the ground. Glyde heard running footsteps behind him. He half turned, saw a white-bearded man carrying a black satchel, coming in his wake. Evidently it was the town doctor. He reached the hushed group and shouldered his way through them. His quick glance picked out three men he had seen earlier that day with Wescott. The remainder appeared to be cowboys, also. Likely, they, too, were Spade riders.

"What's going on here?" he said. He glanced at the still shape lying on the ground. "Who's this?"

He had the answer before he completed the two words. There was no mistaking that white shirt with its pink dots, or the thick yellow hair so badly in need of cutting. A wave of shock passed through him. It was the boy—Heber. At that moment the doctor crowded him aside, kneeled down. He rolled the boy over gently. The dotted shirt front was covered by a dark stain.

The medical man studied Heber's drawn features for a long minute while he probed for pulse. He rose to his feet. "Dead," he announced. "Nothing I can do for him. Couple of you men carry him to my office."

Two of the cowboys moved to comply. In the silence, the discordant notes of a violin, badly off key, carried through the night from a nearby house. It was a harsh, disagreeable sound.

It grated on John Glyde's nerves, inflamed them, like salt on a raw wound, sent a sudden wild fury beating through him. He was no stranger to death, but this wanton, brutal killing appalled him. He whirled, faced the riders.

"Who did it? Who shot that boy?"

There was no immediate reply. Then Otis Canady swaggered forward several steps. His face was pale, but there was a hard grin on his lips.

"Well, would you looky here! A brand new marshal. Seems I recollect Cole telling you to keep riding."

Glyde ignored the redhead's remarks. "You the one responsible for this?"

"It was an accident," one of the cowboys began. "Otis was just having some fun with the kid. . . ."

"Shut up, Hank!" Canady sliced through the man's words. "We don't have to explain nothing to this tin star."

Glyde, fast as light, took two strides forward. He caught Canady by the shoulder, whirled him about. As the cowboy stumbled, Glyde drove him to his knees with a hard chop to the back of his neck. Instantly Glyde was behind him. His shotgun flashed up, began to drift over the surprised Spade riders. The two or three whose hands had dropped instinctively to the pistols at their sides thought better of it.

"First man to make a wrong move," Glyde said in a winter-cold voice, "gets a load of buckshot in his belly."

From where he crouched, Otis Canady said: "It was an accident, Marshal. Just like Hank said. I was only having some fun with that kid, making him jig. Somebody bumped me and the bullet went high."

"Save it for the judge," Glyde snapped. "You're under arrest for murder."

"Arrest?" the cowboy echoed. "Now, hold on a minute. Who the hell do you think you are, anyway?"

170

"I'm the marshal of this town," Glyde said flatly. "Get up on your feet. Do it slow and easy. And don't make any quick moves because I'm just aching to blow your head off with this scatter-gun."

Canady rose slowly, carefully. When he was upright, Glyde lifted the pistol from his holster, thrust it into his own belt. He shifted his attention to the silent line of watching riders.

"I ought to run the rest of you in, too," he said, "for standing around and letting this happen. I would, if I had a jail big enough to put you. Now, move on. Don't let me see you on the street again tonight, unless you want trouble."

The man called Hank laughed. "Expect you already got trouble, mister. Just as soon as we tell Cole what you've gone and done."

"You give Wescott a bit of advice for me. Tell him to stay out of this. It's murder Canady is up against this time, not just a drunken brawl charge. I'll be lucky if I can keep the town from lynching him."

Hank Johnson jeered. "Lynch? Hell, this town ain't got guts enough to whistle 'Dixie' unless Cole tells them it's all right."

"Could be things have changed," Glyde said quietly. "Move on."

"Sure, sure," the cowboy said, and turned for the street. The remaining Spade riders trailed after him. "We'll see you later."

"You know right where I'll be," Glyde replied. He prodded Canady in the back with the muzzles of the shotgun. "Let's go, kid killer. Got a cell waiting for you."

The redhead swore, jerked away from the gun's barrels. "Wasting your time, Marshal. I'll be out quick, soon as Cole hears about this."

"We'll see," Glyde said. "My guess is you'll be there until you hang."

IV

Spade's riders were in the street ahead of them. Glyde, keeping the twin muzzles of his weapon pressed to Otis Canady's spine, allowed them to shamble on toward the hotel where, apparently, Cole Wescott was at that moment. He gauged his pace, setting it so that he and his prisoner would reach the jail at about the same time Hank Johnson and the others arrived at the Great Western. As they moved through the ankle-deep dust, Glyde kept a watchful eye along the way. He half expected a mob to be gathering, to come surging for Canady's life in reprisal for young Heber's murder. But the walks were empty. He saw only a few white faces peering at him and his prisoner from behind shaded windows and through partly open doors. He was relieved that there apparently was to be no trouble—yet, strangely, he had a feeling of disappointment, almost one of shame, also.

Was Cole Wescott's power over the town so absolute that it would ignore the murder of the boy? It hardly seemed possible, yet there was every evidence of it. Maybe Hank Johnson was right. If he were, then he could stop wondering about any help coming from the citizens of Lawless. There would be none.

They reached the jail. He pushed the redhead into a cell, slammed and locked the door. As he hung the keys on their customary peg, Canady snickered.

"Don't you go running off far, Marshal! I don't figure I'll be in here long."

"You got a surprise coming," Glyde said, and began a round of the doors and windows. He secured them all, and, when that was completed, he checked his three weapons—the shotgun, the rifle, and pistol. All were fully loaded and ready. He placed a supply of ammunition on his desk where it would be handy. Satisfied, he settled down in his chair to wait.

He needed to talk to Strickland. The circuit judge must be

located and summoned, so that a trial for Canady could be held. And the sooner that was done, the better for all concerned. He arose, walked to the door and looked out into the street. Perhaps he could send word to the merchant by some passer-by. The town appeared wholly deserted. The citizens of Lawless were taking no chances on an aroused Spade crew.

He started to turn back, froze abruptly when motion, directly opposite, in the dark passageway alongside the Great Western, caught his attention. He reached for the shotgun, caught it up in the cradle of his left arm. A dozen men on foot filed silently into the street. They strung out, came to a halt in a short, ir-regular line.

"Lawman!"

It was Cole Wescott's strident voice. Glyde shifted his weapon around until it pointed at the vague shape of the rancher. He did not trust Wescott or his men at all, so he remained inside the partially opened door, offering them no target.

"Right here!" he called.

"You got one of my boys locked up in there. I want him turned. . . ."

"Forget it, Wescott!" Glyde cut through the rancher's demand. "He stays put. You and your bunch mount up and get out of town."

"You turn him loose or, by heaven, we're coming after him!"

"Try it and he's a dead man. Something you're overlooking, Wescott. I'm no regular lawman. I don't have all the high and mighty principles they're supposed to have. The business I've been in, a man hangs onto his prisoner, even if he has to kill him to do it."

"Meaning what by that?"

"You pull something . . . rush me or try to burn me out, and I'll turn Canady loose and then shoot him down when he tries to escape. He's my prisoner and I aim to keep him, dead or alive. Whichever it will be is up to you."

A murmur swept through the shadowy figures in the street. Glyde grinned to himself in the darkness. The bluff might work. The fact that he had done some bounty hunting in the past lent credence to his threat. The popular conception of a bounty man was that he would as soon kill his prisoner as bring him in alive. It was the opposite of truth, insofar as John Glyde was concerned, but let Wescott and his crew believe it.

"What you figuring to do with Otis?"

It was not the rancher who asked the question, but a voice unknown to Glyde. He said: "Hold him for trial. On a murder charge."

"For shooting that tramp kid?" It was Wescott now. "He was just a bum, belonged to nobody. You can't hold Otis for that, 'specially when it was an accident."

"Well, I am. And he'll hang for it if I have anything to say about it."

Wescott swore loudly. "Glyde, you're a fool to go and mix yourself up in this! You'll regret it. But never mind that now. Spade takes care of its own and I want Otis out of there. How much bail you want? I'll be responsible for him until the judge shows up."

"No bail. This is a murder charge. You might as well climb aboard your horses and move on."

Again there was that low mutter of conversation. It lasted for only brief moments, then Wescott and his men turned away, sifted back into the dark corridor along side the Great Western. Glyde watched them go. His bluff had worked, or it seemed so. He pulled back into the room, closed and locked the door. He moved to the window, drew aside the shade, and looked out. The street was empty. He listened for the thud of horses that would indicate Wescott and his men were taking his advice, were riding out. It did not come.

He was still listening when a knock at the rear door brought him around sharply. He hesitated for a moment, then made his way to the back of the jail.

"Who is it?"

"Strickland. And Daunt."

"See anybody around?"

"No. It's all clear."

Glyde slid the bolt, allowed the two men to enter. They followed him into his office. He lit a lamp, faced them.

"Glad you came by. Know if Wescott's pulling out?"

"Him and his bunch are still over behind the hotel," Strickland said. "Do you think you backed him down?"

"Maybe, but not for long. Wescott won't take anything like this easy. We might get through the night, but tomorrow could be something else. How soon can the judge be here to hold a trial?"

Daunt said: "Was through here three days ago. Told me he would be in Cañon City for a week. Guess he's there now."

"How long will it take to get him back?"

"Send a man now, tonight, and assuming the judge would be willing to ride horseback and start at once . . . he'd be here by noon tomorrow."

"No sooner than that?" Glyde murmured in a disappointed tone. "I was hoping we could have him here by daylight. But I reckon there's no help for it. Are you sure he'll come?"

Strickland nodded. "If we send along a letter and explain the situation, he'll come. The town always has been a sore spot for him."

"Good. You got a man to send that we can trust?"

"My son-in-law," Daunt said. "We can rely on him." The banker paused, looked closely at Glyde. "You dead certain this is the way you want to do this, Marshal? You think you can hold Wescott off?"

"Don't see as I've got any choice. If I'd had my choice, I'd likely have set things up ahead of time. But they started the play. You got any better idea?"

The banker looked down, shook his head. Strickland said: "Like Joe was saying, it has to start somewhere, and sometime. Too bad it had to be that boy, however." He glanced at the preparations Glyde had made. "You figure Cole will lay siege to the place?"

"Maybe not, if I can keep him believing what I said about my prisoner. Beyond that it's anybody's guess."

Daunt studied Clyde's dark, square-jawed face. "You really mean what you said . . . about turning Canady loose and then shooting him down?"

Glyde favored the banker with a tight grin. "Never lost a prisoner yet. Don't figure to break my record now."

The banker turned on his heel, started for the rear exit. Strickland and Glyde followed. The lawman opened the door, listened for a time into the darkness. When it appeared the alleyway was clear, he stepped aside for them to depart.

"What's the feeling around about the boy's murder?" he asked. "Think there'll be any trouble over it?"

Strickland said: "A lynch mob, that what you mean?"

"Been halfway expecting one."

The merchant said: "I don't think you'll have any problems there. Not as long as Wescott and his bunch are in town."

Glyde said: "That's some relief. Get that judge here fast as you can."

"He'll be here, no later than noon," Daunt promised, and stepped into the night.

Strickland paused on the threshold. "I wish there was something the rest of us could do to help. . . ."

"Could be, later on," Glyde said, and watched the merchant move off after the banker.

He closed the door behind them, secured it, and turned back to his office. From his cell, Otis Canady said something, laughed. Glyde ignored the redhead, went to his desk. Matters were proceeding as well as he could expect. He had hoped the judge could arrive sooner, thereby cutting down on the time he would have to guard Canady. But there was no possibility of that. One thing that did make him feel better was Strickland's offer to help, if needed. That was a good sign. Maybe he could fall back on some of the citizens, after all, if things got tight.

A sudden rash of gunshots broke across the night hush. Glyde leaped to his feet, moved to the door. He opened it a narrow crack. The firing was steady. It came, it seemed to him, from down near Joe Moon's Bull River Saloon. He could see no one in the street. And then, from the swinging doors of the saloon itself, he saw a man emerge, duck quickly into the shadows along the edge of the street. Glyde lost him in the darkness at the foot of the buildings, saw him again suddenly when he appeared in front of the hardware store across from the jail. The man halted there, looked about, and then swiftly raced over the open ground. Before he gained the sidewalk, he began to yell.

"Marshal! Hey, Marshal!"

Shotgun in hand, John Glyde stepped partly through the doorway, alert for some trick. The man halted at sight of him.

"What's the trouble?"

"You got to come quick, Marshal! Moon sent me. Them Spade cowboys has got the preacher down there and they're treatin' him somethin' awful! Joe says for you to come in a hurry before they hurt him bad."

Glyde considered. It could be a ruse, a means cooked up by Cole Wescott to draw him away from the jail. But he could not refuse to go. And if Joe Moon sent for him, it must be urgent. He glanced at the man. "This the truth? Moon sent you? If you're pulling a trick on me, I'll. . . ."

177

"It ain't no trick, Marshal! Before God it ain't! Can't you hear that shootin' down there?"

"Who are you?"

"Gulliver . . . the barber."

"Get inside, Gulliver. Lock the door behind you. There's a rifle in the rack. Anybody tries to get in before I come back, shoot."

"No, sir, not me! I ain't about. . . ."

"Inside!" Glyde yelled, and shoved the frightened man into the room. "Lock that door!"

He did not wait to see if his order was complied with. The barber would be little better than no guard at all at the jail, but he might manage to stall Wescott's crowd a few minutes, if he stayed at all. And it would take only a short time to double back if the whole thing was a jail break.

He ran the full length of the street, from the jail to the Bull River Saloon. When he reached the corner of the squat building, the shooting began to fade. He gained the gallery, raced along its length. In the open lot lying at the side of the structure, he saw a scatter of men and horses. He dropped off the porch. Shotgun in hand, he trotted toward the group. Several of the men on horses began to pull away.

In the center of the crowd he saw Damion Paull. He had been stripped of his outer clothing, stood now, a pathetic figure in his white drawers. Spade's crew had been up to its favorite pastime of forcing him to dance to the accompaniment of their guns.

When he saw Glyde, the minister, near exhaustion, sank to the ground. There was a red streak across one cheek, another on his left forearm where bullets had come too close. He swung frustrated eyes to Glyde. "Sorry about this, Marshal. I was a fool. Let them trick me into this. . . ."

"It's all right," Glyde said. "Couple of you help him to the doctor."

"Had to call you," Joe Moon broke in, pushing his way through the dwindling crowd. "They'd have killed him sure, if you hadn't come."

"I can see that. It was all of Wescott's bunch, I take it."

Moon said: "Every last one of them. They started hurrahin' him. . . ."

At that moment a fresh welter of gunshots broke out, this time at the opposite end of the street. Glyde wheeled swiftly. He had guessed right. It had been a scheme to get him away from the jail. He started for the street, running hard. He rounded the corner of Moon's, saw a dozen and more riders milling about in front of the jail. He raced on, reached a point just beyond Lucy Covington's café.

At that moment, Wescott's crew saw him approaching. Guns swung his way, began to blast through the darkness. Bullets dug into the dust around him, droned wickedly by his head. He lifted the shotgun, flung a blind shot into their midst. A yell went up as some of the buckshot found a target. Instantly more guns opened up. He felt searing pain along his ribs, more on his upper arm.

It was like his days in the Army, like charging up a long slope in the face of a steady hail of grape spewing from a cannon. A man didn't have a chance. A bullet plucked at his sleeve. Another smashed into the stock of the shotgun, splintered it. It tore it from his tingling fingers. The impact knocked Glyde off stride, almost drove him to his knees. He clawed out the pistol at his hip, began to use it.

He threw a glance to his right. The two vacant storerooms alongside the café were close by. He wheeled to the nearest. He did not pause to try the door, to see if it were locked. He simply drove it open with the heel of his boot and plunged into its dark interior.

V

He spun, slammed the door shut. In the next moment his foot came up against something lying on the floor. He crashed full length. Outside there was the hard, quick rush of running horses, surging up. Bullets smashed through the single, glass window, sending a shower of fine, sharp splinters. Glyde rolled over, pulled himself to his knees.

A heavy, plank counter stood in the center of the room. He reached for it, jerked. It was nailed to the wall. He went again to his back, kicked savagely at the counter until it came loose. Keeping low, he forced it up against the window and door, effectively blocking both. He lay back, breathing raggedly. He could hear Wescott screaming orders and the steady rap of firing guns. The room was filled with choking dust and the sounds of bullets thudding dully into the counter and the wall behind him. He was safe for the moment—but not for long. And he was pinned down. That irked him most of all for he had no way to fight back with any degree of effectiveness.

He turned onto his stomach, crawled to the rear of the room. There was a door, no window. A wave of hope flooded through him. If he could escape out the back, he could circle around, come in on Wescott from behind. He reached upward for the knob. It turned, but the panel did not open. In the darkness, he searched along the door. Several strips of wood had been nailed across it. He tried the first strip, sought to tear it loose with his fingers. It was tight, nailed flush, and he could find no purchase.

"Marshal!" Wescott's voice came to him through the shattered window. "Marshal! You want to die in there?"

Glyde drew his revolver. He felt along the edge of the lowest crosspiece until he found the narrow crack that separated door from facing. He wedged the tip of the gun's barrel in the small space, pried hard. Nails groaned, gave way. Glyde dropped the pistol. Eagerly he seized the crosspiece and ripped it off.

"Come on out!" Wescott yelled. "No sense of you holing up in there!"

Keep talking . . . just stay a bit longer, Glyde prayed. Just long enough for him to get that door open and reach the street. He yanked another wooden strip away, hurled it to one side. The shooting had ceased. Glyde found the last crosspiece, began to work at it feverishly.

"You been shot, Marshal? That why you ain't talking? Well, you had fair warning. I told you to keep riding but you was bull-headed about it."

The final wood strip was off. Glyde grasped the knob. The door still would not budge. He swore under his breath. He ran his fingers along the edge of the panel. More nails, driven in sideways.

"Now you see how Spade runs this town. And you or nobody else is going to change it!"

With one of the crosspieces he had torn from the door, Glyde began to hammer the nails back. *Just a few more minutes, Wescott. Only a few more.*

"Got my boy out of your jail, so I'm satisfied. I'm willing to forget things. You pack up and get out of the country. Don't want to see you around here again. You got that plain?"

The last nail. Glyde clawed at the knob, jerked hard. The door came open with a rush, slammed him back against the wall. He did not pause to recover his exploded breath but, gun in hand, plunged into the open. The rear of the jail was immediately to his left. He ran past it, came to the back of Strickland's store. He crossed behind it at a dead run, rounded the corner, and raced up its length. Before he was halfway, he saw he was too late. Wescott and his crew had already ridden away, and were disappearing into the night.

He pounded into the street, swung toward Dutch Krieder's. He must have a horse. Men began to appear along the way. Strickland came out onto the porch, shouted at him. "Marshal, you all right?"

"I'm all right!" he shouted back.

He saw Lucy Covington then. She came from the café, hurried into the street to intercept him. "You can't go after them!" she cried, realizing his intentions. "Not alone. And you've been hurt."

Her words brought a measure of reason to him. She was right, of course. It would be suicide to go thundering off boldly after Wescott and his bunch by himself. It would be a dozen or more guns against his one. He came to a halt.

"Come inside," Lucy commanded. "Let me look at that arm."

"In a minute," he snapped, impatient with himself, with his own failures. He looked over the men gathered in front of the storeroom where he had taken refuge.

"I'm forming a posse," he said, loud enough for all to hear. "We're going after Canady and bring him back. I expect every man able to ride a horse and shoot a gun to meet me in front of the jail in fifteen minutes." He hesitated, waited for some sort of response. It did not come, favorable or otherwise. He swept the group with a withering glance. "What's the matter with you people? Do you ride with me or not?"

Again there was only silence. Two men turned, began to walk away. Others followed. Lucy Covington touched Glyde's arm lightly.

"They won't help, John. And you can't blame them. They've tried to oppose Cole Wescott before . . . and always lost. They're afraid this time will be like the others. Come inside now and let me wrap up your arm."

"No time," he said angrily. "If they won't come with me, I'll go it alone."

There were running footsteps behind him. It was Daunt and Joe Moon, and the Dutchman, Karl Krieder.

"You hurt, Marshal?" the saloon man asked.

"No more than a scratch. I need a posse. Any of you able to ride?"

Moon said: "Not much good at it any more."

Nor would the elderly Daunt or the ponderous Krieder be of any help. He realized that as soon as he asked the question. He spun about, stalked to his office. The others trailed along in his wake. Strickland came in a moment later, and finally Sam Vorenberg. Glyde sat down in his swivel chair. Lucy began to fuss with the slight wound in his arm. The scorch along his side he did not think was worth mentioning.

"Glad to see you ain't hurt bad," the hotel man said, lining up with the others in front of the desk. "All that shooting sounded like a war."

"I didn't get to do much of it," Glyde snapped irritably.

"Reckon you were doing all you could," Vorenberg said. "What you figure to do now?"

Glyde lifted his glittering eyes to the hotel owner. "Do? Go after Canady! What else?" A long, uneasy silence followed John Glyde's words. The lawman allowed his hard glance to drift over the townsmen, touch each with its hostile challenge. "That's what you want, isn't it? You hired me to clean up your town, didn't you?"

Sam Vorenberg shifted his bulk. "Well, yes, I reckon you're right, Marshal, on that. Only maybe some of us figured it could be done a little different. Sort of worked up to gradual like instead of blowing the lid off all at once the way. . . ."

"Appears to me this wasn't so much the marshal's doings as it is Cole's," Strickland cut in. "I'd say he called the turn, not Glyde here."

Glyde said: "He did, but I can't see that it makes any differ-ence. The point now is the time to cut Wescott and his outfit down to size. If we don't . . . if we can't make the law stand for something, then we might as well forget it."

"I agree with that," Joe Moon said, "but how you figure to go about doing it? You can't just wade in there single-handed. That's a hard bunch Cole keeps around him. Canady is a killer. Heber wasn't his first. We've heard talk of others, some in the back. And Cole himself is no greenhorn when it comes to handling a six-gun."

"If I can't get any help, then I've got no choice except to go it alone."

"Count me in," Strickland said quickly.

John Glyde waited for more volunteers. When, after a time, there was none, a cold anger began to glow within him. *Same old story,* he thought.

"I still figure it would be a good idea to let things cool off a bit," Vorenberg said. "Wait until Cole has settled down some. Maybe we could talk to him then, make him see things our way."

"What makes you think he would listen now?" Strickland asked. "He never would before. Might as well get this in your head. He's not going to stand by and see this town slip out of his hands . . . not as long as he's got men like Otis Canady and Hank Johnson who will do what he tells them to."

Lucy Covington finished with her dressing of Glyde's slight wound. He glanced at her, gave her a brief smile of apprecia-tion, and stood up. He crossed the room, took up his rifle. Levering it, he assured himself that it was fully loaded.

He faced the committee. "What I should do," he said in a level voice, "is saddle up and ride out of this town. Some of you don't know what you want and a man could get killed, easy, helping you find out. But I took an oath to uphold the law and my word means something to me. What's more, I don't like Cole Wescott and his kind. Maybe that's my strongest reason for sticking around. No, you can stop me right now if you want. If you haven't got the guts for what's ahead, you can take my badge, pay me off, and send me on my way. That will end it, as far as you're concerned. You'll be able to wash your hands of the whole mess and maybe Cole Wescott will forgive you for showing a little backbone. But if you do that, you can kiss your town good bye permanently. I want to know where I stand. You're all here, so make up your minds. Either I'm the law and I see this thing through, come snow or sunshine, or I'm out. Let's hear the answer."

Vorenberg said: "Seems we ought to think a long time before we. . . ."

Lucy Covington's blue eyes flashed. "Think it over!" she exclaimed. "I wish I were a man . . . I'd ride with you, John. What's the matter with all of you? We hired a man to be our marshal. The least we can do is stand behind him."

"My sentiments exactly," Aaron Daunt said. "And I wish I could be of some help, Marshal. With a gun, I mean. But count on me all the way in anything I can do. I knew Cole wouldn't take this lying down when we first thought of it. I expect the rest of you did, too. Why the change now?"

"I haven't changed," Strickland said flatly. "I say we back the marshal. Now that he's got things rolling, the smart thing to do is to keep it going. You can't make me believe Cole isn't worried some about it."

Sam Vorenberg shook his head. "Don't everybody go jumping off the wagon. I'm thinking about the town and the people in it. The way things are headed, a lot of them are bound to get hurt. You vote how you please, but I say no. I say we ought to take it easy at first, build up to it. That's the way I feel."

The hotel man turned abruptly, stalked from the room. The

others watched him go in silence. John Glyde faced them. "What's it to be?"

"Majority rules in this committee," said Strickland. "I'm for it. And I'm ready to ride when you are."

Dutch Krieder slapped his huge hands together. "You do what you figure iss right, Marshal. I am with you. And I go with you, also, if you let me use my buckboard."

"Count me in," Joe Moon added. "I ain't so good on a saddle no more, but I can sit a seat alongside of Dutch. Ought to improve my shooting some, too."

Daunt smiled grimly. "Been a long time since I handled a weapon of any sort but if I may ride with Krieder and Moon on that buckboard. . . ."

Glyde said: "Fine. The main thing I needed was to know how you felt. You're all agreed that you want me to go ahead. All right, that's the way it will be. I give you my word I'll try to keep gun play out of town so as to avoid hurting innocent people. But I can't guarantee much. Cole Wescott's going to figure it just the other way. He'll use it as a means for bringing the town to terms." The lawman paused, swung to Krieder. "Dutch, have your hostler get my horse ready . . ."—"And mine," Strickland interrupted.—"and if you and Joe want to come along in your buckboard, you're more than welcome. A little show of strength won't hurt. Aaron," he continued to the banker, "be better if you stay here in town. Somebody should be here when that judge arrives to tell him what it's all about. Make him stay. We may not have a prisoner right at the moment for him to try, but we will have. You can promise him that."

The stable man was already moving through the doorway. Joe Moon was a step behind him. Strickland followed, saying: "Got to get my gun. Meet you here in ten minutes, John."

"And don't worry about the judge," Daunt said. "He'll be on hand when you're ready for him. That much I can do for the cause. Coming, Lucy?"

"In a few moments," the girl replied.

When the banker had gone, she glanced at John Glyde. He was busy at that moment stuffing rifle cartridges into the pockets of his brush jacket.

"Don't feel too hard toward Sam Vorenberg," she said. "He always has been cautious when it came to opposing Cole."

"A man can't expect to sleep with a rattlesnake and not get bit someday," Glyde commented dryly. "Vorenberg ought to realize that."

"Like most everyone else, he's afraid it will mean a lot of trouble . . . even killings . . . and still end up in a failure just as it has before."

"This time it will come out different," Glyde said quietly.

Lucy studied him for a long minute. Finally she said: "It has become a personal matter with you, hasn't it?"

He had finished supplying himself with shells for the rifle and was now filling the empty loops in his gun belt. "Like I said, I don't like the Cole Wescotts in this world. Maybe that makes it personal."

She stepped nearer to him. Her eyes were filled with sudden concern. "John, don't underestimate Cole. He's a dangerous man, with or without the gunmen he keeps around him. And he's controlled this country for a long time."

He gave her a slanted glance. "One thing I never do is take anything, or any man for granted. A pistol in the hands of a six-year-old kid can kill you just as dead as one fired by an expert."

She nodded but she did not smile. "How long will you be gone?"

"Until I get Canady . . . or they get me."

"I'll be praying. . . ."

From the doorway came Henry Strickland's voice. "I'm ready. Where the devil is Dutch with those horses?" The merchant disappeared immediately, evidently deciding to go to the stable in search of the missing mounts himself.

"I wish there were more going with you," Lucy said. "Just the two of you against all of Spade. You won't have a very good chance."

"None at all in a head-on fight," he said. "But there's other ways to trap a skunk. How's the preacher? Have you heard?"

She shook her head. "All right, I guess."

"I feel sorry for him. Seems to me people around here go out of their way to make it tough for him."

"They do," she agreed. "Religion is a hard thing to sell in Lawless."

"We're ready, Marshal," Strickland's voice sang out from the dark street.

Glyde picked up his rifle. He grinned at Lucy. "Thanks again for the doctoring. Hope it won't happen again. And don't worry about us . . . we'll be back."

"I know you will," she said, "but take care."

He walked out into the night. Henry Strickland was mounted. He held the reins of Clyde's horse in his left hand.

"Dutch and Joe are coming," the merchant said, and handed over the leathers to the lawman.

Glyde stepped to the saddle. There was not much point in the two men accompanying them. A team and buckboard would be unable to travel the route that must be followed. But he would not say it. They wanted to help. Let them do what they could. Moon and the stable man rolled up out of the darkness at that moment, halted.

"What's the plan, Marshal?" Moon asked.

"Strickland and I will go on ahead. You and Krieder stay on the road. We'll take to the brush. When we get close to Wescott's place, haul up. If you hear shooting, come on fast as you can."

"Right," the saloon man said. "You get something started, try to keep it in the open where we can take a hand."

"Sure," Glyde said. "Let's go!"

They rode out immediately. Only Lucy Covington standing in front of her restaurant, and a few men lolling about the saloon, watched them go. Glyde and Strickland pulled away from the men in the buckboard almost at once and soon left them far behind.

"We heading straight for Cole's place?" the merchant asked.

Glyde said: "Only up to a point. We're not looking for any shoot-out. We're out to take Canady and bring him back for trial."

"Then we better keep to the trees and bushes," Strickland said. "We can come in on Spade from the south. Brush runs up pretty close to the buildings on that side."

"Good idea."

"But getting our hands on Canady will be something else. Suppose he's inside the bunkhouse?"

"They won't be expecting us. That should make it fairly easy to walk right in and arrest him, then get out before they can act. May have to do some roping down, but we'll climb that hill when we get to it."

They had pulled off the well-traveled road and were now jogging slowly through a heavily overgrown strip of forest. They topped a small rise. Strickland pointed to a scatter of lights in the distance.

"That'll be Spade," he said. "Looks like everybody's still up."

"Could be we'll take Canady easier than I figured," Glyde murmured.

"Don't quite see how. . . ."

The stillness of the forest suddenly erupted with the crash of guns. Orange flashes bloomed through the thick darkness. Bullets droned past the two men, clipped viciously at the leaves and brush around them.

"Ambush!" Glyde yelled, and drove hard for the nearest stand of cover.

VI

John Glyde, with Strickland crowding the heels of his horse, plunged away from the murderous hail of lead. Someone had forewarned Cole Wescott. Someone had tipped him off. It could be no other way. Wescott would not have expected an immediate pursuit. Glyde swore feelingly, continued to thread his horse in and out the brush and trees at a reckless pace. The crash of guns seemed to come from everywhere. But Wescott and his men were shooting blind. They could see very little in the darkness and were relying more on the noise the two wildly plunging horses were making.

"Don't shoot!" the lawman yelled at Strickland. "They'll spot the powder flash."

He could not tell if the merchant heard or not, but no firing came from the man and he took that as his answer.

"Get after them!"

It was Cole Wescott's harsh voice coming from somewhere to the left and behind them. Instantly Glyde swung in that general direction. It was a bold, dangerous move. But, he reasoned, it would carry them into that area back of Wescott and his Spade riders. If successful, it could confuse them and throw them off the trail for a few minutes. He drew his revolver, held it in his hand to use as a club. There was a chance they had passed beyond the last man in the ambush line and now could cut in behind it without being detected, but there could still be a cowboy somewhere in the brush. If so, he must be silenced and not by gunshot.

"Where the devil you going?" Strickland cried, riding in close.

"Trying to get behind them. Let them think we're still out in front."

The merchant, apparently understanding, crouched lower over his horse. Glyde could hear Wescott and his riders thrashing about in the brush fifty yards to their right. It would appear his maneuver had worked. Dead ahead he saw a thick clump of brush. He rushed for it, pulled up short in its deep shadow. Strickland was only a yard behind him.

"We'll hold here for a few minutes, let them string out and start a search," he explained to the merchant. "Then we'll drift in among them and cut out Canady. That big white hat he wears will make him easy to find. Better stay mounted. We might have to leave sudden-like."

Strickland twisted about uncomfortably. "Forgot a saddle could be so damn' hard. Man gets soft not riding regular." He brushed at the sweat on his weathered forehead, listened into the moonlit night. Sounds of Spade's search seemed to be moving south. "They was just sitting there, waiting for us to show up," he said then in a tight, furious voice. "Dang if I don't think somebody warned Cole."

"I'd make a bet on that," Glyde said. "Somebody's working for Wescott. Somebody we think's with us."

"Could have been some jasper that saw us getting ready to ride out."

"Maybe, but some of us would have seen, or heard, him ride off. Or we could have heard him on the trail ahead of us."

"Seems so," Strickland murmured. "Now, who would be playing the hand from both sides of the table?"

"I wonder," Glyde said thoughtfully. He was reaching back, carefully going over the minutes after Cole Wescott had ridden away from Lawless with his men. No one knew of his intention to follow then, not until he had met with Strickland and the other members of the committee in his own office. Vorenberg had walked out. He knew of the plan and he would have had time to send out a rider. Then there was the Dutchman. And Joe Moon. It had taken an abnormally long time for them to get horses ready. Even Strickland had remarked on that. And what about Strickland? He had been gone a long time, supposedly after his guns. He could have dispatched a messenger. But Strickland was with him now. He hardly would ride straight into an ambush of his own making.

"They're doubling back, sounds like," the merchant said.

Glyde turned his attention to that. The occasional shouts were drawing nearer. He glanced about, sought to make out the dark, shadowy area in which they rested. "Better we separate," he said. "Not so likely to be seen. Watch for Canady's white hat." He put the gelding into motion, and drifted silently to another tall growth of brush a dozen yards away. He wished there were more light. At short distance a horse and rider were visible but scarcely distinguishable. It was a fortunate thing for them that Otis Canady wore such distinctive headgear. He glanced at Strickland. The merchant was bent forward in his saddle, listening into the night.

"They've got away, sure as hell!" A voice startlingly close suddenly broke through the hush. "Who was it, anyway?"

The second man, somewhere near Strickland, coughed, swore. Glyde saw Strickland stiffen at the unexpected nearness of the rider. "That there new lawman the town hired on and some other yahoo. Never got me a look at him."

"He's a stubborn cuss, that lawman. Figured Cole had him scared off."

"Reckon Cole did, too. Hey! What was that?"

Strickland's horse had shaken his head. The sharp jingle of metal was loud in the stillness.

"What was what?"

"Something there behind them bushes . . . look out!"

The night was shattered by the explosion of Henry Strickland's gun. The darkness was ripped by the flash of burning powder. Strickland's horse bolted, plunged off into the forest.

"That's one of them! Get him!" a voice yelled.

The two riders wheeled in after the merchant. Glyde drove spurs into the gelding, sent him racing straight at the pair. Both turned at the sound of his coming. He had a brief look at their startled faces. Neither was Otis Canady but that did not matter now. He snapped a quick shot at the nearest. Both wheeled off, dodged into the brush. He rushed on, trailing Strickland.

"Over here!" Glyde heard one of the pair set up a call for the rest of Spade. "Over here! We got 'em both cornered!"

He could not see Strickland, could only hear the crashing echoes of his flight. He rode on, weaving in and out of the trees and brush. Behind him the sounds of the pursuit getting under way became more definite. The gunshots and yells had been heard by all. He began to curve the gelding, to swing away from Strickland. There was little point in leading Cole Wescott and his bunch right to the merchant.

The undergrowth began to thin out, the trees to become larger, the country more open. He realized he was headed up the slope of a hill and sensed the greater danger it would offer. He now could be seen more easily by Spade. Almost at once guns began to open up. Wescott and the others were still some distance away, but the bullets droned uncomfortably close and he knew they had him in range. He sliced to his right, dropped into a long, narrow ravine. His horse was beginning to tire from the hard run uphill. Favoring the gelding, he cut flat across the slope trusting the easier grade would enable the horse to pick up speed and carry them both beyond danger.

A new flurry of gunshots broke out in the dense forest from which he had just come. Someone had spotted Strickland and was now crowding him hard. Glyde spun the gelding about, rode back down the hill, still keeping to the arroyo that partly masked his movements. He knew the little merchant, nervy as he was, would be no match for Wescott's men. He must locate him, show himself to the Spade riders, and then pull away. They would follow, he was certain. After all, it was he they wanted, not Henry Strickland.

He broke out of the arroyo, crossed a short stretch of open ground, entered the brushy flats once more. A rider abruptly loomed up on his right. They fired together, the two shots almost one. Glyde felt the breath of the bullet fan his cheek, saw the Spade man's dark shape jolt, and then spill from the saddle. He rushed on, not looking back. The shooting had ceased ahead, but it could not have been far off.

He saw motion again in the dusty darkness. He brought up his gun, but the rider was going away from him, had not seen him. He was behind Wescott's men now; they were all scattered somewhere before him or back up on the slope where he had just been. He pulled the heaving bay to a stop, tried to listen. The horse was sucking noisily for breath, but he could still hear the sounds of the search, the crash of brush, the thud of running hoofs, faint, low shouts. And then he heard the unmistakable noise of a horse, walking slowly.

It was nearby. Glyde froze in the saddle and listened intently. His eyes probed the shadowy darkness that surrounded him. He placed the muted *tunk-tunk* of steel shoes moving across the soft floor of the forest a moment later, off to his right. Gun ready, he waited out the long moments. The animal broke into the open, halted at sight of Glyde's bay. The man on the saddle had folded forward. One hand clung to the animal's mane, the other dangled limply alongside its neck. It was Henry Strickland.

Glyde rode forward quickly. He seized the reins of the merchant's horse, leaned toward the man. "Strickland! It's

Glyde. You hit bad?"

"Pretty bad, I think," the merchant muttered. He struggled to sit up. "You all right?"

"I'm all right. Hang on. Wescott's bunch is all around us, but we'll make it. We've got to find a spot where you can hide out for a spell."

"Sure . . . have . . . got to get off this horse . . . for a minute . . . ," Strickland managed, and doubled forward over his saddle again.

Glyde, with the merchant in tow, moved out of the clearing. He rode deeper into the brush, listening as he did so for sounds of Spade men doubling back down the slope, now to the right, or returning from their fruitless chase after Strickland. One thing was clear to him. He and the stricken merchant could not continue the deadly game of hide-and-seek in which they had been engaged. Strickland was hurt badly and needed attention and rest before he could even return to town.

A thick stand of Osage orange loomed up ahead. It was not as far from the scene of the original encounter as he would have liked, but he had no choice. He rode into its tangled depth, halted in the center. He dismounted, moved quickly to Strickland's side. Grasping the merchant under the armpits, he lifted him off the saddle, laid him on the ground. Pulling aside the bloody shirt front, he examined the wound. The bullet had entered his chest on the right side. It had bled considerably, but the bullet evidently had missed the lung.

Glyde stepped to the gelding. From the saddlebags he took several pieces of cloth and one of his spare white shirts. He returned to the merchant, and with the material he fashioned bandages. That done, he sat back on his haunches. "Ought to hold you until we can get to the doctor," he said, making his voice cheerful. "But we'll have to lay out here for a time."

Strickland said: "Where's Wescott's bunch now? Close by?"

"Wandering around out there somewhere. Don't worry. They'll never find us here. Know who shot you?"

Strickland moved his head wearily. "Too dark. I couldn't see him."

Glyde suddenly rose to his feet. "Somebody's coming," he said in a low whisper.

There were several riders in the group, he judged. They were passing only a short distance from the cluster of Osage orange. Their voices at first were little more than unintelligible murmurs, and then became distinct as the men drew abreast.

"You sure you plugged one?" It was Cole Wescott who asked the question.

"Sure, I'm sure! Saw him dang' nigh fall off his saddle. Then that fool horse of his went roarin' off into the dark and I lost him."

Wescott said: "Good. But you're not sure if it was that marshal?"

"Couldn't tell. Happened fast, like I said. And it was dark. . . ."

"All right, all right," Wescott cut the man short. "I'm hoping it was that lawman. But it won't matter much. I figure we've put a crimp in their plans, whoever it was. Might as well call the boys off. That pair, if they're still around, will be holed up so deep we'd never find them. And pass the word along that I want every man jack of the crew in town tonight. Those people are going to know once and for all who's the law around here."

"Sort of rub it in, eh, Cole?"

"Exactly. I'm going to teach. . . ."

The rancher's voice faded and was lost as the riders passed out of hearing distance. Glyde ran Wescott's words slowly through his mind. Spade would return to Lawless that night and demonstrate its contempt for the town's new law. It was like Wescott. It was what could be expected of him. And if he got away with it, Lawless could forget any hope for independence and for a future.

He returned to Strickland, squatting down beside the wounded man. The merchant appeared to be sleeping. Glyde settled back, ears attuned to the sounds of the night. Somewhere in the trees an owl hooted and off in the remote distance a dog barked a lonely beat. An hour dragged by. Two. There were no more sounds of Spade and he had allowed ample time.

He aroused Strickland. "Time we get started. Be a long, hard ride for you. I'll take it as easy as I can. When it gets too rough, sing out and we'll rest for a few minutes."

Strickland said: "I'll make it."

The lawman helped him to his feet, and then onto the saddle. Strickland groaned from the effort. "Want me to tie you on?" Glyde asked.

"I'll make it," the merchant said again. "Never mind."

They rode out of the Osage orange, headed back for Lawless. Glyde, fearing no more trouble from Wescott for the time being, angled across the flats deliberately in an effort to intercept the road. It would be easier going for Henry Strickland—and there was a slim possibility and hope they would come upon Dutch Krieder and Joe Moon in the buckboard.

In that he was disappointed. When he arrived at Lawless around midmorning, after a slow and tedious journey, they had met no one on the trail. He went directly to Dr. Clooney's office, aware of the glances of several townspeople, and aided the medical man in carrying Strickland inside. He waited while the doctor made an examination.

"Serious, but I expect he has a chance," the physician said. "It would have been better if you'd got him to me sooner."

"Better if he hadn't got shot at all," Glyde said, faintly irritated.

He left the building, made his way to his office. As he

dismounted, he saw Aaron Daunt come from the bank and start across the street. Farther along, Dutch Krieder was hurrying toward him. He entered his quarters, sat down wearily in the chair. Daunt came in, his thin face pale. "That Strickland I saw you take into Clooney's?"

The lawman nodded. "Shot in the chest. The doc thinks he'll be all right."

Daunt said nothing for several moments. Then: "Rough time of it?"

Glyde said: "Pretty rough and it got me nothing."

Krieder's bulk darkened the doorway. "Marshal, glad I am to see you back. We heard all that shooting, but we could not find you. Iss Henry bad hurt?"

"Bad enough."

"And the others . . . Wescott's men?"

"I got one of them. Don't know who. Strickland may have downed another. I'm not sure. He's in no shape to talk."

"We try to help," Krieder said apologetically, "but you were in the woods and on the mountain, it sounded like. We couldn't take that buckboard over. . . ."

"It's all right, Dutch," Glyde said. "Maybe it was a fool idea, anyway. But we've got to start making a believer out of Wescott sometime." He glanced up. Lucy Covington came through the doorway. She carried a tray of hot breakfast for him and a pot of steaming coffee. He grinned his pleasure. "Best thing that's happened to me yet," he said.

She placed the food before him, poured out a cupful of the black liquid. "I'm glad you're all right," she said quietly. "Is Henry . . . ?"

"Dead? No, he has a good chance, the doctor says. We were lucky at that. Wescott was expecting us."

"Expecting you," Aaron Daunt echoed. "You mean there was an ambush?"

Glyde took a long swallow of the coffee. "Somebody tipped him off. He knew we were coming."

"It's unbelievable!" Lucy Covington exclaimed. "When . . . how could somebody do it?"

"Had to be during the time we were getting ready to pull out."

He was watching the three narrowly, assessing the surprise they registered. He wished Vorenberg and Joe Moon had been present. He would have liked to see their expressions. The shock appeared genuine enough in the eyes of the banker and Dutch Krieder—and Lucy.

He told them then of the night's events, and of Wescott's last instructions to his men. "They'll be here," he said, "ready to take the town apart as a lesson to us. You might as well get set for it."

"What do you figure to do?" Daunt asked.

"Stay out of sight for the rest of the day. I had hoped to keep my return a secret and maybe give Wescott the idea I'd pulled out, but I couldn't do it. Quite a few saw me ride in with Strickland. If I stay off the street for the rest of the day, it could be the idea will still get around that I rode on."

"Then what happens?"

"Tonight, after Spade gets here, I'll watch my chances and grab Canady again. This time he won't be getting away."

Daunt wagged his head. "I'll say this, Marshal, you don't know when to quit. Anything you want us to do?"

"Not much. And I don't want anybody else hurt. One thing, we don't want to give Wescott's bunch a chance to hurrah somebody like they did the preacher last night. See if you can keep anybody they're apt to pick on off the street."

"We'll do what we can. Where will you be until dark?"

Glyde pointed toward his quarters outside the jail. "In my shack. I'm going to lock the doors and pull the shades and get myself some sleep."

"Looks like you could use some," Krieder observed.

"We'll see that nobody wakes you up," Daunt said. "Not unless it's something important."

"Can't think what it would be," the lawman answered. He turned to Lucy. "I appreciate your bringing me something to eat. I was considerable hungry. Dutch," he added to the stable man, "that horse of mine is about done in. Henry's, too. I'd be obliged if you'd look after them."

"Sure, Marshal, sure. I'll do that," Krieder said, and hurried through the doorway. Daunt followed.

Lucy picked up her tray. She smiled at him, her eyes soft and lovely. "I'm thankful you're back," she said. "But tonight . . . do you think it's wise to go up against Cole and his men again . . . and alone?"

"Canady's only one man," he said. "I don't figure to take them all. Don't worry about it."

VII

John Glyde awoke to an insistent pounding on his door. He sprang to his feet, hurried to the one small window in the front of his shack. He drew the shade aside, glanced out. It was almost dark, but he recognized the features of Damion Paull, the minister.

He stepped to the door and opened it. Paull entered. "Thought I'd better wake you, Marshal. Wescott and his men are in town."

Glyde returned to his cot and sat down. He began to draw on his boots. "Glad you did. He up to anything special?"

"Not yet. Right now he's out in front of the bank, talking to Daunt and some of the other people."

"About what?"

"I don't know."

Glyde looked at the minister curiously. The lean man's face, slightly puffy and marked by his treatment at the hands of Wescott's men, was pale in the diminishing light.

"How long you been there in front of my door?"

"Since the middle of the afternoon, or so."

The lawman stared at him, surprised. "Why?"

Paull shrugged his slight shoulders. "I wanted to help out where I could. Thought it might be a good idea to watch your place while you slept. Felt a little responsible for things, since it was I who sort of let Wescott get the upper hand last night."

Glyde felt his liking for the mild-mannered Paull increase. "Forget that," he said. "If it hadn't been you, it would have been somebody else. You feeling all right now?"

"Guess it was mostly my pride that was injured," the minister said, "and a man is better off without that."

Glyde strapped on his heavy gun and belt. He drew the revolver, checked the cylinder for loads. It was full. "I'm obliged to you for keeping your eyes on me. Know if that judge arrived yet?"

"He hasn't come. Daunt figures he must have been holding court and couldn't get away right then. He's certain he will come, though."

The lawman moved to the doorway, opened it a narrow crack. Full darkness had almost settled in. Lights were beginning to appear along the street.

"Any way I can get to Daunt's bank where I can hear Wescott without being seen?" he asked without turning around.

"Sure. We can go down the alley. Follow me."

The minister slipped by Glyde, stepped into the open. The lawman dropped in behind and together they walked the length of the street in the deep shadows that lay to the rear of the buildings. At the back end of a passageway that separated a print shop from Daunt's place of business they halted. A man lounged at the opposite end of the opening, blocking the street. It was too dark to recognize him or any of the others gathered in front of the bank, but the voice of Cole Wescott reached them clearly.

"You want a lawman, you'll get one. Fact is, I've already sent for a good man who will keep things in line for you. Ought to be here today, maybe tomorrow. There was no need for you to go hiring some gunslinger that'll hightail it out first time real trouble blows in."

John Glyde smiled to himself in the darkness. Evidently Wescott was under the impression that he had ridden on.

"Four-flushers like that only get you in trouble. Like Strickland, shot bad and maybe dying."

Glyde turned to the minister questioningly. Paull shook his head. "He's pretty bad. Lost a lot of blood. But Clooney hasn't given up hope yet."

Aaron Daunt's voice said: "We want our own lawman, Cole, not somebody who works for you. That's the main point of our differences, the root of the trouble between Spade and the town. You agree to our handling it ourselves and we have no problem."

"We've got none, anyway," the rancher replied. "Like I've told you, there'll be a real lawman here to take over."

"What about Canady?" a strange voice asked. "He killed that boy."

"I'm standing good for Otis. When the marshal gets here, he'll turn himself over to him. We'll leave it up to him whether Otis stands trial for an accidental killing or not."

Someone said: "Sounds fair enough to me. Don't see as it makes much difference where the marshal comes from, so long as we got one."

Not much it won't! Glyde thought. Wescott was making the crowd, with the exception of Daunt and a few who knew better, see things his way. Perhaps it was better, he decided, amending his thinking. Allow Wescott to believe he had the town with him. It might put him off guard, make it easier to recapture Canady.

"Now that we've had our little understanding, how about going across the street to Joe Moon's and having a drink on me? All this yammering has sure dried up my throat."

A chorus of agreement lifted at that. The crowd swung about and there was a general movement toward the Bull River Saloon. Glyde drew back from the passageway.

Paull said: "What next, Marshal?"

"Evening's young," Glyde said. "Right now, I'm going to get some supper. Join me?"

"Be a pleasure," the minister said.

They retraced their steps down the alley to the rear of the American Café. The door was closed. Glyde rapped on it softly, and it was opened almost immediately by Lucy Covington. The lawman looked beyond her. The restaurant was deserted.

"Couple of hungry men needing food," he said, grinning at her.

"Come right in, hungry men," she said, smiling as she stepped back.

They moved into the warm, savory kitchen. Lucy pointed to a small table. "You can eat back here if you like," she said. "Aaron told me of your plans, so I know you don't wish to be seen. The town is filled with Spade riders."

"Good idea," Glyde said, and sat down at the table. Damion Paull took a chair opposite.

Lucy at once began to heap two plates with food. She placed them before the men, turned to get cups and saucers for coffee. "You hear Cole's little speech?" she asked.

"Some of it," the lawman replied. He rose, pulled a chair back for her. "Glad you were able to make him think I had pulled out. Makes things easier."

"No one told him you had," she said, filling the cups from a small, granite pot. "You just weren't around to be seen and Dutch kept your horse hidden in his stable. Cole has a colossal conceit. He naturally figures that you ran."

"Any new word on Strickland?"

"Only that he is pretty low."

"Sorry he had to be the one that got shot. An unlucky break for him."

"How did it happen?" Paull asked.

Glyde shook his head. "Don't know exactly. We separated. I heard shooting over in the direction he had gone. I rode that way and came upon him. He'd already been hit."

"Too bad. I heard, too, that you were ambushed. Do you still think so?"

Glyde studied the minister's pinched face for several moments. "It was an ambush," he said. "No doubt of it."

Damion Paull sighed. "Terrible thought . . . that someone in the committee is holding up for Wescott. Could it have been someone outside that warned him?"

"Possible," Glyde said, "but I doubt it. Hardly time for anyone else to do it."

"But who of us would do such a thing?" Lucy broke in. She halted abruptly, more words unsaid on her lips. The front screen door had opened. It remained so for a length of time, then banged shut. The heavy tread of booted feet echoed in the small building. Lucy rose quickly, hurried to the counter.

"Apple pie and coffee, lady," said the unmistakable voice of Otis Canady.

"Same here," a second man added.

Damion Paull laid his knife and fork down with elaborate care. Glyde paused in his eating. He considered the possibilities. It would be simple to step out from behind the partition, challenge the outlaw, and arrest him. Easier yet to take him out the back door, up the alley to the jail. Likely no one would see him. But he shook his head at the minister. It would be too dangerous for Lucy. Canady and whoever was with him might choose to fight. He could not risk Lucy's getting hurt. Once they were out of the building, however, they could try something.

Lucy remained up front, taking no chances on either of the Spade riders coming to the rear for her in the event they desired second helpings. Glyde continued to enjoy his meal, listening as he did to the men's run of conversation. They were going next to the Great Western, he learned, to do a bit of gambling. Canady felt lucky, figured it was his night to buck the tiger.

Glyde grinned at that. Canady felt lucky. He had a big surprise coming to him. He heard the chink of coins as the pair paid their checks. An idea came to him suddenly. If they were going to Vorenberg's first that meant they would likely walk the length of the street, thereby passing the vacant storeroom next to the jail into which he had been driven that previous night. At that point they would cross the street to the hotel. Of course, they could cross over immediately and tread the opposite walk, but human nature being what it was there was a good chance they would keep to the east side until they reached the end of the block.

The lawman got silently to his feet. It was worth gambling on, he concluded. He motioned for Paull to remain seated, waited until he heard the front screen door slam. He turned then, left the restaurant, and ran the short distance to the empty building. He entered, moved quickly to the door. He opened it, peered cautiously around its frame. Canady and his friend were only steps away. They had not crossed over. Glyde drew his pistol. He waited out the moments until they were almost abreast. He stepped suddenly before them.

"What the . . . ?" Canady blurted, completely startled.

Glyde shoved him hard, sent him stumbling and reeling into

the black depths of the storeroom. He jammed his gun into the second man's spine, pushed him at Canady. They collided in the darkness, went down in a heap. Glyde was upon them like a cat. He jerked their guns, thrust them into his belt, and stepped back.

"Get up," he ordered in a cold voice.

"What the hell's all this . . . ?" Canady began, but the lawman cut him off harshly.

"You know what it's all about. You're going back into jail to await trial. And you," he said to the other rider "are going with him so's you won't go tattling to Wescott."

"You ain't lockin' me up!" the cowboy yelled, and lunged for the door.

The lawman grabbed for him, caught only a fingertip of his shirt. The cloth ripped. At that same instant Otis Canady leaped to his feet. Glyde swung on him, drove him to his knees with a hard blow to the ear. Canady lay still, but it was too late then to stop his companion.

Glyde prodded the Spade rider to his feet, out through the back door. Everything had gone too well, been too easy. If he could only have held onto Canady's friend and placed them both under lock, there was a good chance the night would pass with no incident. The pair's absence would have gone unnoticed for a while. Now Wescott would know and come again.

He marched the gunman into the jail, locked him in a cell. His original plan had been to wait until it was very late, until most of Wescott's men had returned to the ranch or were occupied elsewhere, and then arrest Canady. There would have been fewer Spade riders to cope with then. Perhaps it would have been better, but there was no point in thinking of it now. He had acted as he saw fit.

From the dark depths of his cell Canady said: "I'm going to kill you for this, lawman. No matter what Cole says, I'll kill you this time when I get out."

"If you get out," Glyde answered coolly.

"Don't you worry none about that. Soon as Burke gets word to Cole where I am, he'll be here with the boys. Then it'll be my turn."

Glyde knew he could depend on that. The thing to do was to get ready for the rancher and his men. They would come soon. An idea flashed into his mind. Why wait for Wescott? Why be there when he arrived? A good thought, but where could he take his prisoner? *The church!* It came suddenly to John Glyde, like a shaft of white light spearing through the darkness. No one—Cole Wescott least of all—would think to search the forlorn, neglected little church building that Damion Paull occupied. He hurried to his desk. From one of the drawers he procured a rusty pair of handcuffs. He unlocked them, tested their strength. They were in good working order despite long disuse.

He continued to go through the desk, came up finally with a thick, wool scarf. It would serve as an effective gag. Otis Canady must not be permitted to make any outcry. Glyde went to the cell, opened it. Canady watched him with narrowed, hating eyes.

"Stand up," the lawman ordered. "Turn around and put your hands behind you."

"The hell with you . . . !"

"Do it," Glyde snarled, "unless you want me to bend this gun barrel over your head! Makes no difference to me."

Canady complied sullenly. The lawman snapped the cuffs about his wrists, slipped the ratchet until they were snug.

"What do you think you're doing?" Canady said in rising alarm.

"Going to take you where we can have a nice, quiet night," Glyde said, and drew the scarf about the rider's face. Canady

207

struggled briefly but with no success. The lawman bound his lips tightly and, when he was finished, only Canady's nose and eyes and the upper part of his head were visible. As a final precaution, Glyde took a short length of rope, fashioned a loose slip noose in it, and dropped it about Canady's neck.

"Just in case you try to run," Glyde said.

Canady raged beneath his gag, but the sounds that came forth were only smothered grunts. Glyde secured the front entrance of the jail, placed the lighted lamp on his desk. The shades were already drawn.

"Out the back," he said, and motioned to Canady.

The Spade rider muttered under the scarf, but moved through the doorway into the night. Glyde followed, set the lock, and paused to listen. The sound of voices in the street was swelling. Wescott apparently had been advised of the arrest. He tugged lightly on the leash around Canady's neck. They left the shadows behind the jail and angled across the open ground to the church. The door was not fastened and they entered. It was dark inside the small structure, and they halted in a narrow, hall-like vestibule. Glyde looked around. He feared to strike a light. One showing might be noticed and invite investigation.

A door opened off to his left. He swung it back. It led to the bell tower. A ladder was fastened to one wall. Glancing upward, he could see, by means of faint moonlight filtering through the slatted cupola, a small landing. It offered the perfect hide-out and he turned to Canady. "We're going up that ladder," he said, unlocking the cuffs. He directed Canady to hold his hands in front of him and reshackled him. "That's so you can climb. But don't get any ideas. I'll still have this rope around your neck and a gun pointed at your back. Start climbing."

Otis Canady presented no trouble. They mounted the crude ladder, crawled onto a narrow platform. There was no bell and that afforded them ample room in which to stretch out. Their position, high above the town, also provided a vantage point from which Glyde could observe the street. It was impossible, of course, to determine the identity of persons because of the darkness, but their movements were apparent.

Glyde, looking between the slats, watched the milling knot of men in front of the jail. Several more, two of whom carried flaming torches, were at the rear.

"We got out of there just in time," he said to Canady. "Your friends are going to be some surprised when they break in and find you missing." The gunman muttered. Glyde said: "Might as well settle down. We'll be right here until I see that judge ride in . . . and your bunch leaves."

A rectangle of light suddenly flared through the darkness behind the jail. They had broken in the door. Glyde watched the spur of activity, and then the lessening as the structure was discovered empty. The crowd formed again in the street. More torches blazed into the night. After a few minutes they scattered and began a slow procession along the stores and buildings. The search was on. It probed slowly to the end of the street, paused. It began again, spread out to the houses that stood beyond and back of the town itself. Two men, one bearing a light, split off from the others, slanted toward the church. Glyde watched them approach, vague shadows peaked by a flickering flame. He cocked his revolver, the sound loud in the hushed bell tower.

"One move out of you," he said to Canady, "and you're dead . . . along with them."

Canady, his face only partly visible in the bars of weak moonlight, nodded. The two men reached the church. Glyde heard the door open below, caught their voices as they entered, paused in the vestibule. Their boot heels rapped hollowly on the bare floor when they walked along the rows of wooden pews. The minutes dragged. And then John Glyde heard the door slam shut. He swung his attention to the slats. Below the two riders were returning slowly toward town.

He took a deep breath, glanced at Canady. "You were smart that time," he murmured.

The outlaw shrugged. It was evident he deemed it foolish to chance certain death when deliverance by Cole Wescott was only a matter of time.

VIII

Sometime after midnight Spade gave up the quest. Glyde saw the torches go out, heard the sound of running horses as several of Wescott's crew hammered northward on the road out of Lawless. Some were remaining, he realized—Wescott and a picked few. He saw the town grow quiet after that, watched the lights wink out, one by one, until, at last only Sam Vorenberg's Great Western Hotel showed evidence of life. He considered briefly the advisability of returning his prisoner to the jail; doing so would allow him to rest, get a few hours sleep as he would no longer be faced with the necessity for maintaining a vigil. He decided against it. They were better off where they were. There was little wisdom in inviting trouble.

Faint snores came from Otis Canady. Glyde glanced across the landing to where his prisoner lay. Whether the sleep was feigned or not, he was unsure. But it didn't matter. He was wide awake himself. The fact that he had spent most of that day catching up on his rest had put him in good condition for the long watch.

He saw the dawn break over the low hills to the east, watched the first stirrings of the town as it came alive to a new day. He was right about Cole Wescott. Around 8:00 he saw the rancher, with three of his riders, emerge from Vorenberg's and strike for Lucy Covington's café, apparently going for breakfast. Later they left the restaurant, went to Aaron Daunt's bank.

The banker, with Wescott and his men, came out into the

street. They crossed over, entered the jail. Lucy Covington made an appearance, hesitated in front of her establishment, and then walked the short distance to Henry Strickland's store. Going to check on the merchant's condition, Glyde surmised. Canady awoke, grumbled into his gag, and stretched.

The morning hours, steadily growing warmer, wore on. The stage rattled in, halted before the Great Western in a swirling cloud of dust. Three prisoners got out, moved about for the allotted ten minutes, climbed back into the vehicle, and were off again in a jangle of harness metal and boiling gray powder. Daunt, Wescott, and the others returned to the street. The banker headed back to his place of business. The rancher and his crew moved slowly down the street for the hotel.

At noon the heat in the tiny cubicle of a bell tower was intense. Canady fumed and muttered, cursed Glyde steadily with his eyes. He finally managed to displace the gag.

Glyde studied the outlaw intently. "All right, leave it off. But you know what happens if you yell."

"I can hardly breathe under that damn' thing," Canady said. "Like to choked. How long you going to keep me here?"

"Until I see the judge ride in. . . ."

Canady swore again. "Could be all day. Hell, man, I'm hungry. I need some water."

"You'll live through it," Glyde said. "Could be that's the judge coming in now."

Canady twisted about so he could look through the wooden grillwork. Two riders were entering Lawless from the south road. One wore a dark suit, the coat of which was long and hung down below his saddle skirts.

"One of them is Daunt's son-in-law," Canady said. "Don't reckon I know the other."

"He'll be the judge then," the lawman said. "All right, we'll go down and back to the jail. You follow me on the ladder. Just in case you move too slow, keep in mind I'll have that rope ready to yank.".

"I'm coming," Canady grumbled. "I figure the sooner I'm back in your jail, the sooner Cole will get me out. Then you and me have got something to settle, Mister Tin Star."

Glyde only smiled. He descended the ladder quickly. Canady followed obediently. Once on the ground floor, the lawman changed the outlaw's handcuffs, shackling his arms behind his back once more. He replaced the gag.

"We'll go in the back way," he said. "I'd just as soon nobody saw us. Move out."

There may have been some in Lawless who saw John Glyde escort his prisoner across the open ground to the rear door of the jail, but they would have been those in the houses back of the town. Strickland's store and other buildings along the street effectively screened their movements.

Once inside the jail, Glyde deposited Canady in a cell, removing the handcuffs and gag. He gave the rider a drink of water from the bucket. "Get you something to eat as soon as I get set," he said.

He propped a chair against the back door, which had been booted in; he left the front standing open just as he had found it. He blew out the lamp, and then stood for a time and studied the weary horses waiting in front of Aaron Daunt's place. They were hard ridden. The judge was inside, talking matters over with the banker, he guessed. And Wescott, hearing of the jurist's arrival, would undoubtedly be along soon.

"How about them eats?" Canady called from his cell. "Man's a prisoner, he's supposed to be fed."

"You'll eat," Glyde answered.

Cole Wescott strode into view at that instant. He was trailed by the same three men. They went into the bank. Five minutes later they reappeared, accompanied by Daunt and a short, heavy-set man in a dusty, black frock coat.

"I figure he took my boy out and shot him down, murdered him," Wescott's words came to Glyde. "Then he rode on. He wasn't no real marshal, just a gunman they hired to cause trouble."

The group reached the jail. Glyde stepped into the doorway. The men came to an abrupt halt. Relief flooded across Aaron Daunt's face. Wescott's mouth dropped open in surprise.

" 'Morning," Glyde said easily. He placed his gaze on the man in the frock coat. "You're the judge, I take it."

"Benjamin Venn, Marshal Glyde," the jurist said. He had a round, flabby face but his eyes were bright and sharp and there was a grimness to the small mouth. "I came as fast as I could. There was a case in Cañon City I had to see through."

"Where the hell you been all night?" Wescott demanded, recovering his voice.

"Had me penned up in the church with a rope around my neck!" Otis Canady yelled from the depths of the jail. "Had me so's I couldn't do nothing."

Judge Venn smiled slowly. Daunt nodded in admiration for the strategy. Beyond them other men had begun to gather. Lucy Covington had come from the interior of her café, stood now in the brilliant sunshine on the walk.

"If you'll step aside, Marshal," Venn said, "we'll talk matters over."

Glyde nodded. "You and Daunt. The rest stay outside."

"Now, wait a minute . . . ," Wescott began angrily.

"Mister Wescott represents the prisoner," Venn said mildly. "He is entitled to be in on the preparations for the trial."

Glyde said: "All right. But the others stay out." He stepped back into the jail. Venn, Daunt, and Cole Wescott entered. The three remaining Spade riders made no effort to follow.

"Sure mighty glad you got here, Cole!" Canady called from

his cell. "Hurry up and get me out of here. I got something I figure to. . . ."

"Don't worry," the rancher said. "Nobody has ever yet hung a Spade man."

Venn flicked Wescott with a cold glance. He moved around Glyde's desk, settled himself in the chair. He studied the palms of his square hands for a time. Then: "I suppose it is in the interests of all that we hold this trial immediately. You have witnesses available, Marshal?"

"None that will testify," Wescott cut in smugly.

Glyde said: "There may be one or two who will speak up. The main thing is the prisoner admitted the killing to me in the presence of a dozen other men."

"Good enough," Venn said. He drew a thick, nickeled watch from his vest pocket. "It's now two-fifteen. I'll set the trial for four o'clock. We shall hold it here in the jail. The fewer spectators we provide for, the better, I believe."

"This is no place for it," Wescott protested. "We've got a right to an audience. I say we hold it in the lobby of the hotel. Plenty of room there."

"The trial will take place here in this jail, promptly at four o'clock," Venn repeated calmly. "I will allow you and four friends to be present. Mister Daunt, you have the same privilege."

"All a waste of time," Wescott fumed. Anger colored his face. "Damn it all, I'm not going to let you railroad one of my boys. . . ."

Venn swung his sharp eyes to the rancher. "Are you threatening this court, Mister Wescott? If so, you will quickly find yourself in that empty cell alongside your boy, as you choose to call the prisoner."

The rancher made no reply. He stared at the jurist for a long moment, spun on his heel, and stomped out of the room.

Judge Venn sighed. "These kings topple hard," he murmured.

"Gentlemen, we are likely to be in for a busy afternoon." He rose to his feet. "I think I'll go to the hotel and rest for a while. It was a long ride from Cañon City and that young man you sent for me wouldn't let me tarry. I will see you again at four o'clock."

Glyde stepped aside, allowing the jurist to depart. When he was gone, Aaron Daunt turned to him.

"I was never happier in my life than when I saw you standing there in the door," he said. "I'll confess, you had us all worried a bit."

"I wasn't going to lose my prisoner a second time," Glyde said. "You think Venn will be all right at the hotel?"

Daunt said: "I'm sure of it. He's too big a man in the territory for Cole to fool with. What about the trial? You figure you can manage things?"

Glyde nodded. "Somehow. Glad it's to be held right here in the jail. Meanwhile, I think I'd better ride herd on Canady, just in case he's got some friends who want to help. I'd appreciate it if you will have some grub sent over, and a man to fix that back door. I'll feel easier when it's bolted."

"I'll take care of it," the banker said. He turned for the street, halted. "Strickland's no better. I thought you would want to know."

"Too bad," Glyde commented. "Another good reason why this trial has to come off."

"For a fact," Daunt said, and stepped outside.

Otis Canady had no defense. Readily, almost defiantly he admitted the killing of young Heber, seeming to think it was all a huge joke. When a witness was called for by Venn, Damion Paull was the only one to offer himself. His testimony, plus that given by John Glyde, convinced the judge. Cole Wescott had presented his version of the incident, claiming it was all an accident, that the boy was a willing participant in the affair. Paull's words refuted this, and despite the baleful, threatening glares of Wescott and the men with him, he set forth the facts as he had witnessed them. It was enough for Benjamin Venn.

"Otis Canady," he said, his sharp old eyes drilling into the cowboy's face, "I find you guilty of the charge of murder. You are hereby sentenced to be hanged by the neck until you are dead. Said sentence is to be carried out by the town marshal tomorrow morning, at dawn, at a place suitable for the execution."

Glyde seized Canady by the arm, hustled him back into his cell. There was no sudden rise of conversation in the hot, packed room, only a crackling stillness. His prisoner safely away, Glyde stood in the doorway that led to the rear of the jail, arms folded across his chest, his face stern.

"That's all of it," he said. "Everybody out."

Cole Wescott rose slowly. He threw an angry glance at Venn, another at Glyde. "Let's go, boys," he said in a low, promising voice. "We got some figuring to do."

They filed out into the street. Vorenberg, Dutch Krieder, and Joe Moon followed. Only Daunt, Damion Paull, and the judge remained with the lawman. The banker stepped forward, extended his hand to the jurist.

"The town thanks you and congratulates you, Ben. We've taken a long step toward being a better town today."

The judge smiled, accepted the tribute. He nodded at Glyde. "There's the man to pat on the back, Aaron. Not many would buck an outfit like Cole Wescott's."

"We know that, and we're not forgetting it," the banker said. "You know how we feel, Marshal."

Glyde's face was serious. "Sure, but I would feel a hell of a lot better if this wasn't going to string out so long. It would be better if we could carry out the sentence and get it over with today. The longer we wait, the better chance there is for trouble."

"You're right there," Daunt said. He faced Venn. "What about it, Judge? Any possibility of going ahead with the execution today . . . at sundown?"

Venn said: "No, it wouldn't be right. I appreciate your problem, gentlemen, but a man condemned to death is entitled to a few hours in which he can make his peace with his God. It's only a few minutes until sundown. You will have to wait until morning."

"It could be inviting trouble," the lawman said. "I don't think Wescott will give it up."

"You'll have no more trouble with him, once he realizes what has taken place," the jurist said in a confident tone. "He'll not risk tampering with the law at this stage."

"I hope you're right," Glyde said doubtfully.

"I am," Venn said, and moved for the doorway. "I'll be here overnight. If anything arises, you can reach me at the hotel."

The judge stepped into the fading sunlight, swung off down the street. Daunt said: "Looks like you've got a long night ahead of you. Anything you need?"

Glyde smiled grimly. "A little good luck," he said. "And maybe some help from the town. One thing I need right away is a couple of shotguns."

Damion Paull said: "I'll go get them."

Glyde laid his hand on the minister's shoulder. "No. After your testimony, I think you'd better stay out of Spade's way, at least until it's all over with. I don't think you'd be safe on the street."

Daunt said: "I agree. Let me get them. I'll pick them up at Strickland's and be right back. Anything else?"

"That's all I can think of. What about the town? Do you feel that people will back us up, now that we've actually made a start at breaking Wescott's hold?"

A man appeared in the doorway. He said—"Mister Daunt."—and waited while the banker stepped out into the street. They conversed for a few moments after which Daunt, his face stiff, came back into the building. He met Glyde's questioning gaze with solemn eyes. "To answer your question . . . a few minutes ago I would have ventured a guess that they would. Now I am not so sure. Henry Strickland just died."

IX

In the hush that followed, Damion Paull said: "I must go to Missus Strickland." He saw the frown that gathered on Glyde's face and added: "I know, Marshal, but it is my duty. She will need me. And I'm not afraid."

"Go through my bank and down the alley," Daunt suggested. "Less chance of your being seen."

Paull said—"Good idea."—and started for the door. "When you're finished," Glyde called after him, "stay out of sight!"

The minister nodded, continued on his way.

"Now, I'll go after those guns," Daunt said. "Back in a few minutes."

"Fine. And if you don't mind, I'd appreciate your telling Missus Strickland how sorry I am about Henry. I doubt if I'll get a chance myself very soon."

The banker departed on his errand, and Glyde, beginning now to feel the drag of long hours awake, settled himself in his chair.

"What's the matter, Marshal?" Otis Canady called from his cell. "You about petered out?"

Glyde gave him no answer. He was thinking of Henry Strickland, feeling deeply the loss of his new friend. The merchant had been one man in Lawless he was certain of, except Aaron Daunt and, of course, Lucy. But neither of those could be of any help to him, Daunt with his crippled arm and Lucy being a woman. Someone should be made to pay for Strickland's death. Executing Otis Canady was not enough; it was a different score he was being called to account for. Cole Wescott had led the men who had shot Strickland. Why not bring him to justice for the crime? He decided he would talk it over with Judge Venn when next he saw him.

"You'll get your sleep tonight, Marshal," Canady said in that dry, sneering way of his. "Could be it will be a permanent one. Cole and the boys will be back, you can sure figure on it. You heard what Cole said about nobody going to hang a Spade man."

Glyde rose, walked to the outlaw's cell. He stood for a time just looking at the cowboy. Finally he said: "Otis, you don't mean a thing to me, but take a little advice. You're living your last hours right now. Tomorrow you will be a dead man. Quit fooling yourself about Cole Wescott. He'll never get you out of this, not while I'm alive and I'm hard to kill. Best thing you can do is face up to what's ahead, and if you've got anything on your soul, square it up. That's why the judge made me wait until the morning, to give you that chance. If you'd like to talk to the preacher, I'll send him in."

Canady's face had paled. It was as if he had suddenly realized there was a very real possibility he was looking at death with no hope of escape. But after a minute he shrugged. "Aw, the hell with that kind of talk. I know Cole better than you. He ain't forgetting me. You'll see."

There was a knock at the door. Glyde wheeled, walked to it. Aaron Daunt stood outside. The lawman opened the panel and the banker handed him the two new shotguns and a box of shells. He did not enter.

"Time I was getting home," he said. "Anything more I can do?"

"Thanks. This takes care of it. Might pass the word to Lucy

to stay inside her place tonight."

"I'll do that," Daunt said. "See you in the morning."

Glyde watched the banker fade into the darkness. He wished he might again take Canady from the jail and hide him in a safe place for the night. But the outlaw himself had voided the one possible place when he told Wescott about the church. There was no other place to which they could go.

It would be a matter of converting the jail into a fortress, for despite Judge Benjamin Venn's conviction that Cole Wescott would hesitate to interfere, he was certain Spade was planning to strike. He wished he had spoken to Daunt about deputies, a half a dozen men who could stand guard with him—and he knew in the next moment that it would have been a useless request. Daunt would have agreed, but where would the men come from? Who would accept such a job, even for pay? Strickland's death, the direct result of opposing Spade, would intimidate any who might have harbored a faint spark of courage.

He began to move about the jail, placing the shotguns at strategic points, checking his other weapons and generally getting things ready. The threat of buckshot flaring from a scattergun was a powerful deterrent, he knew; almost any man would quail and hesitate to face such a blast. But if they rushed him from the front and rear at the same moment, he could not expect to hold out. Even one deputy would be a tremendous help.

He paused at the window, drew aside the shade, and glanced out. It was dark and a definite hush lay over the town, like the stillness before a storm. He saw a man come from Lucy Covington's, a napkin-covered tray in his hands. It was Damion Paull. Glyde hurried to the door and opened it to admit the minister.

"Little something to eat," Paull said, and placed the tray on the desk. "Enough coffee to last us the night."

Glyde looked at the man. "Us?"

Paull smiled wryly. "You said to stay out of sight. I can't think of a better place than this. Besides, I figured you might need a little help before morning. I'm offering my services, for what they're worth."

It was a strange thing, Glyde thought, the only person in the entire town willing to stand by him and fight was a man of peace, a minister. He reached for Paull's hand. "I'm obliged to you," he said.

He took a plate of food to Otis Canady, returned to his desk where Paull awaited him. They began to eat and conversation between them was sporadic during that time. When the meal was finished and they were enjoying coffee, Glyde leaned back in his chair.

"Where you from, Reverend?"

Damion Paull gave him a quick smile. "Thank you. Been a long time since anyone addressed me that way. Usually it is Holy Joe or Soul Saver or maybe Preacher, but never that. But to answer your question, I'm from Pennsylvania. A little town called Carlisle."

"That country is a bit different from this, I expect."

"Like another world entirely."

"What brought you out here? Why did you come to a place like this, I mean?"

"A man goes where there is a need. The same as in your profession."

"I'd say you picked a tough one to crack. From what I see, you haven't been able to make much headway. Probably due a lot to Wescott."

Damion Paull sighed. He ran his long, tapered fingers through his hair. "It takes time. And I can't hope to get far with Cole Wescott and his men always a threat over the town. But I do feel I should have made better progress than I have. The people around here have never really accepted me for some reason. Instead of accomplishing something of value, I've succeeded only in making myself an object of ridicule, a complete failure. I suppose that is the story of my life."

"It could be you're going at it wrong," Glyde said kindly. "This is a tough country and the people in it are tough . . . and hard. These values you speak of aren't the same out here as they are back East. People look at things, at a man, in a different light. You say our professions are alike since we go where we are needed. They're the same in another way, too. A man first has to prove himself, earn the respect of others."

Paull said: "I suppose that's the answer. However, conditions are hardly the same. A man such as you gains it with a gun and by sheer courage. Those are not the weapons of my trade. In fact, violence is the exact opposite of what I am supposed to teach."

"Words can be mighty powerful sometimes. Words and belief in a conviction."

"But first you must have people to speak such words to. A man doesn't get far preaching to a handful of old women and small children."

"It's a start," Glyde said. "Maybe, after this night, things will be different."

The lawman rose, walked to the window. He pulled the shade back, looked out upon the dark, silent street. "I figured we'd hear from Wescott before now. I wonder what's holding him back? You see anything of him and his bunch when you were at Strickland's?"

"They were in the hotel, I think. I did see a half a dozen of his men ride in. There was a new man with them. One I've never seen before."

"There sure must be some reason for his stalling."

"It could be he's decided to wait until morning to make his move. And there's also the possibility the judge is right, that he's going to keep hands off."

"I'd like to believe that," Glyde answered. He turned away from the window. A need for sleep was pressing him. The meal had only increased the desire. He yawned, stretched, shook his head to throw off the drowsiness.

Paull said: "As long as things are quiet, why don't you take a nap? I'll wake you if Wescott or any of his crowd shows up."

"I could use a few winks," the lawman said. "It's been about twenty-four hours since I closed my eyes. If you don't mind keeping watch, I think I'll stretch out there in that empty cell."

"Go ahead," Paull said.

Glyde walked to the rear of the jail. Canady lay on his cot, appearing to be asleep. The lawman sat down in the adjoining cell, weariness dragging at him like iron chains. He lay back. A couple of hours' rest would make a world of difference, put him in good condition for Wescott when he did come. And there was no danger. Paull would awaken him at first sign of the rancher and his crew. He sighed, closed his eyes.

It was only moments. Or, at least, it seemed so to John Glyde. He felt a hand on his shoulder. Then, someone slapped him, hard. He sat up, and the first face he looked into was that of Cole Wescott. Damion Paull had failed again.

X

Glyde's hand dropped automatically to the holster at his hip. It was empty, of course.

Cole Wescott laughed. "We've already pulled your claws, mister."

There were other men present. They clustered about the rancher, grinning down at Glyde in a triumphant sort of way. Canady—Hank Johnson—the one they called Cal—two he had seen dogging the footsteps of Wescott—and a stranger. He was a stocky man, dark-eyed, with a black mustache and black wedge beard. He wore a star on his dusty vest. Glyde felt his own breast.

Spade's owner laughed again. "Yeah, it's yours, bucko. We pulled that, too. Let me introduce you to the new marshal of Lawless . . . Mister Dan Clagg. He took over while you were catching up on your sleep."

Glyde swung his legs over the edge of the cot, started to rise. Clagg reached out a thick hand, pushed him back. "You ain't going no place. This town wanted a hanging in the morning. Reckon you're it."

"That man of mine you shot the other night isn't doing so good," Wescott said. "Fact is, he'll maybe die. That makes you a killer. And we hang killers in this town."

Glyde glanced to the front of the jail. The room was empty. He brought his eyes back to Wescott. "What did you do to Paull? Where is he?"

"That psalm singer? Oh, he's all right. Couple of my boys are looking after him. We didn't hurt him any, if that's what's worrying you. We just don't want him and a couple others underfoot come morning."

Glyde relaxed. He hoped he could believe Wescott. He wanted no harm to come to the minister because of himself. He said: "This is the biggest mistake you'll ever make, Cole. You're overstepping yourself. Judge Venn will see you hang for this."

The rancher's grin broadened. "Old Ben? What can he do? He knows better than to fool with me. Long road to the next town and accidents can happen." Wescott swung away. "Come on, boys we got things to do. Clagg can take care of the prisoner. I mean to teach this town a lesson it won't ever forget. Get the crew together and then tree the town like it's never been done before. Understand? I intend to make these people around here

224

think twice before they latch on to any more cute ideas again."

There was a wild yell of approval for the rancher's instructions. Canady and the others rushed for the door, poured out into the street with Wescott in their midst. Gunshots broke out immediately. Somewhere glass tinkled as a bullet shattered a window.

"Be a high old time around here tonight," Clagg said dryly.

More shouts lifted from across the street as the rest of Spade's crew were informed of the rancher's wishes. A fresh volley of gunfire ripped through the night.

"Get some horses!" a voice yelled.

Glyde stirred restlessly on his cot. Lawless was in for a bad time and he was powerless to do anything about it. Wescott would have his way now and by morning the hopes of the town would be dead—as would he! That thought jarred him. He studied the dark-faced man who stood in the doorway of his cell, listening absently to the rising din in the street. He was vaguely familiar.

"We met before?" Glyde asked.

Clagg shifted his flat, bitter gaze to Glyde. "Maybe. Been a lot of places. Why? You going to say that we're friends, or maybe related?"

"Doubt that," Glyde answered. "Just seems I've seen you some place."

"Reckon there's a few pictures of me scattered about."

Glyde remembered then. Reward posters. The face was the same but the name was different. He could not recall where he had seen the dodger or what the charge was. "Change for you, wearing a badge."

He watched the man closely, seeking an opening that might lead to freedom. But Clagg was too far away to permit a sudden attack. He would have ample time to draw and shoot before Glyde could reach him.

"Don't mean anything to me," Clagg said, and flicked the star with a fingertip. "This Wescott hired me to do a job. Wearing a badge is part of it."

The racket in the street had turned to bedlam. Horses thundered back and forth. Gunshots set up a deafening uproar. The shattering of glass, the crash of falling timber as gallery roof supports were jerked down testified to the damage being visited upon Lawless.

Clagg stepped back, swung the cell door shut. He locked it, tossed the keys onto the desk. "No reason why I got to hang around here," he said. "Might as well join the celebration and have some fun myself. See you in the morning, Marshal . . . for the hanging."

Glyde watched him move off into the street, pulling the door closed behind him. He settled back on the hard cot, trying to think of a way out of his desperate situation. Wescott would carry out his intention, he knew. Spade would thoroughly chastise the town and then cap it off by ruthlessly hanging him—the symbol of resistance. And he could expect no help from the citizens of Lawless. After this night they would fear even to show themselves on the street. He couldn't find it in his heart to blame Aaron Daunt and the rest of the committee if they backed down now. Cole Wescott appeared to be invincible.

He rose, began to pace about his small cell, seeking some weakness, some means for escape. After a time he gave it up. The only way out was through the door. He resumed his seat on the cot. The keys lay on the desk. If someone friendly would drop by he could, perhaps, attract their attention. But who would be out except Spade? The people of Lawless would all stay well out of sight while Wescott and his crew ravaged the town.

Time dragged. The confusion and violence in the street swelled, reached a peak, and began to die off. No more horses raced madly back and forth. There were fewer gunshots. Spade was tiring of the sport, settling down to the less strenuous diversions of drinking and gambling. Around midnight Glyde heard several riders move out, taking the north road. Some of Spade going back to the ranch to attend to their regular duties, he supposed. He wondered if Wescott were with them. Not likely. Spade's owner would want to be present for his final triumph at dawn.

His thoughts came to a sudden halt. He heard the distinct scrape of a boot upon the dry, hard-packed ground outside the jail. He rose quickly, moved to the door of his cell. There was a metallic click at the rear door as someone tried the latch, found it locked. Glyde remained silent. It was evident whoever the person might he, he was avoiding the front entrance, apparently fearful of being seen by Wescott's men; therefore, it was logical to assume it was a friend.

He waited, listened. He heard no more. And then suddenly Sam Vorenberg slipped through the doorway and was inside.

"Back here," Glyde called in a hoarse whisper.

The hotel man seized the ring of keys, walked hastily to the cell where the lawman was imprisoned. "Couldn't let Cole do this to you, Marshal," he said. "Figured you was just trying to do the job we hired you for. That didn't call for getting murdered. Told Cole that, but he feels mighty hard toward you and wouldn't listen."

Vorenberg fitted the thick key into the lock and pulled open the door. Glyde stepped out. He watched the big man closely, mentally reviewing the words he had spoken. "You said that to Wescott? Does that mean you're the one next to him . . . that you've been doing the tipping off?"

"Not much time, Marshal," Vorenberg said, ignoring the question. "Better get out the back. Get yourself a horse at Krieder's and ride on while there's still time."

"What about it?"

Vorenberg shook his head impatiently. "You're wasting time. Sure, I sided with Cole on what was best for the town. I did it because it was smart . . . because I wanted to stay in business. But I didn't agree to no murder like he's got planned for you. That's why I came. Couldn't stand by and let them do it."

So it had been Vorenberg. Glyde had considered him suspect, but had never given it much thought. He could see it clearly now. He should have known it was the hotel man. He brushed by Vorenberg to his desk. He yanked open the drawers until he found his gun. He checked the weapon, jammed it into its holster.

Vorenberg said: "Out the back, Marshal. Nobody will see you that way."

"I'm not leaving, Sam," the lawman said in a low voice. "It's not the time to pull out. I've got to see what I can do about stopping Wescott. And there's still an execution to carry out in the morning."

Vorenberg was aghast. "You're plumb loco! You haven't got a chance. . . ."

"Maybe," Glyde said, and again crossed the room. It would be smart to use the back door of the jail as the hotelkeeper had suggested. Not as a means to leave town, but as one to enter it unseen, and work his way along the buildings where he could take stock of the situation.

"Obliged to you for unlocking that cell," he said, pausing at the rear exit. "No, you'd better get away from here before somebody spots you."

Vorenberg wagged his head. "I didn't figure you'd look at it this way. I thought I'd be doing you a favor, saving your neck. You ought to be glad for a chance to get out of town."

"I am . . . but I've still got a job to do."

Glyde stepped into the darkness. He left the door open, not

certain if Vorenberg would follow or use the front opening.

"What the hell are you doing here?"

Glyde halted sharply at the sound of Dan Clagg's harsh question.

"What you doing with those keys?"

"Just came in . . . ," Vorenberg stammered, fear rising in his voice.

"You damn' double dealer!" Clagg yelled. "You've gone and turned that lawman loose! I figured you for a chicken-livered. . . ."

"Wait! Wait . . . !"

Before Glyde could reach the doorway, the jail rocked with the explosion of Clagg's pistol. He saw Sam Vorenberg stagger back, fall heavily. Glyde hesitated for a brief instant, then, bending low, he circled the building, came to the front. He glanced down the street. The gunshot apparently had passed unnoticed. He moved swiftly into the jail, halted just within the doorway. Clagg, bent over the slain Vorenberg, was methodically going through the hotel man's pockets for money and other valuables.

"Clagg," the lawman called quietly.

The gunman spun, his reflexes automatic. His gun came up in a swift blur. Glyde drew and fired. The bullet from his pistol caught Clagg dead center, killing him instantly, and sent him sprawling across the body of Vorenberg.

XI

John Glyde spun, stepped to the door, and surveyed the street. Again a gunshot had aroused no attention. He closed the thick panel, locked it. He must get the bodies of Vorenberg and Clagg out of sight. As long as Spade thought he was in a cell and their private marshal was alive and on the job, all would go well. If the gunman's body were found, Cole Wescott and his crew would start hunting him all over.

The shack. That was the answer. He hurried to the rear of the jail, crossed to the small structure that had been assigned to him as living quarters. He propped open the door, returned to the jail. He loaded Clagg across his shoulders, carried him the short distance, and deposited him on the floor in one corner. He placed Vorenberg beside him.

He locked the shack and reëntered the jail. He felt better, now the bodies of the two men were out of sight. He selected one of the shotguns from the rack, thrust a handful of shells into his pocket. The next thing was to see if Canady were still in town—and how many of Spade's riders were with him.

He paused to blow out the lamp, then left the building by the rear, again taking the precaution to turn the lock. He hoped any Spade crew member, stopping by and finding the place locked and in darkness, would assume those inside were asleep and continue on his way.

He entered the empty building that lay next to the jail and stood for a time in the darkened doorway, looking into the street. He suspected most of Wescott's men, and the rancher himself if he were still in town, would be in the Great Western's gambling room and small bar. But there seemed to be considerable noise and activity at Joe Moon's place at the opposite end of town.

He dropped back through the vacant storeroom, walked down the alley until he reached the bank. There he made his way along the passageway to the sidewalk. He halted just within the deep shadows. A great amount of loud talking, punctuated with coarse laughter issued from the Bull River. Glyde listened, endeavoring to distinguish the voices. None was familiar, and after a time during which he checked the street to be certain it was clear, he crossed over.

He worked his way along the south wall of the building to a window. Removing his hat, he looked in. Except for the bartender at his customary station and four men gathered about a circular table upon which they played cards, the Bull River was deserted. Glyde examined them carefully. Canady was not one of them. It was a noisy game, and while the lawman watched, one of the riders drew his revolver and fired a bullet into the line of bottles shelved back of the bar. The barkeeper leaped to one side, his mouth working angrily. The quartet of Spade men roared.

Where was Joe Moon? That Wescott was taking it out on the saloon owner for his participation in the town's revolt was evident. But what had they done with him? Was he dead, killed by accident or by intent? That Cole Wescott was easily capable of the latter had become clear to Glyde.

The lawman moved on. He circled the building, listening for any sounds. All was deathly quiet and the remaining windows were dark. He continued on, crossed behind Krieder's stable, the barbershop, and several other small stores that lined that side of the street, until he reached the hotel. There he halted, taking up a stand behind a broadly spreading cottonwood tree that arched over the wagon yard.

The lower floor of the Great Western was ablaze with lights despite the late hour. He heard no laughter, only an occasional mutter of voices. It set him wondering whether Cole Wescott and most of his crew were staying the night or had ridden on, leaving only a token band to occupy the town. It could be so. Regardless of outside activities, a ranch must be operated, the daily chores and duties must be taken care of. He thought then of the stable behind the hotel. He could learn much there simply by counting the number of Spade branded horses that would be in the corral. He moved away from the cottonwood, circled the yard to avoid exposure on the open ground, and entered the barn. A lantern burned at low wick in the hostler's quarters. Glyde eased silently along the wall to a point where he could look into the small, tack-burdened room. It was empty. *Likely he's in the hotel's bar,* Glyde decided. He moved deeper into the stable, located the corral. Seven saddled horses dozed patiently in the pale moonlight. All bore Wescott's brand.

That answered his question. There were seven Spade men in Lawless; the rest had returned to the ranch. There were four at Joe Moon's; three would be inside the Great Western. Who were they? Was Cole Wescott one of them? Otis Canady? He hoped the outlaw was one of the trio, and smiled grimly at the thought. This time, if he could get his hands on his prisoner, there would be no escaping. But there was only one way to know who was present—go and see.

He started back up the runway, moving quickly through a band of yellow light thrown by an overhead lantern. He gained the far wall, kept to the dark shadows along its base. A sound off to his left brought him to an abrupt halt. The hostler was returning. Or possibly it was one of Cole Wescott's men, coming for his horse. Glyde flattened himself against the rough boards and waited for the man to come into sight.

Again he heard the noise. It seemed now to arise from within the stable, from a room just ahead. He rode out another long minute, concluded no one was actually approaching but, instead was moving about in the room he had just looked in. He went on, taking short, careful steps. He reached a door, halted. It was open. All was dark within the area and he could see nothing. He dropped to a crouch, prepared to cross over.

"Marshal. It's me . . . Paull."

At the sound of the minister's husky whisper, Glyde straightened up. He stared into the black depths of the room, seeking to locate the man.

"Over here. In the corner. They got me trussed up." When the lawman did not immediately respond, the minister added: "It's all right. There's nobody else around."

Glyde entered, stepped quickly to Paull's side. The minister was propped against a wall, his ankles and wrists bound tightly. Glyde set to work at the hard-drawn knots.

"Saw you when you passed under the lantern," Paull said. "Couldn't attract your attention at first. I was afraid somebody would hear me."

"How long have you been here? What happened?"

"Ever since Wescott and his bunch took over the jail. Glad you managed to get away."

The minister's ankles were free. Glyde turned him about, started in on the rope that locked his wrists together.

"Saying I'm sorry about what happened won't help much," Paull said, his voice low. "It was plain stupidity on my part. They fooled me . . . or, rather, Vorenberg did. Couple of hours after you fell asleep, somebody knocked on the door. I got up and looked out. It was Vorenberg and I figured it was all right to let him in. When I opened the door, Wescott and a half a dozen of his crew pushed in with him. He's the one that's been carrying tales, Marshal. Sam Vorenberg."

"I know," Glyde said. "But it's finished for him now. He's dead." The rope about Paull's wrists fell free. The lawman stood up. "That's it. You hurt?"

Paull got to his feet. "No, I'm all right. They slapped me around a bit, but I've gotten used to that. You say Vorenberg's dead?"

Glyde related the incident at the jail. When he was finished, Paull said: "Guess that proves the power of prayer. I am ashamed for what happened. I had failed again . . . and probably was going to cost you your life. I asked for help . . . for Divine help, a miracle or something that would set you free. Apparently my prayers were answered."

There was silence between the two men for a time. Finally Glyde said quietly: "We'd better get out of here. This'd be a bad

233

place to get pinned down."

They started up the runway for the wide double-door entrance. Paull said: "What's next, Marshal?"

"Otis Canady is under sentence to be hung for murder," Glyde answered. "That means I've got to find him and carry it out. If he's gone back to the Spade Ranch, then I've got a tough job ahead. If he's one of the three men inside the hotel, it won't be such a problem."

They reached the yard, moved along its edge, and came again to the huge, old cottonwood. Paull laid his hand on Glyde's arm, halted him. "Guess I've proved I'm not much good at anything, Marshal, but I'm still willing to try and help if you'll let me. Seems like I have to say something like that to you every time we meet, but. . . ."

"Forget it," the lawman said. "Anybody would have made that mistake with Vorenberg. Let's see who's in the hotel."

XII

In the dark silence, Glyde and Damion Paull crossed the narrow strip of open ground that lay between the tree and the building, and stepped up onto the wide gallery fronting the Great Western. They stopped just outside the open door. Somewhere within they could hear voices, but it was only occasional conversation of sorts, a dry comment, a dropped observation.

"They're in the gambling room, just off the lobby," Paull said.

Glyde drifted softly to the doorway. He could see the entire lobby. It was empty. "Wait here," he murmured to the minister, and stepped into the cluttered reception area.

He crossed to a broad archway that led into an adjoining room. At its edge he paused. Using great care, he threw his glance through the heavy portières. In a far corner four men were assembled about a table upon which cards and a considerable amount of money were scattered. A sigh of relief slipped from Glyde. The player facing him was Otis Canady. The others were a gambler who regularly worked for Vorenberg, and the two Spade riders, Cal Wolff and Hank Johnson. Nearby, watching the game with interest, were the hotel desk clerk and the hostler.

Glyde thought for a time, then returned to where Damion Paull awaited him. "We're in luck," he said. "Canady's in there and it looks like an all night game."

"You going to arrest him now?"

Glyde shook his head. "Safer to leave him right where he is. When we're ready for him, we'll come after him."

Paull said: "I've been thinking about that, about what you said back there in the stable. You think you'll be able to go through with the execution? What about Cole and the rest of Spade . . . they're not going to let you do it."

"Wescott's not in the hotel," Glyde said. "That means he's gone back to his ranch, which also means he plans to be back by dawn. Far as he knows I'm still in a cell and Dan Clagg holds the keys. I think I know how we can fool the whole bunch and still get the job done."

He moved off the porch, closely followed by Paull, and returned to the alley. There, in the darkness, away from the hotel, it was easier to talk.

"A few things have to be done. It's not going to be easy, naturally, where Spade's concerned, it will be dangerous. . . ."

"John," the minister cut in, "give me a chance to help. You set me to thinking when you said a man had to prove himself in this country. So far I know I haven't done a very good job of it . . . of anything . . . but I need this chance. If I fail you again, then I've failed myself and that ends it. But I've got to try. I've got to know."

There was no denying the appeal in the man's voice. Glyde said: "Sure. And you'll be all right. You'll make it."

"Thank you," Paull said quietly. "What do you want me to do?"

"First we got a small chore at Joe Moon's to take care of."

They started down the alley, walking fast. They came to the Bull River at its rear side, circled around to the front. They halted. Glyde handed the keys to the jail to Paull.

"Open up the back door and have a cell ready. I'll be there shortly with four customers. Better do your traveling in the alley."

He waited until the minister had crossed over and was lost in the darkness beyond the bank, then entered the saloon. The four Spade riders still sat at their table. The bartender dozed behind his counter. Glyde, shotgun leveled, strode boldly into the room.

"On your feet!" he barked. "Put your hands over your heads."

The quartet paused uncertainly, their faces mirroring surprise. At sight of the shotgun's twin muzzles they rose slowly.

"What's this all about?"

"Turn around!" Glyde ordered. "And watch those hands unless you want a load of buckshot. You," he added to the bartender, "get their guns."

The man behind the counter did not move. A sudden fear had sprung into his eyes. "Marshal . . . I don't want to get mixed up. . . ."

Glyde shook his head impatiently. "All right, forget it," he snapped. He moved in behind the riders. One by one he pulled their pistols, threw them into a far corner of the room. "Where's Moon?"

"Search me," the bartender said. "He left with a couple of Mister Wescott's men. Never did come back."

Glyde jabbed the rider nearest him with the end of the

shotgun. "Where is he? Where did they take him?"

"I don't know," the man growled. "I wasn't even here myself when that happened. You're makin' a big mistake, friend. When Cole. . . ."

"Keep looking the other way!" Glyde said, and jabbed the man again in the spine. "I'd as soon blow all of you to hell as fool with you. Now, we're marching out of here. The four of you will walk close together, and you'll keep your hands up high. I'll be six feet behind you with both hammers of this gun cocked."

"Where we goin', anyway?"

"Jail."

"Good," one of them said in a weak show of humor. "Was gettin' a mite sleepy. Won't have to pay no room rent now."

"Law's supposed to have a reason for juggin' a man," said another. "What you taking us in for, Marshal?"

"Disturbing the peace. Destroying property. Move out. And watch your step."

"Sure, sure. How'd you get away from that new man Cole hired?"

"I killed him," Glyde said flatly.

Conversation ended abruptly with that. They left the saloon, circled the bank, and passed down the alley to the jail. Paull was waiting for them. Glyde put the once garrulous riders into a cell, secured the lock.

He walked back to his desk where Paull waited. Glancing at the clock on the wall, he said: "Not much time left. It'll be dawn about five o'clock."

He stood for a long minute, lost in deep thought. He turned then to the minister. "Think you can get by Canady and those other men and talk to the judge? He's got a room in the hotel, somewhere."

"Sure. I'll go in the back way. I can even get to the desk and look at the register without them seeing me."

"Fine. Tell Venn I'd like for him to be here at four-thirty. That'll be a half hour before dawn. Then see if you can find Krieder and Aaron Daunt. Give them the same message. They are to be here, at the jail, no later than four-thirty."

"What about Moon?"

"You can try to locate him. Wescott had two men take him off somewhere. Could be he's done the same for Dutch and Aaron."

"Got them out of the way, same as they did me," Paull said. "I'll hunt them down."

He left immediately. Glyde followed, locking the door as he did. In the alley behind the jail, he paused. There was no scaffold upon which Canady's execution could take place. He would have to improvise. He crossed to Krieder's stable. The doors were closed, bolted. He could not arouse anyone. He remembered then the horses in the barn behind the Great Western.

He procured one of the seven, choosing one that carried a coiled rope on the saddle. He led it to a tree a short distance beyond Moon's saloon. There he tied the animal so it would not stray. He fashioned a knot in the rope, tossed it over a low limb; he left it hanging there where it would be quickly available.

Those necessary chores completed, he returned to the jail. The four Spade riders were hammering on the cell bars, doing their best to attract attention. When Glyde entered, the noise ceased. He grinned at them. "You're going to a lot of trouble for nothing," he said. "Who do you figure will hear you?"

"Cole and the rest of the boys will be showin' up soon," one of them replied. "Won't take them long to get us out of here."

"When they come," Glyde said, "they'll be welcome to you."

He moved to his desk, sat down. He poured himself a cup of coffee. It was cold but strong, and he drank it all.

"Reckon you got some other reason for puttin' us in here,

Marshal. You just gettin' us out of the way so's you can string up Otis?"

"That's a good guess," Glyde answered. "The judge sentenced him to hang for murder. My job is to see that he does."

"You're forgettin' one thing. We ain't the only ones around. And Cole will be comin' with a lot more, about daylight."

"I'll be expecting him."

There was a knock on the door. Glyde, gun in hand, stepped to it. "Who is it?"

"Venn," the judge's voice replied.

Glyde opened the panel quickly. The jurist, heavy-eyed and only partly dressed, entered. "What's this all about, Marshal?"

"I need your help in carrying out the execution. I'm going to do it thirty minutes early."

Venn nodded his understanding. "Guess you were right about Wescott and I was wrong. The preacher told me all that's happened. Sorry about it." He walked back, looked into the cells. "Where is Canady? I don't see him here."

"He's over at the hotel, in a poker game. I'll get him when it's time." He stopped, glanced at the jurist sharply. "Didn't you see him when you came through the lobby?"

Venn said: "Didn't go out the front. Used the back. There was a card game going on in the saloon, however. I heard them talking."

Glyde relaxed. "I thought for a minute things had gone wrong."

Venn came back to the desk. "Got some more help lined up?"

"Paull is out trying to round up Krieder and Moon and Aaron Daunt. I'm not sure he'll find any of them. Wescott got them out of the way."

"We'll need all the help we can get," Venn said. "Too bad a few more people in this town haven't got a little courage. But that's the way it goes. Somebody else has to make the break for them. When it's done with, they'll all come piling onto the band wagon."

"Not mine," Glyde said. "When this is over, I'm pulling out. If this is the kind of thing a regular lawman is up against, I don't want any part of it. I need the money to pay off a ranch I'm trying to buy, but I'll make it some other way."

"Could be there's a reward for that gunslick Wescott brought in . . . that you had to shoot. The preacher described him to me. Sounds like an outlaw named Pete Hervey. I'll take a look at him, come daylight. What's your plan for the execution, Marshal?"

"Just get it over with early, before Wescott and the rest of Spade rides in. I figure you, Paull, Krieder, Moon, and Daunt can serve as guards. Just in case somebody shows up a little sooner than I expect them."

Venn picked up one of the shotguns. "Six men. Not many if it comes down to holding off Wescott's entire crew." He fondled the twin-barreled weapon absently. "Been a long time since I used one of these. Guess a man never really forgets how."

Paull and Aaron Daunt arrived a few minutes after that. Glyde let them into the room, looked questioningly at the minister.

"What about Krieder? And Joe Moon?"

"Can't find either of them. Looked every place I could think of. Want me to keep at it? They must be around somewhere."

Glyde glanced at the clock. "No time left," he said. "And Wescott could have taken them out of town, to his ranch maybe." The loss of the two men was a serious blow to his plan, but there was no help for it. He would have to proceed without them. He turned to Daunt, outlined what was to be done. Finished, he said: "Without Krieder and Joe Moon we couldn't offer much of a fight if things don't work out right. I won't blame any of you if you decide to back out."

There was a silence. The banker said: "I still feel the same about it. If we're ever to have law here, this is the time to get it. I can't offer you much help with only one good hand . . . that's probably why Wescott didn't have me hauled off with the others . . . but I can handle a pistol."

Venn chuckled. "Never heard of a judge being a hangman, but I'm with you, Marshal."

They all looked to Damion Paull. The minister was standing at the window, looking into the street, now growing steadily lighter.

"Otis Canady is a criminal. He has been sentenced to punishment by the law. I do not stand for violence nor do I believe we have the right to take another man's life. God alone has that power. But this is a different matter. The strength of the law must be proven, otherwise there will come only more violence and killing. I am a man of peace, but I am willing to do what is required of me."

Glyde said: "You've helped a lot in this, Reverend. I won't ask you to do any more. It would mean you'll be carrying a gun and the chances are good that you will have to use it."

Paull did not take his eyes from the street. "If it is required of me, then I shall have to do it."

Aaron Daunt stepped to the minister's side. He thrust out his hand. "Guess I never really took time to know you, Reverend. You're a stronger man than any of us."

Paull smiled at him. "There comes a time in a man's life when he must do something he knows is right . . . but feels is wrong. Guess this is that time for me. I'm ready to go when the rest of you are."

The lawman handed a shotgun to the minister. "This will be easier to manage. The judge is carrying the other."

Daunt said: "I brought my own pistol, Marshal."

Glyde nodded. He glanced at the clock—4:25. "Let's get started. Ought to have this job over with before Wescott rides in. If we don't. . . ."

The judge said: "I guess we understand, Marshal."

XIII

At Vorenberg's Glyde stationed Venn and Damion Paull on the front gallery as look-outs. He did not expect the owner of Spade and his crew until dawn, but he was in no mood to take chances. With Daunt, he then entered the hotel, crossed to the side room where Canady and the three other men still played at their game of cards. The clerk was asleep in a chair but the hostler saw them and straightened with an exclamation.

Canady leaped to his feet, his dark face pale. Glyde and the banker covered the surprised men with their guns. The two Spade riders, hands above their heads, rose slowly.

To the gambler and the hostler Glyde said: "Keep out of this."

They moved their heads slightly in understanding.

Glyde said: "Get Canady's gun, Aaron. And the others', too. Keep clear. Don't walk in front of me."

The banker moved in behind the trio, relieving them of their weapons. "I'll leave them at the jail," he said.

"Head for the door," the lawman ordered. "And keep your hands up high."

Canady, with the man named Johnson at one shoulder and Cal Wolff on the other, started across the room. He entered the lobby, slowed his steps.

"I don't know what you think you're pulling, Glyde, but you won't get away with it. Cole will be here in a few minutes and he'll. . . ."

"That'll be too late for you to worry about," the lawman murmured. "Keep walking."

Canady came to a firm halt. A realization of what was happening seemed to dawn upon him suddenly. "What are you going to do, Marshal? Where's Clagg?"

"Clagg won't be around any more. And you're on your way to be hung for murder, just as the law decided."

A wild fear ripped through the outlaw. "You can't do this to me! It ain't right!"

"Judge Venn is outside," Glyde said. "Tell him that."

"But I don't want . . . I can't swing! Don't hang me, Marshal! I'm sorry about that kid. And them others. I didn't mean to shoot. . . ."

"Keep moving," Glyde said.

"Please, Marshal. . . ."

Hank Johnson half turned, favored Canady with a disgusted glance. "Cut out the bawlin', Otis. You asked for this, you and that fast gun of yours. You was always braggin' about what a big man you are. Sure don't see none of it now."

They reached the door, stepped out onto the porch. The sky to the east was streaked with gray and yellow and things along the street were becoming more distinct.

"No sign of anyone," Venn said. "Where does this take place?"

"Beyond Moon's. Got everything ready there," Glyde said. "Put your gun on the prisoner while I lock up these others."

"Hank . . . Cal . . . don't leave . . . don't let them do this to me!" Canady's voice was a rising scream.

The two Spade riders moved off ahead of Glyde. They crossed to the jail, entered, and filed into the empty cell. Behind him Glyde heard Daunt toss the three guns he had collected onto the desk.

"What's going on out there, Hank?" one of the men in the other cell demanded. "What's all the yelling about?"

"Otis's on his way to a hangin' . . . his," Hank Johnson said.

"*A hanging!* What about Cole?"

243

"Reckon he ain't goin' to be around to do anythin' about it."

Glyde and Aaron Daunt returned to the street. The lawman had picked up his steel cuffs and now manacled the outlaw's hands behind his back.

"Let's go," he said, and shoved the man into the center of the street, taking up a position behind the condemned Canady. Daunt, Damion Paull, and the judge fell in, a step to the rear.

"Spread out and watch sharp," Glyde said. "Don't think Wescott will hit town for another fifteen minutes, but we can't be sure."

The street was deathly still in the pre-dawn hush. Here and there Glyde saw a shade pull back an inch or two, a door open cautiously as those of the early risers, hearing the small procession, peered out to see what was taking place. *A cripple, a minister of the gospel, and an elderly judge! A hell of a fine representation to back the law's might,* John Glyde thought grimly. But at least they had some convictions—and the courage to back them up. That was more than could be said of the rest of Lawless.

They reached the corner of the Bull River Saloon. Ahead stood the horse, waiting patiently beneath the tree. The prepared rope swayed gently in the faint breeze. Otis Canady caught one glimpse of the scene, dropped to his knees in the dust.

"No! No, Judge! You can't! It ain't right . . . !"

Benjamin Venn studied the groveling outlaw scornfully. "Not right? What do you know or care about rights? Were you thinking about rights when you murdered that poor, harmless boy? Or any of the others whose deaths you are responsible for?"

"But I didn't mean. . . ."

"A poor reason for murder. You are a cold-blooded, heartless killer, Otis Canady. And the law finally caught up with you. You were fairly judged and found guilty of murder. You are to die for it. That is the law. My only regret is that you were not brought to justice long before now. A young boy might have been alive today, if you had."

Glyde pulled Canady to his feet, forced him to the horse. He boosted him onto the saddle and placed the rope about his neck, adjusting the knot below the ear so that death would be as quick and painless as possible. That done, he stepped back, threw his glance up the street. It was still empty.

Damion Paull moved up beside the outlaw. "If you would like for me to say a prayer. . . ."

"Hell with it!" Canady screamed. "Get away from me!"

Paull lowered his pale face, stepped back. Canady seemed to wilt again. He looked down at the minister. "Maybe, preacher, you ought to. . . ."

Paull closed his eyes, murmured a few words. Venn said: "I'll handle it from here. The rest of you keep watching that street."

Glyde, Aaron Daunt, and Paull faced toward the town. The sun was just breaking over the eastern horizon, bathing the dusty street with its twin rows of weather-beaten buildings in a golden glow.

"Here they come," Daunt said suddenly. A half a dozen riders had entered the far end of Lawless.

There was a slap of leather behind Glyde, the sudden rush of a horse. He heard the taut creak of rope fiber as it rubbed harshly against the tree limb. And then silence.

"May God have mercy on his soul," Damion Paull said softly.

"And on ours," Daunt added, as more Spade riders filed into the far end of the street.

XIV

John Glyde was conscious of Venn's moving up to his side, taking up a position to his left. He did not remove his eyes from the horsemen, now halted before Vorenberg's. Cole Wescott was not among them. That accounted for their evident indecision. But a moment later the rancher appeared. He rode out ahead of the others, halted.

"We stay here?" Aaron Daunt asked in a tight voice.

Glyde said: "No. We walk straight down the middle of the street. Right at them."

"Good," Venn said. "This is going to be the moment of truth. Either the law is bigger than Cole Wescott, or it isn't. Now we shall find out."

"Split up," Glyde said. "We'll stay in a line, about six feet between us. I'll do the talking. If Wescott and his bunch open up, make a run for the nearest building."

"Going to be like Pickett's charge," Venn said. "Hope we have better luck than he did."

The four men drifted apart, formed a short line. Glyde kept his attention on Wescott. The rancher was talking matters over with his men. That he could see Canady's body was certain. And that the town was coming alive to the tense situation, was also evident. He could see partly open doors all along the street and vague, shadowy faces in the windows. He wondered if Lucy were watching. He hoped not.

"Here they come," Daunt said.

Wescott had dismounted. His men, a dozen or more of them, had followed his example. They ranged up beside him. In a line that extended almost the width of the street, they started forward.

"Let me try to talk to Wescott," Venn suggested. "Maybe I can make him listen."

"Wouldn't do any good," Glyde answered. "He's already proved he has no respect for your position. I'm the law and I'm the one responsible for it. You three stay in the background and, if shooting starts, do like I said, get off the street fast."

The lawman moved out a half a dozen paces. At a point opposite Dutch Krieder's stable, he halted. The three men with him took up positions a few steps to his rear. Glyde, legs straddled, hands hanging loosely at his sides, waited. He watched the slow approach of Wescott and his men. Again he had the hope that Lucy Covington was not watching; matters could get bad.

The rancher and his riders drew abreast of the jail. A sudden clamor arose from within the small building. Wescott and his crew came to a halt. Two men broke away from the group, headed for the door.

"Far enough!" Glyde warned. "Those men are prisoners. I'll consider any move to free them a jail break and I'll arrest every man that has anything to do with turning them loose!"

The two Spade riders hesitated uncertainly. Wescott half turned, said something to the men behind him. The two riders rejoined the others. A moment later Cole Wescott, with a man at either side, resumed his approach, leaving the remainder of the crew in front of the jail.

"Now what?" Venn muttered. "Cole's a man who likes good odds. Can't see him leaving his bunch behind and coming on with just two men."

"Two gunmen," Daunt corrected. "I take it he's showing the town his contempt for us. Himself and a couple more. That's all he needs."

"Guess you're right," the jurist said. "Cole's got a big pride. He has to keep the town believing in him and his power."

Wescott and the two men at his shoulders came to a slow halt. Glyde watched them narrowly. Somewhere along the street a child began to cry fretfully.

"Marshal!" Cole Wescott's voice was loud in the hushed cañon between the buildings. "Marshal, looks like this thing has melted down to something between just us. Either you or me is going to run this town."

"You're through running it, Wescott."

"Maybe. I say we ought to decide it ourselves. Just you and me."

Glyde said: "Just me and you . . . and two gunslicks. That's what you mean?"

"I don't need them!" the rancher said. "They're no better than me with a gun. I brought them along to keep an eye on your friends there."

"Don't worry about my friends," Glyde said, and added to the three men behind him, "Move out of the street. Get on the sidewalk."

He waited until Venn had reached the front of the building on the left and Paull and Daunt had gained the edge of the street to the right. He said: "All right, Wescott."

The two men that accompanied the rancher did not move. Wescott took three or four steps forward, settled himself firmly on his feet.

"This is a fool's way to settle this," Glyde said in a quiet, distant tone. "The smart thing for you is to turn around and ride out of here. No matter how this comes out, you lose. I'll see to that."

"Maybe," Wescott said, and clawed for his gun.

The rancher was fast. Glyde realized that as he swept up his own weapon. Wescott fired first. Glyde felt the bullet pluck at his sleeve as he squeezed off his own careful shot. He saw Wescott stagger under the impact of the heavy slug, go to one knee. The gunman at the rancher's right heaved forward, bent down. Early sunlight glinted against the pistol suddenly in his hand. The deafening blast of the shotgun in Judge Venn's hands rocked the town. As if swept by some gigantic hand, the gunman went backward into a sprawling heap as the charge of buckshot caught him.

Glyde stared at the third man, waiting for him to make a move. The Spade rider was half crouched, his right hand, fingers splayed, hovered near the gun at his hip.

"Make your try," the lawman said softly. "It's you and me."

The gunman rode out a long breath, slowly straightened. He shook his head. "No thanks," he said, and started to turn away.

"Shoot him! Draw on him!" Cole Wescott screamed from where he lay in the dust. "I'm paying you to do what I tell you . . . !"

The rider looked down at the rancher. "Not me, Cole. I'm through around here . . . and so are you."

Glyde watched the man walk on down the street. He did not take his glance away, not trusting the gunman at all. It was only when he reached the others and was out of effective range that the lawman swung his attention to the rancher. He moved slowly to Wescott.

"You want to let it end here?"

The rancher glared at the marshal. And then suddenly the hard line of his mouth broke. "Let it end," he said. He brushed at the sweat beading his forehead. "Get me that sawbones, will you?"

"In a minute," Glyde answered. He motioned to Venn and the other two who still stood on the sidewalk. "Let's finish this," he said.

They covered the remaining distance that separated them from the rest of the Spade riders. When they reached the jail, Glyde said—"Hold it here."—and went inside.

He released the prisoners, handed them their weapons, and herded them back into the street. He waited until they had rejoined the others, and then stepped before them.

"Spade no longer owns this town," he said. "You're welcome to visit it whenever you like . . . so long as you behave yourselves. If there's any of you who don't figure you're going to like it that way, now's the time to ride on."

"Reckon that means me," the gunman who had been one of

those that had sided Wescott said. "Was gettin' sort of fed up with this country, anyway."

He pulled his horse about, headed out of town. Two others followed him.

Glyde said: "Anybody else? I'm reminding you that if you come into town and forget there's law here, you'll mighty quick find yourself in a cell. And Cole Wescott won't be able to get you out. Never again."

"You've made it plain, Marshal," Hank Johnson said. "Ain't none of us goin' to be looking for trouble."

Glyde said: "Good. Get down there and look after your boss. He needs a doctor. And haul off that other man."

The lawman turned abruptly, walked into the jail. Tension still gripped him in a vise-like squeeze. He heard Spade ride off down the street. He moved to his desk, leaned up against it. He was still standing there, moments later, when the small office began to fill with people.

He accepted their congratulations with little enthusiasm. Only a few short minutes ago they had feared even to speak to him; now everyone was his friend. But he supposed he shouldn't condemn them too much. Wescott and Spade had been the power in Lawless. The same situation had existed other places before—and likely would continue to happen elsewhere.

Damion Paull, Daunt, and Judge Venn had come into their share of appreciation, also. Glyde glanced to where the minister was the center of an admiring group. Paull would have no trouble filling his church pews now.

"Marshal," a man he did not know pressed up to him. "Dutch and Joe Moon are all right. Wescott held them at his ranch all night. Turned them loose to walk to town this morning. They're mighty tired, but Wescott didn't hurt them none."

Glyde thanked the man. He was happy that the two men were unharmed. He looked about the crowded room, searching for a face he had not seen. Lucy Covington. She still was not there.

"Marshal," Judge Venn broke in on his thoughts. "I told these people what you said . . . about moving on, I mean. You still got that in mind?"

"You can't do that, Marshal!" a protesting voice broke in before Glyde could reply. "You just got this here town straightened out. You can't leave now."

"Sure would be a shame," said another.

Glyde said: "There are plenty of men around who'll take the job. I got myself a ranch bought over on the eastern side of the territory. You don't need me."

He hadn't thought much about that ranch these last few days. It had almost slipped his mind. And he still had to earn the rest of the money that was due.

"I don't think you're cut out to nurse cows," Venn said. "You're doing the thing now that you're best at."

Aaron Daunt shouldered through the doorway into the packed room. He pushed his way to the lawman's side. "Got a message for you," he said with a smile. "Lucy says she'd prefer to do her congratulating where there's not so many people around. She's waiting for you at her place."

John Glyde grinned broadly. Although he had just, at that moment, realized it, it was Lucy he had been looking for and hoping to hear from all the time. He started for the door, paused at Benjamin Venn's side.

"I'll do some thinking about this marshal's job," he said. "Could be, if things turn out the way I'm hoping, I'll stay right here. A man can always get in the ranching business."

ABOUT THE AUTHOR

Ray Hogan was an author who inspired a loyal following over the years since he published his first Western novel, *Ex-Marshal*, in 1956. Hogan was born in Willow Springs, Missouri, where his father was town marshal. At five the Hogan family moved to Albuquerque where they lived in the foothills of the Sandia and Manzano Mountains. His father was on the Albuquerque police force and, in later years, owned the Overland Hotel. It was while listening to his father and other old-timers tell tales from the past that Ray was inspired to recast these tales in fiction. From the beginning he did exhaustive research into the history and the people of the Old West, and the walls of his study were lined with various firearms, spurs, pictures, books, and memorabilia, about all of which he could talk in dramatic detail. "I've attempted to capture the courage and bravery of those men and women that lived out West and the dangers and problems they had to overcome," Hogan once remarked. If his lawmen protagonists seem sometimes larger than life, it is because they are men of integrity, heroes who through grit of character and common sense are able to overcome the obstacles they encounter despite often overwhelming odds. This same grit of character can also be found in Hogan's heroines, and in *The Vengeance of Fortuna West* (1983) Hogan wrote a gripping and totally believable account of a woman who takes up the badge and tracks the men who killed her lawman husband by ambush. No less intriguing in her way is Nellie Dupray, convicted of rustling in *The Glory Trail* (1978). One of his most popular books, dealing with an earlier period in the West with Kit Carson as its protagonist, is *Soldier in Buckskin* (Five Star Westerns, 1996). Above all, what is most impressive about Hogan's Western novels is the consistent quality with which each is crafted, the compelling depth of his characters, and his ability to juxtapose the complexities of human conflict into narratives always as intensely interesting as they are emotionally involving. *Wanted: Dead or Alive* will be his next Five Star Western.